Advance praise for

THE DEAD HOURS OF NIGHT

'Lisa Tuttle is, quietly and unsensationally, the finest practitioner of unsettling fiction writing today. She can make you doubt reality, she can chill your flesh and walk you into the darkness with gentle, perfectly constructed prose. Her authorial voice is so sensible that it's easy to forget, over and over, in story after story, that she's one of the dangerous ones, the kind of writer that somebody really should have warned you about, and now it is (as it so often is is in Tuttle's fiction) much, much too late.'

– Neil Gaiman

'The tales are intense and character-driven, exploring women's lives and realities, and the inherent terror therein. Filled with complicated, fully realized women – not just "final girls" – Tuttle's captivating protagonists narrate dark, unsettling stories with a direct tone, immediately drawing readers into their weird worlds, immersing them in the dread until the inevitable, emphatic last line that leaves readers gasping, yet eager to dive back in to the next story and experience it all over again. These dark emotions gloriously build throughout the collection, never disappointing.'

– *Booklist* (starred review)

Also available by Lisa Tuttle

A Nest of Nightmares
Familiar Spirit

VALANCOURT BOOKS

The Dead Hours of Night
First edition February 2021

Published by Valancourt Books, Richmond, Virginia
http://www.valancourtbooks.com

ISBN 978-1-948405-82-9 (hardcover)
ISBN 978-1-948405-83-6 (trade paperback)

Also available as an electronic book.

Cover by M. S. Corley
Set in Bembo Book MT Pro

CONTENTS

Introduction

What is it about certain stories that captures the imagination? The horror genre is full of tales of cursed objects, of haunted spaces, of buried secrets. These stories are circulated around campfires, whispered at sleepovers, and written down, repackaged in new frightening forms. Every horror author has their own version, their own unique spin on the classic tropes. Lisa Tuttle is no different. In this collection, readers will encounter a book that is haunted by the ghostly figure of a man, a lover with a deadly secret (in an update on the Bluebeard lore, with the added element of alchemy), a woman 'cursed' by a spiritualist, and ancient stones that can kill if someone simply looks at them. Tuttle expertly takes these plot details and weaves them into wonderfully weird stories, stories that often begin firmly rooted in the mundane 'real' world and swiftly open doors to fantastic adventure.

Tuttle's writing career began to earn her accolades in the 1970s and 1980s. In 1974, she won the Astounding Award for Best New Writer (then named the John W. Campbell Award for Best New Writer) and steadily collected wins and nominations for British Science Fiction Association (BFSA), Nebula, and Locus Awards in the years to come. One Locus nomination came with her novel *Windhaven* (1981), a collaboration with *A Song of Ice and Fire* author George R. R. Martin. I feel it is worth a mention that she wrote so prolifically during these decades. After all, the '70s and '80s are an interesting time period for the development of the horror genre. In film, slashers reigned supreme, their legacy so powerful that, for some, slashers are synonymous with the genre as a whole. The formula is simple: a masked killer takes down a group of people (usually teens) with some sort of sharp-bladed weapon. I'll put a disclaimer here: I love slashers. Wholeheartedly. But I have heard criticism that they don't always allow for much character development. And that is fair. Sometimes, especially in the land of the endless sequels, it can feel like the characters are simply fodder for the killer to mow down, rather than fully-fleshed out characters.

In this landscape, I find Tuttle's stories all the more fascinating. Her characters are fully designed, with rich interior lives. The characters who tell these stories are dealing with trauma of all kinds: the loss of parents, sexual abuse, divorce. Tuttle's writing style allows for the reader to not just empathize with the characters' traumas, but to experience them. Here, there are no stories of killers taking down faceless victims. While there are stories that are blood-filled, stories with brutal killers, stories with gore and viscera, enough to turn a reader's stomach, the main characters are never fodder. They have wants, desires, needs – even if those desires aren't always what polite society deems 'normal'.

Tuttle's talent soars, however, when she writes women characters, particularly how women's experiences (as well as their bodies) remain secretive and mysterious in the patriarchal outer world. All of the stories in this collection are worth reading, but there are a few that stand out, at least to me. 'My Pathology' is a story about love and relationships, and about the secrets that we keep from each other. Bess, the narrator, is in love with Daniel, a would-be alchemist. He is ever secretive about 'The Work', as he calls it. He deliberately keeps a curious Bess in the dark about what happens in his secret room. There are shades of Bluebeard here, but also of *Rosemary's Baby*, as his mother becomes a meddling presence as soon as Bess becomes pregnant. These elements alone make for a thrilling horror story, but what is truly special is how Tuttle highlights the danger that men are willing to put women in – if it will further their 'work', an idea reaching all the way back to writers like Nathaniel Hawthorne and the early Gothics. Daniel, like many men in these stories, is willing to use women's bodies as he sees fit. One line, in particular, stands out to me: 'He's got such strange ideas about women's bodies.' Daniel sees the female body as both a mystery and something sacred – a space he can exploit to make literal magic in the real world. The woman's body, in Tuttle's world, therefore, is a magical and secretive space.

In the stories that follow, Tuttle explores the secretive space of women, taking their sometimes mysterious realm (including things like pregnancy, birth, and menopause) and weaving in elements of the weird and the supernatural. In 'Born Dead', a woman named Florida McAfee finds herself 'accidentally pregnant' at 40. As a powerful and successful career woman, Florida never expected to have a child – and certainly not one that would be born dead yet continue to grow. In 'A Birthday', a man witnesses his mother's 'hysterical bleeding', which he is told is a product of 'the change of life'. Not understanding menopause, he misunderstands what his mother is actually going through, which is something supernatural (I'll save the details for fear of spoiling the story). His misunderstanding at the basics of a woman's biology is both humorous and horrific, but it underlines a true horror in the real world. A woman's body is a thing of mystery to most men (and by extension, to some women even). In all these stories, the feminine space is one that eludes understanding. Tuttle's female characters choose to become plants, or they have erotic relationships with men made of discarded food waste. They give birth to (and choose to raise) strange 'blood babies' or dead children who continue to grow. This may seem a puzzling choice to the reader, but the choice always makes sense to the protagonist. And in the end, that is what matters. After all, a woman's decision is not for someone else to make. It is for her – and her alone.

Enter these stories with reverence, then, as you are entering the sacred space of someone else's inner thoughts, desires, and yes, even inner horrors.

Enjoy.

Lisa Kröger
August 2020

Lisa Kröger, Ph.D., is the Bram Stoker Award and Locus Award winning author of *Monster, She Wrote*, as well as co-host of the *Know Fear* and *Monster, She Wrote* podcasts. She's contributed fiction and nonfiction to *Lost Highways: Dark Fictions From the Road*, *EcoGothic*, *The Encyclopedia of the Vampire*, and *Horror Literature through History*. Her essay collections include *Shirley Jackson: Influences and Confluences* and *Spectral Identities: The Ghosted and the Ghostly in Film and Literature*. You can find out more at www.lisakroger.com.

For my friend Betty Binz Ericson Jones with happy memories of the scares, dares and fun we shared when we were young.

Objects in Dreams May Be Closer Than They Appear

'One had supposed that the ghost story itself was already an obsolete form, that it had been killed by the electric light,' wrote Edmund Wilson in 1944, reflecting on the continuing popularity of the horror story. But ancient spectres were not banished by brighter, more reliable sources of light, and developments in new technology, rather than wiping out primitive superstition, have simply created new horrors, like those beloved yet sinister smart devices that guide us and spy on us in our daily life, logging our daily footsteps, reminding us where we're supposed to be and telling us how to get there. Like the narrator of this story, I once received an email from my ex-husband with a link to a Google Street View picture of the house we'd owned decades ago. This not-entirely-welcome blast from the past sent me on a journey into the uncanny valley of virtual tourism from which I emerged disorientated, but with an idea for a different sort of haunted house story.

SINCE WE DIVORCED TWENTY YEARS AGO, my ex-husband Michael and I rarely met, but we'd always kept in touch. I wish now that we hadn't. This whole terrible thing began with a link he sent me by e-mail with the comment, 'Can you believe how much the old homestead has changed?'

Clicking on the link took me to a view of the cottage we had owned, long ago, for about three years – most of our brief marriage.

Although I recognized it, there were many changes. No longer a semi-detached, it had been merged with the house next door, and also extended. It was, I thought, what we might have done ourselves given the money, time, planning permission and, most vitally, next-door neighbours willing to sell us their home. Instead, we had fallen out with them (they took our offer to buy as a personal affront) and poured too much money into so-called improvements, the work expensively and badly done by local builders who all seemed to be related by marriage if not blood to the people next door.

Just looking at the front of the house on the computer screen gave me a tight, anxious feeling in my chest. What had possessed Michael to send it to me? And why had he even looked for it? Surely he wasn't nostalgic for what I recalled as one of the unhappiest periods of my life?

At that point, I should have clicked away from the picture, put it out of my mind and settled down to work, but, I don't know why, instead of closing the tab, I moved on down the road and began to discover what else in our old neighbourhood was different.

I'd heard about Google Earth's 'Street View' function, but I'd never used it before, so it took me a little while to figure out how to use it. At first all the zooming in and out, stopping and starting and twirling around made me queasy, but once I got to grips with it, I found this form of virtual tourism quite addictive.

But I was startled by how different the present reality appeared from my memory of it. I did not recognize our old village at all, could find nothing I remembered except the war memorial – and that seemed to be in the wrong place. Where was the shop, the primary school, the pub? Had they all been altered beyond recognition, all turned into houses? There were certainly many more of those than there had been in the 1980s. It was while I was searching in vain for the unmistakable landmark that had always alerted us that the next turning would be our road, a commercial property that I could not imagine anyone converting into a desirable residence – the Little Chef – that it dawned on me what had happened.

Of course. The Okehampton bypass had been built, and altered the route of the A30. Our little village was one of several no longer bisected by the main road into Cornwall, and without hordes of holidaymakers forced to crawl past, the fast food outlet and petrol station no longer made economic sense.

Once I understood how the axis of the village had changed, I found the new primary school near an estate of new homes. There were also a couple of new (to me) shops, an Indian restaurant, wine bar, an oriental rug gallery, and a riding school. The increase in population had pushed our sleepy old village slightly up-market. I should not have been surprised, but I suppose I was an urban snob, imagining that anyone living so deep in the country must be several decades behind the times. But I could see that even the smallest of houses boasted a satellite dish, and they probably all had broadband internet connections, too. Even as I was laughing at the garden gnomes on display in front of a neat yellow bungalow, someone behind those net curtains might be looking at my own terraced house in Bristol, horrified by what the unrestrained growth of ivy was doing to the brickwork.

Curious to know how my home appeared to others, I typed in my own address, and enjoyed a stroll around the neighbourhood without leaving my desk. I checked out a few less-familiar addresses, including Michael's current abode, which I had never seen. So *that* was Goring-by-Sea!

At last I dragged myself away and wrote catalogue copy, had a long talk with one of our suppliers, and dealt with various other bits and pieces before knocking off for the day. Neither of us fancied going out, and we'd been consuming too many pizzas lately, so David whipped up an old favourite from the minimal supplies in the kitchen cupboard: spaghetti with marmite, tasty enough when accompanied by a few glasses of Merlot.

My husband David and I marketed children's apparel and

accessories under the name 'Cheeky Chappies'. It was exactly the sort of business I had imagined setting up in my rural idyll, surrounded by the patter of little feet, filling orders between changing nappies and making delicious, sustaining soups from the organic vegetables Michael planned to grow.

None of that came to pass, not even the vegetables. Michael did what he could, but we needed his income as a sales rep to survive, so he was nearly always on the road, which left me to take charge of everything at home, supervising the building work in between applying for jobs and grants, drawing up unsatisfactory business plans, and utterly failing in my mission to become pregnant.

Hard times can bring a couple together, but that is not how it worked for us. I grew more and more miserable, convinced I was a failure both as a woman and as a potential CEO. It did not help that Michael was away so much, and although it was not his fault and we needed the money, I grew resentful at having to spend so much time and energy servicing a house I'd never really wanted.

He'd drawn me into *his* dream of an old-fashioned life in the country, and then slipped out of sharing the major part of it with me. At weekend, with him there, it was different, but most of the time I felt lonely and bored, lumbered with too many chores and not enough company, far from friends and family, cut off from the entertainments and excitement of urban existence.

Part of the problem was the house – not at all what we'd dreamed of, but cheap enough, and with potential to be transformed into something better. We'd been jumped into buying it by circumstances. Once Michael had accepted a very good offer on his flat (*our* flat, he called it, but it was entirely his investment) a new urgency entered into our formerly relaxed house-hunting expeditions. I had loved those weekends away from the city, staying in B&Bs and rooms over village pubs, every moment rich with possibility and new discoveries. I would have been happy to go on for months, driving down to the West Country, looking at properties and imagining what our life might be like in this house or that, but suddenly there was a time limit, and this was the most serious decision of our lives, and not just a bit of fun.

The happiest part of my first marriage now seems to have been compressed into half a dozen weekends, maybe a few more, as we travelled around, the inside of the car like an enchanted bubble filled with love and laughter, jokes and personal revelations and music. I loved everything we saw. Even the most impossible, ugly houses were fascinating, providing material for discussing the strangeness of other people's lives. Yet although I was interested in them all, nothing we viewed actually tempted me. Somehow, I couldn't imagine I would ever really live in the country – certainly not the practicalities of it. I expected our life to continue like this, work in the city punctuated by these mini-holidays, until we found the perfect house, at which point I'd stop working and start producing babies and concentrate on buying their clothes and toys and attractive soft furnishings and decorations for the house as if money was not and could never be a problem.

And then one day, travelling from the viewing of one imperfect property to look at another which would doubtless be equally unsatisfactory in its own unique way, Blondie in the cassette player singing about hanging on the telephone, we came to an abrupt halt. Michael stopped the car at the top of a hill, on one of those narrow, hedge-lined lanes that aren't even wide enough for two normal-sized cars to pass each other without the sort of jockeying and breath-holding manoeuvres that in my view are acceptable only when parallel parking. I thought he must have seen another car approaching, and taken evasive action, although the road ahead looked clear.

'What's wrong?'

'Wrong? Nothing. It's perfect. Don't you think it's perfect?'

I saw what he was looking at through a gap in the hedge: a distant view of an old-fashioned, whitewashed, thatch-roofed cottage nestled in one of those deep, green valleys that in Devonshire are called coombs. It was a pretty sight, like a Victorian painting you might get on a box of old-fashioned chocolates, or a card for Mother's Day. For some reason, it made my throat tighten and I had to blink back sentimental tears, feeling a strong yearning, not so much for that specific house as for what it seemed to promise: safety, stability, family. I could see myself there, decades in the future, surrounded by children and grandchildren, dressed in clothes from Laura Ashley.

'It's very sweet,' I said, embarrassed by how emotional I felt.

'It's exactly what we've been looking for,' he said.

'It's probably not for sale.'

'All it takes is the right offer.' That was his theory: not so much that everything had its price, as that he could achieve whatever goal he set himself. It was more about attitude than money.

'But what if they feel the same way about it as we do?'

'Who are "they"?'

'The people that live there.'

'But you feel it? What I feel? That it's where we want to live?'

I thought about the children – grandchildren, even! – in their quaint floral smocks – and nodded.

He kissed me. 'All right!' he cried, joyously, releasing the handbrake. 'Let's go!'

'Do you even know how to get there?'

'You've got the map. Direct me.'

My heart sank. Although I had the road atlas open in my lap, I never expected to have to use it. Michael did not understand that not everyone was like him, able to look at lines and coloured patches on a page and relate them to the real world. His sense of direction seemed magical to me. Even when the sun was out, I had no idea which way was north. On a map, it was at the top. In the world, I had to guess at right or left or straight ahead.

'I don't know where we are *now*,' I objected. 'We need to stop and figure it out.'

Fortunately, we were approaching a village, and it offered parking space in front of the church, so that was easily done. Michael had no problem identifying which of the wriggly white lines was the road we'd been on, and where we'd stopped and seen the house, and with that and the location of the village we were in, he was able to perform some sort of mental triangulation that enabled him to stab a forefinger down on a blank place within the loops of spaghetti representing the nameless country roads. 'There,' he said with certainty. 'It's got to be there. An OS map would show us exactly, but anyway, it shouldn't be hard to find. We'll just drive around until we spot it.'

We drove around for the next two or three hours. Round and round and round. The same route, again and again, up and down the narrow roads, some of them like tunnels, they were so deep beneath the high-banked hedges, until I was dizzy, like a leaf swept away in a stream. Deep within those dark green lanes there was nothing to see except the road ahead, the deep, loamy earth with roots bursting through on either side, and the branches of trees overhead, through which I caught pale, gleaming shards of sky. The house remained hidden from view except when Michael drove up to higher ground, and found one of the few places where it was possible to see through, or over, the thick, ancient hedgerows that shielded nearly every piece of land from the road.

There it was, so close it must be just beyond the next curve of the road, yet forever out of our reach. The faint curl of smoke from the chimney inspired another yearning tug as I imagined sitting cosy and warm with my dear husband beside a crackling fire. I could almost smell the wood smoke, and, closer, hot chocolate steaming in a mug.

I was hungry, thirsty and tired of stomping my foot down on an imaginary brake every time we met another car. There was a chill in the air as afternoon began to fade towards evening, and I wondered if we'd be able to get lunch anywhere, and made the point aloud.

He was impatient with my weakness. 'We'll get something afterwards. Surely they'll invite us in for a cup of tea when we get there. They can't have many visitors!'

'If we could find that house by driving around, we would have found it already. You've already taken every turning, and we've seen every farmyard and tumbledown shed and occupied house in the whole valley.'

'Obviously we have missed one.'

'Please, darling. It'll be dark soon. Look, we need to try something else. Why not go to Okehampton and ask an estate agent?'

'So now you're assuming the house is for sale.'

'No. I assume it was for sale some time in the past and will be again in the future, and it is their business to know the local market. It's a beautiful place. We can't be the first people to have asked about it.'

'No, but we will be the ones who get it!'

No one knew the house in the offices of the first two estate agents, and the man in the third one also stated there was no such cottage in the valley where we claimed to have seen it – that area was all woods and fields, he said – but there was something in his manner as he tried to fob us off with pictures and details of ever more expensive houses located twenty miles away that made me think he was hiding something, so we persisted, until, finally, he suggested we go see Mr Yeo.

Mr Yeo was a semi-retired property surveyor who had been in the business since before the War, and knew everything worth knowing about every house in this part of Devon. He lived still in the village where he had been born – Marystow – a name we both recognized, as it was one of the places we'd passed through a dozen times on our futile quest. So off we went to find him.

He was an elderly man who seemed friendly, happy to welcome us into his home, until Michael revealed what we had come about, and then, abruptly, the atmosphere changed, and he began to usher us out again. The house was not for sale, we would not be able to visit it, there was no point in further discussion.

'But surely you can give us the name of the owners? An address to write to?'

'There b'ain't owners. He's not there.'

I thought at first 'he' referred to the owner, unused to the way that older inhabitants of rural Devon spoke of inanimate objects as 'he' rather than 'it'. But Mr Yeo made his meaning clear before sending us on our way: the perfectly desirable house we'd seen, nestled in a deep green coomb, did not exist. It was an illusion. We were not the first to have seen it; there were old folk and travellers' tales about such a house, glimpsed from a hilltop, nestled in the next valley; most often glimpsed late in the day, seemingly near enough that the viewer thought he could reach it before sunset, and rest the night there.

But no matter how long they walked, or what direction they tried, they could never reach it.

'Have you ever seen it?'

Mr Yeo scowled, and would not say. ''Tis bad luck to see 'im,' he informed us. 'Worse, much worse, to try to find 'im. You'm better go 'ome and forget about him. 'Tis not a good place for you'm.'

Michael thanked the old man politely, but as we left, I could feel something simmering away in him. But it was not anger, only laughter, which exploded once we were back in our car. He thought Mr Yeo was a ridiculous old man and didn't buy his story for an instant. Maybe there was some optical illusion involved – that might explain why we hadn't been able to find the house where he'd expected it to be – but that was a real house that we'd seen, and someday we would find it.

Yet we never did. Not even when Michael bought the largest scale Ordnance Survey map of the area, the one for walkers that included every footpath, building and ruin, could we find evidence that it had ever existed. Unless he'd been wrong about the location, and it was really in a more distant coomb, made to look closer by some trick of air and light . . . Even after we moved to Devon – buying the wrong house – we came no closer to solving the mystery. I think Michael might have caught the occasional glimpse of it in the distance, but I never saw it again.

I shouldn't pretend I didn't know what made Michael's thoughts return to our old home in Devon, because I had been dreaming about it myself, for the same reason: the Wheaton-Bakers' Ruby Anniversary Celebration. We'd both been invited – with our respective new spouses, of course – to attend it at their house in Tavistock in four weeks' time. I didn't know about Michael, but I had not been back to Devon in over twenty years; not since we'd sold the house. The Wheaton-Bakers were the only friends from that period of my life with whom I'd kept in touch, although we saw each other no more often than Michael and I did.

I'd been pleased by the invitation. The party was in early October. David and I had booked a room in an inn on Dartmoor and looked forward to a relaxing weekend away, with a couple of leg-stretching, mind-clearing rambles on Dartmoor book-ending the Saturday night festivities. And yet, although I looked forward to it, there was also a faint uneasiness in my mind attached to the idea of seeing Michael again, back in our old haunts; an uneasiness I did not so much as hint at to David because I could not explain it. It was irrational and unfair, I thought. My first marriage had not worked out, but both of us, or neither, were responsible for that, and that failure had been come to terms with and was long in the past. There was no unfinished business between us.

When the weekend of the party arrived, David was ill. It was probably only a twenty-four-hour bug (it was going around, according to our next-door neighbour, a teacher) but it meant he couldn't consider going anywhere farther than the bathroom.

I should have stayed home and tended to him, like a good wife – that is what I wish I had done. But he insisted I go. The Wheaton-Bakers were my friends. They would be sorry not to see me. We wouldn't get our money back for the hotel room – that had been an internet bargain. And he didn't need to be tended. He intended to sleep as much as possible, just lie in bed and sweat it out.

So I went. And I did enjoy myself. It was a lovely party; the Wheaton-Bakers were just as nice as I remembered, and they introduced me to other friendly, interesting people, so I never felt lonely or out of place for a moment. Michael was there, but he'd been seated at a different table, and struck up conversations with a different set of people, so although we'd exchanged greetings, we'd hardly done more than that. It was only as I was preparing to leave that he cornered me.

'Hey, you're not leaving!'

' 'Fraid so.'

'But we've hardly spoken! You're driving back to Bristol tonight?'

'No, of course not.' I told him where I was staying.

'Mm, very posh! I'm just up the road, nylon sheets and a plastic shower stall. Want to meet and have lunch somewhere tomorrow?'

I was happy to agree. We exchanged phone numbers, and

he offered to pick me up at my hotel at ten. 'If that's not too early? It'll give us time to drive around a bit, see how much the scenery has changed, before deciding what we want to do.'

There was a familiar glint in his eye, and I was suddenly certain he meant to take me back to look at our old house, and maybe one or two other significant sites from our marriage. I didn't know why he felt the need to revisit the past like that – the past was over and done with, as far as I was concerned – but I didn't say anything. If he needed to go back and see with his own eyes how much time had passed, to understand that we were no longer the people who had fallen in love with each other, then perhaps I owed him my supportive, uncomplaining companionship.

Anyway, I thought it would be more fun than going for a walk by myself or driving straight back home.

The next morning, I checked out, and left my car in the car park. There was no question that we'd go in his: I remembered too well that he'd always disliked being a passenger. His car was better, anyway: a silver Audi with that new car smell inside, soft leather seats and an impressive Sat-Nav system. Something by Mozart issued softly from hidden speakers as we headed down the A386 before leaving the moor for the sunken lanes I remembered, winding deep into a leaf-shadowed coomb.

'Remember this?' he asked, as the car raced silently along. It was a smoother ride than in the old days.

'I'm glad they haven't dug up all the hedgerows,' I said. 'I was afraid Devon might have changed a lot more.'

He frowned, dissatisfied with my answer. 'Didn't you click on that link I sent you?'

'Yes, I did. I saw our old house – didn't I send a reply?'

He shrugged that off. 'I thought you might have explored a bit more widely. Not just the village, not just the street view, but moving up and out, looking at the satellite pictures.'

'It's a busy time of the year for us, with Christmas coming. I don't have much time to play around on the internet. Although I'm sure it's very interesting.'

'It's more than just "interesting". You can see things that aren't on other maps. The aerial shots – do you remember how we had to go up to the top of the hill to see it?'

I understood. 'You're not talking about our house.'

'You know what I'm talking about.' He touched the screen of his navigation system and a calm, clear female voice said, 'You are approaching a crossroads. Prepare to turn right.'

'You found it?' I asked him, amazed. 'How?'

'Turn right. Follow the road.'

'Satellite view on Google. I zoomed in as much as I could – it wasn't easy to get a fix on it. Street View's no good – it's not on a road. But it's there all right; maybe not in exactly the place we kept looking for it. Anyway, I have the coordinates now, and I've put them into my system here, and – it will take us there.' He grinned like a proud, clever child.

'How, if it's not on a road?'

'Prepare to turn left. Turn left.'

'It will take us as close as it can. After that we'll walk. Those are good, sturdy boots you have on.'

'Take the first turning to the right.'

'Well done, Sherlock,' I said. 'Just fancy if we'd had GPS back in those days – we'd have found it, and . . . do you think they'd have accepted our offer?'

'Bear left. At the next crossroads, turn right.'

Despite the smoothness of the ride, as we turned and turned again – sometimes forced to stop and back up in a *pas de deux* with another Sunday driver – I began to feel queasy, like in the old days, and then another sort of unease crept in.

'Haven't we been along here already? We must be going in circles,' I said.

'And when did you develop a sense of direction?'

'Prepare to turn right. Turn right.'

The last turn was the sharpest, and took us off the road entirely, through an opening in a hedge so narrow that I flinched at the unpleasant noise of cut branches scraping the car, and then we were in a field.

There was no road or path ahead of us, not even a track, just the faint indication of old ruts where at some point a tractor or other farm vehicle might have gone, and even they soon ended.

'Make a U-turn when possible. Return to a marked road.'

Michael stopped the car. 'So that's as far as she'll take us. We'll have to rely on my own internal GPS the rest of the way.'

We got out. He changed his brown loafers for a pair of brilliant white sports shoes that looked as if they'd never been worn, took an OS map out of the glove box, and showed me the red X he had marked on an otherwise blank spot. 'And this is where we are now.'

'Why isn't it on the map?'

He shrugged. I persisted. 'You must have thought about it.'

He shrugged again and sighed. 'Well, you know, there are places considered too sensitive, of military importance, something to do with national security, that you're not allowed to take pictures or even write about. There's an airfield in Norfolk, and a whole village on Salisbury Plain – '

'They're not on maps?'

'Not on any maps. And those are just the two examples I happen to know. There must be more. Maybe this house, or the entire coomb, was used for covert ops in the war, or is owned by MI5, used as a safe house or something.'

My skin prickled with unease. 'Maybe we shouldn't go there.'

'Are you kidding? You're not going to wimp out on me now!'

'If it's so secret that it's against the law – '

'Do you see any "No Trespassing" signs?' He waved his arms at the empty field around us. 'It's a free country; we can walk where we like.'

I took a deep breath, and thought about that airfield in Norfolk. I was pretty sure I knew the place he meant; it was surrounded by barbed wire fences, decorated with signs prohibiting parking and picture-taking on the grounds of national security. It was about as secret as the Post Office Tower. I nodded my agreement.

It was a good day for walking, dry and with a fresh, invigorating breeze countering the warmth of the sun. For about fifteen minutes we just walked, not speaking, and I was feeling very relaxed when I heard him say, 'There it is.'

Just ahead of us, the land dropped away unexpectedly steeply, and we stopped and stood gazing down into a deep, narrow, wooded valley. Amid the turning leaves the golden brown of the thatched roof blended in, and shadows dappled the whitewashed walls below with natural camouflage. If we hadn't been looking for it, we might not have seen it, but now, as I stared, it seemed to gain in clarity, as if someone had turned up the resolution on a screen. I saw a wisp of smoke rise from the chimney, and caught the faint, sweet fragrance of burning wood.

Michael was moving about in an agitated way, and it took me a few moments to realize he was searching for the best route down. 'This way,' he called. 'Give me your hand; it's a bit tricky at first, but then I think it should be easier.'

I was suddenly nervous. 'I don't think we should. There's someone there.'

'So? They'll invite us in. We'll ask how long they've had the place and if they'd consider selling.'

I saw that the notion of an MI5 safe house was far from his mind, if he had ever believed it. He wasn't even slightly afraid, and struggled to comprehend my reason for wanting to turn back.

'Look, if you want to wait for me here . . .'

I couldn't let him go by himself. I checked that my phone was on, and safely zipped into my pocket, and then I let him help me down to the first ledge, and the one after that. Then it got easier, although there was never anything as clear as a path, and on my own I'm certain I would have been lost, since my instinct, every time, was to go in a direction different from his. He really could hold a map in his head. At last we emerged from a surprisingly dense wood into a clearing from which we could see a windowless side wall.

I fell back and followed him around towards the front. Pebbles rolled and crunched gently underfoot on the path to the front door. I wondered if he had a plan, and what he would say to whoever answered the door: was he really going to pretend we were interested in buying?

Then I looked up and as I took in the full frontal view, I knew I had been here before. It was the strongest wave of *déjà vu* I'd ever felt, a sickening collision between two types of knowledge: I knew it was impossible, yet I remembered this visit.

The memory was unclear, but frightening. Somehow, I had come here before. When my knock at the door had gone unanswered, I'd peeked through that window on the right, and saw something that made me run away in terror.

I could not remember anything of what I had seen; only the fear it had inspired was still powerful.

Michael knocked on the door, then glanced over his shoulder, impatient with me for hanging back.

I wanted to warn him, but of what? What could I say? I was in the grip of a fear I knew to be irrational. I managed to move a little closer to Michael and the door, telling myself that nothing could compel me to look through that window.

We waited a little while, but even after Michael knocked again, more loudly, almost pounding, there was no reply. I relaxed a little, thinking we were going to get away with it, but when I spoke of leaving, he insisted, 'Not until I find out who lives here, what it's all about. There is someone here – I can see a light – look, through that window – '

I moved back; I wouldn't look.

'I think I can smell cooking. They're probably in the kitchen. Maybe a bit deaf. I'm going to try the back door. You coming? Suit yourself.'

I didn't want to stay, but wanted even less to follow him around the back, so I waited, wrapping my arms around myself, feeling a chill. The sun didn't strike so warmly in this leafy hollow. I checked my phone for the time and was startled to see how much of the afternoon was gone. I wondered if I should call David to warn him I'd be late, but decided to wait for Michael.

I didn't like to keep checking the time because it made me more nervous, but at least five minutes had passed when I felt I had no choice but to walk around to the back of the house to look for him.

I had no sense of *déjà vu* there; I was certain I'd never seen the peeling black paint that covered the solidly shut back door, or the small windows screened by yellowish, faded curtains that made it impossible to see inside.

'Michael?' I didn't like the weak, wavering sound of my voice, and made myself call out more loudly, firmly, but there was no reply. Nothing happened. I knocked as hard as I could on the back door, dislodging a few flakes of old paint, and as I waited I listened to the sound of leaves rustling in the wind; every once in a while one would fall. I felt like screaming, but that would have been bloody stupid. Either he had heard me or he hadn't. Either he was capable of reply – could he be hiding just to tease me? – or he wasn't. And what was I going to do about it?

As I walked back around to the front of the house I was assailed by the memory of what I had seen when I looked through the window the last time I was here – if that had ever happened. I'd seen a man's foot and leg – I'd seen that there was someone inside the house, just sitting, not answering my knock, and the sight of some stranger's foot had frightened me so badly that I'd run away, and then repressed the memory of the entire incident.

Now I realized it must have been a dream that I recalled. It had that pointless, sinister atmosphere of a bad dream. Unfortunately, it now seemed like a precognitive dream.

Nothing had changed in front of the house. I got out my phone and entered the number Michael had given me. As I heard it ringing in my ear, I heard the familiar notes from the *William Tell* Overture sounding from inside the house. I clenched my teeth and waited. When the call went to his voicemail, I ended it and hit redial. Muffled by distance, the same tinny, pounding ringtone played inside the house, small but growing in volume until, once again, it was cut off by the voicemail program.

I knew what I would see if I looked through the window, so I didn't look. I wanted to run away, but I didn't know where to go. It would be dark soon. I had to do something.

The front door opened easily. Tense, I darted my gaze about, fearful of ambush although the place felt empty. To my right, I could see into a small, dark sitting room where an old man sat, or slumped, in an armchair.

He was a very, very old man, almost hairless, his skin like yellowed parchment, and appeared to have been dead for some time. It would have been his foot I had seen if I'd looked through the window: his feet in brand new, brilliantly white sports shoes. But even as I recognized the rest of the clothes – polo shirt, jeans, soft grey hooded jacket, even the phone and car keys in his pockets – I clung to the notion of a vicious trick, that someone had stolen Michael's clothes to dress an old man's corpse. How could the vigorous fifty-eight-year-old that I'd seen a few minutes ago have aged and died so rapidly?

I know now that it is what's left of Michael, and that there is no one else here.

I am not able to leave. I can open the door, but as soon as I step through, I find myself entering again. I don't know how many times I did that, before giving up. I don't know how long I have been here; it seems like a few days, at most, but when I look in the mirror I can tell by my hair that it must be two months or more.

There's plenty of food in the kitchen, no problems with plumbing or electricity, and for entertainment, besides all the books, there's an old video player, and stacks of videos, as well as an old phonograph and a good collection of music. I say 'good collection' because it might have been planned to please Michael and me, at least as we were in the '80s.

Having found a ream of paper in the bottom drawer of the desk in the other parlour (the room where Michael *isn't*) I decided to write down what has happened, just in case someone comes here someday and finds my body as I found his. It gives me something to do, even though I fear it is a pointless exercise.

While exploring the house earlier – yesterday, or the day before – I found evidence of mice – fortunately, only in one place, in the other sitting room. There were droppings there, and a nest made of nibbled paper, as if the mouse had devoted all its energy to the destruction of a single stack of paper. One piece was left just large enough for me to read a few words in faded ink, and recognize Michael's handwriting, but there was not enough for me to make sense of whatever he was trying to say.

Closet Dreams

I read this aloud at World Fantasy Con in 2006. I was a little nervous, because although I enjoy reading my stories to an audience, I'd only finished writing it a couple of days before the convention, and was still too close to a story no one else had seen to know if it really worked. I only knew that it did when the room, almost as one, gasped in surprise . . . and their stunned pause at the end, before the applause, made me very happy. After publication, it was picked up by Ellen Datlow for her 'Year's Best', and won the International Horror Guild Award for Outstanding Achievement in Mid-Length Fiction. But the spontaneous reaction from that first audience – so rare for a writer to get such immediate and in-person feedback – is what meant the most.

SOMETHING TERRIBLE happened to me when I was a little girl.

I don't want to go into details. I had to do that far too often in the year after it happened, first telling the police everything I could remember in the (vain) hope it would help them catch the monster, then talking for hours and hours to all sorts of therapists, doctors, shrinks and specialists brought in to help me. Talking about it was supposed to help me understand what had happened, achieve closure, and move on.

I just wanted to forget – I thought that's what 'putting it behind me' meant – but they said to do that, first I had to *remember.* I thought I did remember – in fact, I was sure I did – but they wouldn't believe what I told them. They said it was a fantasy, created to cover something I couldn't bear to admit. For my own good (and also to help the police catch that monster) I had to remember the truth.

So I racked my brain and forced myself to relive my darkest memories, giving them more and more specifics, suffering through every horrible moment a second, third and fourth time before belatedly realizing it wasn't the stuff the monster had done to me that they could not believe. There was nothing at all impossible about a single detail of my abduction, imprisonment and abuse, not even the sick particulars of what he called 'playing'. I had been an innocent; it was all new to me, but they were adults, professionals who had dealt with too many victims. It came as no surprise to them that there were monsters living among us, looking just like ordinary men, but really the worst kind of sexual predator.

The only thing they did not believe in was my escape. It could not have happened the way I said. Surely I must see that?

But it had. When I understood what they were questioning, it made me first tearful and then mad. I was not a liar. Impossible or not, it had happened, and my presence there, telling them about it, ought to be proof enough.

One of them – her name escapes me, but she was an older lady who always wore turtleneck sweaters or big scarves, and who reminded me a little of my granny with her high cheekbones, narrow blue eyes and gentle voice – told me that she knew I wasn't lying. What I had described was my own experience of the escape, and true on those terms – but all the same, I was a big girl now and I could surely understand that it could not have happened that way in actuality. She said I could think of it like a dream. The dream was my experience, what happened inside my brain while I was asleep, but something else was happening at the same time. Maybe, if we worked with the details of my dream, we might get some clues as to what that was.

She asked me to tell her something about my dreams. I told her there was only one. Ever since I'd escaped I'd had a recurring nightmare, night after night, unlike any dream I'd ever had before, twice as real and ten times more horrible.

It went like this: I'd come awake, in darkness too intense for seeing, my body aching, wooden floor hard beneath my naked body, the smell of dust and ancient varnish in my nose, and my legs would jerk, a spasm of shock, before I returned to lying motionless again, eyes tightly shut, trying desperately, against all hope, to fall back into the safe oblivion of sleep. Sometimes it was only a matter of seconds before I woke again in my own bedroom, where the light was always left on for just such moments, but sometimes I would seemingly remain in that prison for hours before I could wake. Nothing ever happened; I never saw him; there was just the closet, and that was bad enough. The true horror of the dream was that it didn't seem like a dream, and so turned reality inside-out, stripping my illusory freedom from me.

When I was much younger I'd made the discovery that I guess most kids make, that if you can only manage to scream out loud when you're dreaming – especially when you've started to realize that it *is* just a dream – you'll wake yourself up.

But I never tried that in the closet dream; I didn't dare. The monster had taught me not to scream. If I made any noise in the closet, any noise loud enough for him to hear from another room, he would tape my mouth shut, and tie my hands together behind my back.

I knew I was his prisoner. Before he did that, it wouldn't have occurred to me that I still had *some* freedom.

So I didn't scream.

I guess the closet dream didn't offer much scope for analysis. She tried to get me to recall other dreams, but when I insisted I didn't have any, she didn't press. Instead, she told me that it wouldn't always be that way, and taught me some relaxation techniques that would make it easier to slip into an undisturbed sleep.

It wasn't only for my peace of mind that I kept having these sessions with psychiatrists. Anything I remembered might help the police.

Nobody but me knew what my abductor looked like. I'd done my best to describe him, but my descriptions, while detailed, were probably too personal, intimate and distorted by fear. I had no idea how an outsider would see him; I rarely even saw him dressed. I didn't know what he did for a living or where he lived.

I was his prisoner for nearly four months, but I'd been unconscious when he took me into his house, and all I knew of it, all I was ever allowed to see, was one bedroom, bathroom and closet. Under careful questioning from the police, with help from an architect, a very vague and general picture emerged: it was a single-storey house on a quiet residential street, in a neighbourhood that probably dated back to the 1940s or even earlier. (Nobody had used bathroom tiles like that since the 1950s; the small size of the closet dated it, and so did the thickness of the internal doors.) There were no houses like that in my parents' neighbourhood, and all the newer subdivisions in the city could be ruled out, but that still left a lot of ground. It was even possible, since I had no idea how long I'd been unconscious in the back of his van after he grabbed me, that the monster lived and worked in another town entirely.

I wanted to help them catch him, of course. So although I hated thinking about it, and wanted only to absorb myself back into my own life with my parents, friends and school, I made myself return, in memory, to my prison and concentrated on details, but what was most vivid to me – the smell of dusty varnish or the pictures I thought I could make out in the grain of the wood floor; a crack in the ceiling, or the low roaring surf sound made by the central air conditioning at night – did not supply any useful clues to the police.

Five mornings a week the monster left the house and stayed

away all day. He would let me out to use the bathroom before he left, and then lock me into the closet. He'd fixed a sliding bolt on the outside of the big, heavy closet door, and once the door was shut and he slid the bolt home, I was trapped. But that was not enough for him: he added a padlock, to which he carried the only key. As he told me, if he didn't come home to let me out, I would *die* inside that closet, of hunger and thirst, so I had better pray nothing happened to him, because if it did, no one would ever find me.

That padlock wasn't his last word in security, either. He also locked the bedroom door, and before he left the house I always heard an electronic bleeping sound I recognized as being part of a security system. He had a burglar alarm, as well as locks on everything that could be secured shut.

All he left me with in the closet was a plastic bottle full of water, a blanket and a child's plastic potty that I couldn't bear to use. There was a light fixture in the ceiling, but he'd removed the light bulb, and the switch was on the other side of the locked door. At first I thought his decision to deprive me of light was just more of his meaningless cruelty, but later it occurred to me that it was just another example – like the padlock and the burglar alarm – of his overly cautious nature. He'd even removed the wooden hanging rod from the closet, presumably afraid that I might have been able to wrench it loose and use it as a weapon against him. I might have scratched him with a broken light bulb; big deal. It wouldn't have incapacitated him, but it might have hurt, and he wouldn't risk even the tiniest of hurts. He wanted total control.

So, all those daylight hours when I was locked into the closet, I was in the dark except for the light which seeped in around the edges of the door; mainly from the approximately three-quarters of an inch that was left between the bottom of the door and the floor. That was my window on the world. I thought it was larger than the gap beneath our doors at home; the police architect said it might have been because the carpet it had been cut to accommodate had been removed; alternatively, my captor might have replaced the original door because he didn't find it sturdy enough for the prison he had planned.

Whatever the reason, I was grateful that the gap was wide enough for me to look through. I would spend hours sometimes lying with my cheek flat against the floor peering sideways into the bedroom, not because it was interesting, but simply for the light and space that it offered in comparison to the tiny closet.

When I was in the closet, I could use my fingernails to scrape the dirt and varnish from the floorboards, or make pictures out of the shadows all around me; there was nothing else to look at except the dirty cream walls, and the most interesting thing there – the only thing that caught my eye and made me think – was a square outlined in silvery duct tape.

I knew what it was, because there was something very similar on one wall of my closet at home, and my parents had explained to me that it was only an access hatch, so a plumber could get at the bathroom plumbing, in case it ever needed to be fixed.

Once that had been explained, and I knew it wasn't the entrance to a secret passage or a hidden room, it became uninteresting to me. In the monster's closet, though, a plumbing access hatch took on a whole new glamour.

I thought it might be my way out. Even though I knew there was no window in the bathroom, and the only door connected it to the bedroom – it was at least an escape from the closet. I wasn't sure an adult could crawl through what looked like a square-foot opening, but I knew I could manage; I didn't care if I left a little skin behind.

I peeled off the strips of tape, got my fingers into the gap and, with a little bit of effort, managed to pry out the square of painted sheetrock. But I didn't uncover a way out. There were pipes revealed in a space between the walls, but that was all. There was no opening into the bathroom, no space for a creature larger than a mouse to squeeze into. And I probably don't need to say that I didn't find anything useful left behind by a forgetful plumber; no tools or playthings or stale snacks.

I wept with disappointment, and then I sealed it up again – carefully enough, I hoped, that the monster would never notice what I'd done. After that, for the next thirteen weeks or so, I never touched it.

But I looked at it often, that small square that so resembled a secret hatchway, a closed-off window, a hidden opening to somewhere else. There was so little else to look at in the closet, and my longing, my need, for escape was so strong, that of course I was drawn back to it. For the first few days I kept my back to it, and flinched away even from the thought of it, because it had been such a let-down, but after a week or so I chose to forget what I knew about it, and pretended that it really *was* a way out of the closet, a secret that the monster didn't know.

My favourite thing to think about, and the only thing that could comfort me enough to let me fall asleep, was home. Going home again. Being safely back at home with my parents and my little brother and Puzzle the cat, surrounded by all my own familiar things in my bedroom. It wasn't like the relaxation techniques the psychiatrist suggested, thinking myself into a place I loved. That didn't work. Just thinking about my home could make me cry, and bring me more rigidly awake on the hard floor in the dark narrow closet, too aware of all that I had lost, and how impossibly far away it was now. I had to do something else, I had to create a little routine, almost like a magic spell, a mental exercise that let me relax enough to sleep.

What I did was, I pretended I had never before stripped away the tape and lifted out that square of sheetrock in the wall. I was doing it for the first time. And this time, instead of pipes in a shallow cavity between two walls, I saw only darkness, a much deeper darkness than that which surrounded me in the closet, and which I knew was the opening to a tunnel.

It was kind of scary. I felt excited by the possibility of escape, but that dark entry into the unknown also frightened me. I didn't know where it went. Maybe it didn't go anywhere at all; maybe it would take me into even greater danger. But there was no real question about it; it looked like a way out, so of course I was going to take it.

I squeezed through the opening and crawled through darkness along a tunnel which ended abruptly in a blank wall. Only the wall was not entirely blank; when I ran my hands over it I could feel the faint outline of a square had been cut away – just like in the closet I'd escaped from, only at this end the tape was on the other side.

I gave it a good, hard punch and knocked out the piece of sheetrock, and then I crawled through, and found myself in another closet. Only this one was ordinary, familiar and friendly, with carpet comfy underfoot, clothes hanging down overhead, and when I grasped the smooth metal of the doorknob it turned easily in my hand and let me out into my own beloved bedroom.

After that, the fantasy could take different courses. Sometimes I rushed to find my parents. I might find them downstairs, awake and drinking coffee in the kitchen, or they might be asleep in their bed, and I'd crawl in beside them to be cuddled and comforted as they assured me there was nothing to fear, it was only a bad dream. At other times I just wandered around the house, rediscovering the ordinary domestic landscape, reclaiming it for my own, until finally I fell asleep.

My captivity continued, with little to distinguish one day from another until the time that I got sick. Then, the monster was so disgusted by me, or so fearful of contagion, that he hardly touched me for a couple of days; his abstinence was no sign of compassion. It didn't matter to him if I was vomiting, or shaking with feverish chills, I was locked into the closet and left to suffer alone as usual.

I tried to lose myself in my comfort-dream, but the fever made it difficult to concentrate on anything. Even in the well-rehearsed routine, I kept mentally losing my place, having to go back and start over again, continuously peeling the tape off the wall and prying out that square of sheetrock, again and again, until, finding it unexpectedly awkward to hold, I lost my grip and the thing came crashing down painfully on my foot.

It was only then, as I blinked away the reflexive tears and rubbed the soreness out of my foot, that I realized it had really happened: I wasn't just imagining it; in my feverish stupor I'd actually stood up, pulled off the tape and opened a hole in the wall.

And it really *was* a hole this time.

I stared, dumbfounded, not at pipes in a shallow cavity, but into blackness.

My heart began to pound. Fearful that I was just seeing things, I bent over and stuck my head into it, flinching a little, expecting to meet resistance. But my head went in, and my chest and arms . . . I stretched forward and wriggled into the tunnel.

It was much lower than in my fantasy, not big enough to allow me to crawl. If I'd been a couple of years older or five pounds heavier I don't think I would have made it. Only because I was such a flat-chested, narrow-hipped, skinny little kid did I fit, and I had to wriggle and worm my way along like some legless creature.

I didn't care. I didn't think about getting stuck, and I didn't worry about the absolute, suffocating blackness stretching ahead. This was freedom. I kept my eyes shut and hauled myself forward on hands and elbows, pushing myself ahead with my toes. Somehow I kept going, although the energy it took was immense, almost more than I possessed. I was drenched in sweat and gasping – the sound of my own breathing was like that of a monster in pursuit – but I didn't give up. I could not.

And then I came to the end, a blank wall. But that didn't worry me, because I'd already dreamed of this moment, and I knew what to do. I just had to knock out the bit of plasterboard. Nothing but tape held it in. One good punch would do it.

Only I was so weak from illness, from captivity, from the long, slow, journey through the dark, that I doubted I had a good punch in me. But I couldn't give up now. I braced my legs on either side of the tunnel and pushed with all my might, pushed so hard I thought my lungs would burst. I battered it with my fists, and heard the feeble sound of my useless blows like hollow laughter. Finally, trembling with exhaustion, sweating rivers, I hauled back, gathered all the power I had left, and launched myself forward, using my head as a battering ram.

And that did it. On the other side of the wall the tape tore away, and as the square of sheetrock fell out and into my bedroom closet, so did I.

I was home. I was really and truly home at last.

I wanted to go running and calling for my mother, but first I stopped to repair the wall, carefully fitting the square of sheetrock back into place, and restoring the pieces of tape that had held it in, smoothing over the torn bits as best I could. It seemed important to do this, as if I might be drawn back along through the tunnel, back to that prison-house, if I didn't seal up the exit.

By the time I finished that, I was exhausted. I walked out of the closet, tottered across the room to my bed, pulled back the sheet and lay down, naked as I was.

It was there, like that, my little brother found me a few hours later.

★

Even I knew my escape was impossible. At least, it could not have happened in the way I remembered. Just to be sure, my parents opened the plumbing access hatch in my closet, to prove that's all it was. There was no tunnel; no way in or out.

Yet I had come home.

My parents – and I guess the police, too – thought the monster had been frightened by my illness into believing I might die, and had brought me home. Maybe he'd picked the locks (we didn't have a burglar alarm), or maybe – because a small window in one of the upstairs bathrooms turned out to have been left unfastened – he'd carried me up a ladder and pushed me through. My 'memory' was only a fevered, feverish dream.

Did it matter that I couldn't remember what really happened? My parents decided it did not, and that the excruciating regime of having to talk about my ordeal was only delaying my recovery, and they brought it to an end.

The years passed. I went to a new junior high, and then on to high school. I learned to drive. I started thinking about college. I didn't have a boyfriend, but it began to seem like a possibility. I'm not saying I forgot what had happened to me, but it was no longer fresh, it wasn't present, it belonged to the past, which became more and more blurred and distant as I struck out for adulthood and independence. The only thing that really bothered me, the real, continuing legacy of those few months when I'd been the monster's prisoner and plaything, were the dreams. Or, I should say, dream, because there was just the one, the closet dream.

Even after so many years, I did not have ordinary dreams. Night after night – and it was a rare night it did not happen – I fell asleep only to wake, suddenly, and find myself in that closet again. It was awful, but I kind of got used to it. You can get used to almost anything. So when it happened, I didn't panic, but tried practising the relaxation techniques I'd been taught when I was younger, and eventually – sometimes it took just a few minutes, while other nights it seemed to take hours – I escaped back into sleep.

One Saturday, a few weeks before my seventeenth birthday, I happened to be in a part of town that was strange to me. I was looking for a summer job, and was on my way to a shopping mall I knew only by name, and somehow or other, because I wanted to avoid the freeways, I got a little lost. I saw a sign for a U-Tote-Em and pulled into the parking lot to figure it out. Although I had an indexed map book, I must have been looking on the wrong page; after a few hot, sweaty minutes of frustration I threw it down and got out of the car, deciding to go into the store to ask directions, and buy myself a drink to cool me down.

I had just taken a Dr Pepper out of the refrigerator cabinet when something made me look around. It was him. The monster was standing in the very next aisle, a loaf of white bread in one hand as he browsed a display of chips and dips.

My hands were colder than the bottle. My feet felt very far away from my head. I couldn't move, and I couldn't stop looking at him.

My attention made him look up. For a moment he just looked blank and kind of stupid, his lower lip thrust out and shining with saliva. Then his mouth snapped shut as he tensed up, and his eyes kind of bulged, and I knew that he'd recognized me, too.

I dropped the plastic bottle and ran. Somebody said something – I think it was the guy behind the counter – but I didn't stop. I didn't even pause, just hurled myself at the door and got out. I couldn't think about anything but escape; it never occurred to me that *he* might have had more to fear than I did, that I could have asked the guy behind the counter to call the police, or just dialled 911 myself on my cell. All that was too rational, and I was way too frightened to reason. The old animal brain, instinct, had taken over, and all I could think of was running away and hiding.

I was so out of my mind with fear that instead of going back to my car I turned in the other direction, ran around to the back of the store, then past the dry cleaner's next door, and hid myself, gasping for breath in the torrid afternoon heat, behind a dumpster.

Still panting with terror, shaking so much I could barely control my movements, I fumbled inside my purse, searching for my phone. My hands were so cold I couldn't feel a thing; impatient, I sank into a squat and dumped the contents on the gritty cement surface, found the little silver gadget and snatched it up.

Then I hesitated. Maybe I shouldn't call 911; that was supposed to be for emergencies only, wasn't it? Years ago the police had given me a phone number to call if I ever remembered something more or learned something that might give them a handle on the monster's identity. That number was pinned to the bulletin board in the kitchen where I saw it every single day. It was engraved on my memory still, although I'd never used it, I knew exactly what numbers to press. But when I tried, my fingers were still so stiff and clumsy with fear that I kept messing up.

I stopped and concentrated on calming myself. Looking around the side of the dumpster I could see a quiet, tree-lined residential street. It was an old neighbourhood – you could tell that by the age of the trees, and the fact that it had sidewalks. I was gazing at this peaceful view, feeling my breath and pulse rate going back to normal, when I caught another glimpse of the monster.

Immediately, I shrank back and held my breath, but he never looked up as he walked, hunched a little forward as he clutched a brown paper bag to his chest, eyes on the sidewalk in front of him. He never suspected my eyes were on him, and as I watched his jerky, shuffling progress – as if he wanted to run but didn't dare – I realized how much our encounter had rattled him. All at once I was calmer. He must know I would call the police, and he was trying to get away, to hide. That he was on foot told me he must live nearby; probably the clerk in the convenience store would recognize him as a local, and the police would not have far to look for him.

But that was only if he stayed put. What if he was planning to leave? He might hurry home, grab a few things, jump in the car and lose himself in another city where he'd never be found.

I was filled with a righteous fury. I was not going to let him escape. He'd just passed out of sight when I decided to follow him.

I kept well back and off the sidewalk, darting in and out of the trees, keeping to the shade, not because I was afraid, but because I didn't want to alert him. I was determined to find out where he lived, to get his address and the license number of his car, and then I'd hand him over to the police.

After two blocks, he turned onto another street. I hung back, looking for the name of it, but the street sign was on the opposite corner where the lacy fronds of a mimosa tree hung down, obscuring it.

That didn't really matter. All I had to do was tell the police his house was two blocks off Montrose – was that the name? All at once I was uncertain of where I'd just been, the name of the thoroughfare the U-Tote-Em was on, where I'd left my car. But I could find my way back and meet the police there, just as soon as I saw which house the monster went into.

So I hurried after, suddenly fearful that he might give me the slip, and I was just in time to see him going up the front walk of a single-storey, pink-brick house, digging into his pocket for the key to the shiny black front door.

I made no effort to hide now, stopping directly across the street in the open, beneath the burning sun. I looked across at the raised curbstone where the house number had been painted. But the paint had been laid down a long time ago and not renewed; black and white had together faded into the grey of the concrete, and I couldn't be sure after the first number – definitely a 2 – if the next three were sixes, or eights, or some combination.

As he slipped the key into the lock the monster suddenly turned his head and stared across the street. He was facing me, looking right at me, and yet I had the impression he didn't see me watching him, because he didn't look scared or worried any more. In fact, he was smiling; a horrible, familiar smile that I knew all too well.

I raised the phone to summon the police, but my hand was empty. I grabbed for my purse, but it had gone, too. There was no canvas strap slung across my shoulder. As I groped for it, my fingers felt only skin: my own, naked flesh. Where were my clothes? How could I have come out without getting dressed?

The smells of dust and ancient varnish and my own sour sweat filled my nose and I began to tremble as I heard the sound of his key in the lock and woke from the dream that was my only freedom, and remembered.

Something terrible happened to me when I was a little girl.

It's still happening.

Born Dead

'Born dead' is such a creepy phrase, not just for the inherent sadness of what it means, but because there's a sort of linguistic disconnect between the two words. Birth is about the beginning of life – death comes at the end – so how can anyone be 'born dead'? I often find the inspiration for a story in a turn of phrase, and so it was here, as I tried to imagine a newborn baby that could be both dead and alive, in a liminal state between life and death – undead without being a vampire or a zombie, and with the ability to inspire love. As the story developed, I found myself thinking about the ideas people have about what life should *be – our fantasies about what we think is lacking, what is normal, expected, or necessary to make one's life complete.*

FLORIDA MCAFEE WAS ABOUT THE LAST PERSON I would have imagined getting pregnant by accident, or, to be honest, in any other way, for although she was beautiful – even when she was over sixty her tall, willowy figure, large lustrous eyes and high cheekbones attracted admiring looks – there was something *noli me tangere* about her, and while she had dated an impressive variety of men over the years, she hadn't married or lived with any of them.

I assumed she preferred to live alone, that it had been a positive choice, rather than it being something that had just happened while she'd been so busy with her career. If she'd wanted a family, I reasoned, surely she could have managed that emotional juggling act with the same skill she'd brought to establishing an internationally famous clothing brand.

She was my heroine. Her example declared it was possible

for a woman to become rich and powerful entirely by her own efforts, and without compromising her beliefs. I needed to believe she was single and childless by choice, not because her kind of success was incompatible with family life. Not every woman wanted children – I still wasn't sure myself – and if marriage was really so wonderful, why did so many of them end in divorce?

I'd been working for her for seven years – not directly, but climbing the corporate ladder in a way that had attracted her notice, until I was the head of division, London-based in theory but actually spending most of my life in other parts of the world. It was fun, exciting, rewarding, exhausting, all those good things, and as much as I was enjoying myself, I knew it couldn't last forever.

Crunch-time was coming, and I was going to have to make decisions that would affect the rest of my life.

By many standards I was successful – I made good money, I liked my job, what I did made a difference. But I was not yet where I wanted to be. If I was to make my youthful dreams come true I had to cut loose and start up my own business. It would be risky, and lots more hard work, but neither of those things scared me. I even had an idea that I knew I could turn into a marketable business plan, and the time seemed right to launch it.

But even as I was aware of the opportunities opening up in the business world, I saw the entrance to another world shrinking. I was well into my thirties, young and fit in terms of work, many productive years ahead of me, but the window to motherhood – maybe even to marriage – was narrowing by the day, and if I didn't do something about it soon it would close, and I would end up by myself. Maybe that suited Florida, but it gave me a chill to think of growing old alone. And it was looking more likely by the day: I might have been too busy to care, but the simple fact was that I hadn't had so much as a date in nearly a year. More and more, the men I met through work were married – recently, happily, smugly, sporting their new, gold rings. Not that they were better, smarter, or luckier than me, but they had been quicker off the mark, realizing what they wanted, and going after it. It had taken me so long to notice that life's dance floor was almost filled with couples, and I was going to have to put some serious effort into finding a partner, if that's what I really wanted.

The obvious thing to do, if I was serious about wanting to meet someone, was to go out more, to places where that might happen. Join a club, try something different, spend less time working . . .

Exactly the opposite, in fact, of what was required for my start-up. For that, I needed to concentrate on wooing investors, a different pool from potential husbands.

The thought of putting my business plans on hold made me even more uneasy. What if somebody else took my idea and ran with it? Things can change awfully fast, and if you drop out for a couple of years, nobody holds your place. You have to start all over again. And if I came back from my sabbatical a bride, people would wonder how soon I'd get pregnant, and how I'd manage to divide my attention between home and business. Of course it wasn't fair, since a man getting married proved how solid and dependable and *bankable* he was, but there was no sense whining about that.

Florida always took a mentoring interest in her employees, especially the most ambitious, workaholic females. Her latest invitation to lunch arrived in the midst of my soul-searching, and while I didn't want to let her know I might be leaving her employ, I had hopes that she'd provide the answer.

I'd made some vague remark about the difficulty of balancing outside work with childcare when she suddenly asked me if I'd ever been pregnant.

'No,' I said. 'But I'm keeping my options open. I'm on the pill.'

'So was I.' She gave me a long, measuring look before going on. 'I thought it was making me bloated. And when I stopped, and didn't get a period, I thought it was just my body readjusting.' She looked down and toyed with her salad. 'It never once occurred to me that I might be pregnant.'

I felt shocked, and a little queasy, wondering why she'd decided to confide in me, but said nothing.

'I was nearly forty,' she went on. 'So, the fact that I'd put on a little weight, that I wasn't having periods, that I felt strange . . . I put it down to the menopause. I didn't go to a doctor; why should I? No one else noticed anything odd. Something about the way the baby was lying meant I never looked pregnant.'

'When did you realize?'

'After I gave birth.'

This was so unexpected, I could do nothing but gape.

'I know, it sounds mad,' she said calmly, taking a tiny bite of her salad. 'But I never guessed. I had been feeling constipated for several days, and then one evening, just as I got home, I started getting pains, low in my belly. I thought it must have been something I ate. The pain came and went through the night, but it wasn't until the baby actually came out of me that I realized. And by the time I understood I was pregnant – well, I wasn't anymore.'

She fell silent, looking weary, and for the first time I saw her as an old woman.

'So what did you do then?'

'Well, I picked him up, I cuddled him . . . I thought how strange he looked. It still seemed unreal to me, what had happened. I got a knife to cut the cord – I didn't sterilize it; how could I, on my own, holding a baby, still attached to me . . . it was a clean knife, from the kitchen, and I just had to hope it was clean enough. I guess it was. I couldn't think what to do with the cord, or the other stuff – placenta – it seemed wrong to just stuff it all in the bin, but that's what I did. I cleaned up as best I could, although there was a spot on the carpet I never could get out – I finally had to get new carpet laid – and then I ran a bath . . .'

Impatient with all this detail, the pointless obsession with carpeting, I interrupted: 'But what about the baby?'

'Oh, I took him into the bath with me, of course. I got him all nice and clean, and then I used a hand towel, the softest one I had, to dry him. I wished I had some clothes for him, but of course I didn't, why would I, when I'd never expected . . . ? I thought I could make a nappy out of a square of cloth, but the tea towels were too rough, and I had only a few silk scarves, and they weren't the right shape. I thought about cutting up a pashmina, which was certainly soft enough, but one was black and the other pink . . .' She met my gaze and made an ironic mouth. 'Of course, it was absurd, but people do often focus on irrelevant details when they've had a shock. I thought about going out to buy something, but I was so tired, and it was so late at night . . . In the end, I just cleared out a drawer, and lined it with both pashminas, and laid him down in that, just pulling the edge of the pink one up to his chin. He looked so sweet lying there, so peaceful, I could almost believe he was asleep.'

I felt a sickening pang as I understood. 'He wasn't? He died? Or . . . he was born dead?'

'He never made a sound, never opened his eyes. Never took a breath.'

I wondered, with an odd, internal lurch, half excitement, half fear, if I was hearing the confession of an old crime.

'What did you do?'

She gave the tiniest shrug, as if to say I should have known. 'I went to bed. I slept, so deeply that in the morning it all seemed like a dream. I was still tired when the alarm went, too tired to think, really. I got dressed and went to work as usual.'

'But the baby?'

She shot me a look that said I wasn't paying attention. 'I told you, I put him in a drawer.'

I'd been imagining that drawer pulled out. I shut my mouth and nodded.

The waiter arrived to ask if everything was all right. Florida indicated that he should take away her largely untouched salad, and, having lost my appetite, I did the same.

'Would you like something else?'

'Just coffee, thank you.'

When we were alone again, she continued her story. 'Two days later, I flew to New York. We were in the middle of negotiations, hoping to establish the brand in America, and so, for the next few months, I was hardly at home at all, rarely for more than a few nights. It was one of those nights, or early mornings, when I was so jet-lagged I hardly knew what time it was, and so wired on the excitement of building my own company into a global brand that I didn't care, that I happened to notice that small, dark patch on my bedroom carpet, and suddenly all the details rushed back, and I broke out in a cold sweat.

'I opened the drawer and there was my baby, looking just as sweet and peaceful as the day he was born, and yet . . . not exactly. Even before I picked him up I could see signs of change.'

My stomach clenched as I anticipated the gory details to come, and wondered about the smell. But she surprised me again.

'He was bigger, plumper than when I'd last seen him, almost too big for the drawer. When I lifted him out, I could tell that he'd gained weight. I held him close and kissed him, and although his skin was cool to the touch, and he didn't breathe, he had that wonderful new baby smell. You know what I mean?'

'He was alive? After – how long since you left him there? A month?'

'Closer to three. No, he was still dead.'

'But you said that he'd grown, put on weight – that's impossible.' She had to be winding me up, but I couldn't imagine why, and it was totally out of character for the woman I knew.

The waiter arrived with our coffee, and she waited until he'd gone away again to say, quietly, intently, 'I know it's impossible, but it happened. I still can't explain it except to call it a miracle.'

I thought that was no explanation at all. 'So what did you do?'

'There was a twenty-four hour Asda or something not far away, so I went there and bought a cot and some clothes. After the end of the year, when I had more time at home, I redecorated the guest room for him. It was all right for a tiny baby to share my room, but he would need his own space as he was growing up.'

'You mean, he kept growing?'

'Yes. Just like a live baby.'

Maybe one thing was no more or less impossible than the other, but I was shocked. 'You mean, he didn't *stay* a baby? He grew into a little boy?'

'And then a bigger one.'

'Did you tell anyone?'

'Of course not.'

'Why not? If it really happened?'

'You don't believe me.' She looked amused. 'Of course not. What sane person would believe such an outrageous tale? Does that answer your question?'

'You could have taken him to a doctor.'

Her expression hardened. 'Take my dead boy to a doctor? Why?'

'To find out the reason – '

She shook her head at me. 'There is no reason, or not one that science can accept. If I turned up with a dead body of an unknown man, what do you suppose would happen?'

I shrugged as if I didn't know, but of course, I knew as well as she did that she'd have fallen under suspicion of murder, whether the body was that of a baby, or a young man.

'At the very least, they'd take him away from me. And if I told the truth, they'd lock me up. And bury David. Even if someone believed me, and decided to *observe* him for a few weeks, and saw he wasn't an ordinary corpse – what would be gained by that? We'd be a public freak show. I don't want that. Not for David, not for me. I thank my lucky stars that I've always been able to take care of him, that I have enough money.' She stopped abruptly and took a drink of coffee.

David. It was a nice name, I thought, Biblical, not exactly unusual, but kind of old-fashioned; I had the idea that it meant 'beloved'. It made the subject of Florida's story much more real to me, and I found myself wondering if other babies, born dead, had the potential to continue to grow, if Florida wasn't the first this had happened to, only the first to notice . . .

I caught myself, shocked by how easily I was sliding into belief. Was this some kind of weird test?

'And you've never told *anyone*?'

She had a pretty good poker face, did Florida, but that was a game I played, too. I saw something in her expression respond to my question; just the quickest, tiniest flicker, but when she assured me that she'd never told anyone but me, I knew she was lying. And as that occurred to me, I realized that nothing else she'd told me had felt like a lie. At the very least, *she* believed.

'So why are you telling me, now?'

She put down her cup and folded her hands together in front of her. 'I think you know I've always been impressed by your performance. You are a positive asset to the company, and I should be very sorry to lose you, if . . . well, I can understand if you are considering moving on, striking out on your own.'

I sat very still. I hadn't said a word to *anyone* about my plans. How could she know what I was thinking?

She grimaced. 'Maybe I'm projecting. You see, you rather remind me of myself at your age, and although my situation was quite different, if I were you, I'd be thinking that now was the time to aim higher, and that would have to mean striking out on my own.

'I'm nearly seventy,' she said. 'And although I'm not eager to retire, I can't keep working at the same pace. I know I will have to hand over to someone else.'

She didn't say 'That could be you,' but she paused, and my mouth went dry with excitement and apprehension.

She went on, 'Then there's David's welfare to consider. What happens to him when I die? I've made plenty of money, but he has special needs. I can't put the money into trust for him, or even open a bank account for him because, as far as the outside world is concerned, *he doesn't exist*.'

She sighed. 'If there were only someone I could trust to look after him when I'm gone . . . It wouldn't be difficult. He's so undemanding. Of course, if the two were tied in together – unofficially, of course – the running of the business, caring for my son – I've always known that I couldn't pass it on to him, but as long as he benefits from my success, I'd be happy.' She gave me a look I'd never expected or imagined to see from my boss, the famously powerful, self-sufficient Florida McAfee, a look that was anxious and hopeful and almost pleading.

I said, 'I'd like to meet this son of yours.'

We both made calls to reschedule our afternoons. It took her longer than me, not because she had more scheduled, but because her personal assistant was still very new to the job, and needed to be talked through it all. The woman who'd worked for her in that capacity for over a decade had left a few months earlier, to start a new life in Australia after coming into an unexpected inheritance or winning some lottery – I wasn't sure of the exact details, just that she was now rich and somewhere far away.

When we were done, Florida's driver took us to her house in Holland Park. The journey passed without conversation; she was busy with her iPhone, and I was too nervous to speak. This was a first for me, and I'd never heard of anyone being invited to her home. When she entertained, she rented some appropriate venue, a nightclub in central London or a villa in Italy.

The house was smaller than I'd expected, just an ordinary house on a quiet street. After entering, she took me straight upstairs.

The room behind the locked door was small, no bigger than my own walk-in wardrobe, kitted out like a home office with built-in shelves, desk and filing cabinet. But this was only a front: as she explained, 'I was afraid that I might get a cleaner for whom a locked door was just too tempting to resist. And the more difficult I made the lock, the more likely it would seem there was something worth stealing, worth gossiping about, and attracting the attention of burglars.'

She pulled out a book in the middle of the third shelf down, revealing an electronic keypad. She keyed in a number and the bookshelf-wall opened to reveal a bedroom.

There was a window, on the back wall, curtains open, letting in the soft light of late afternoon. If a burglar had looked in, he'd see a few things worth stealing, although they were no more than the electronic goodies any reasonably well-off young man might own: the sleek laptop, the iPod in a Bose docking system. But if he saw those things, he'd also see their owner, stretched out, fully clothed, on top of the bed, as if asleep. It would take a little while, or a much closer inspection, to recognize the sleeper as a dead man.

'David,' said Florida, in a peculiarly gentle voice I'd never heard her use before. 'Darling, I've brought someone to meet you. I've told you about her. It's Leslie . . . you remember, I've told you about the clever girl I put in charge of R&D?'

Part of me wanted to turn and run like hell. And if I had, I have no doubt there would have been a handsome severance package in my near future, and maybe that would have been just the spur I needed to get out and start up my own company, although it's likely there would have been some sort of non-competition clause to encourage me to go to New Zealand or Canada, or at least far enough from London so Florida wouldn't have to see my face again.

But I was curious. I had to see him for myself, had to confront Florida's secret. I would have to stare down at his closed, handsome face, and touch his cool skin; hold his unresponsive hand in mine; spend time with him, trying to know him, to figure out who he was and what was meant by his existence.

Later, in the weeks and months to come, Florida answered my questions as best she could, as she described her attempts to be a good mother to a child who could not respond, but she could never explain the mystery of their relationship to my satisfaction. Unlike David, I kept asking for more.

But she didn't mind. My questions, my refusal to go away, confirmed that she'd been right in her choice, and that both her business and her son would be safe with me. Just as, in the past, she'd bought him new clothes when he outgrew the old ones, bought him toys and games and books and music, trying to give him what every boy should have, redecorating his room every few years so that it better reflected his age, and filling it with all the latest things, all the treasures she had purchased, as if they were offerings left in the tomb of a young prince, now she had brought him her final gift, me.

Reader, I married him.

Replacements

This must be one of my best-known short stories. It was first published in Dennis Etchison's outstanding 1992 anthology MetaHorror, *then included in two "best of the year" anthologies in addition to more than half-a-dozen other anthologies over the next two decades, including that impressive compendium of dark and imaginative fiction,* The Weird, *edited by Ann and Jeff VanderMeer. It was also the basis for an episode of the Canadian TV series* The Hunger *(not that I could see much resemblance). It is one of the stories that really seems to strike a chord with many readers ("Flying to Byzantium" in* A Nest of Nightmares *is another.) It began with my reflecting on how strange it is that something one person finds irresistibly attractive could provoke outright disgust in another. And it is surely not insignificant that at the time of writing, I was still adjusting (a few months post-partum) to new motherhood.*

WALKING THROUGH GREY NORTH LONDON to the tube station, feeling guilty that he hadn't let Jenny drive him to work and yet relieved to have escaped another pointless argument, Stuart Holder glanced down at a pavement covered in a leaf-fall of fast food cartons and white paper bags and saw, amid the dog turds, beer cans, and dead cigarettes, something horrible.

It was about the size of a cat, naked-looking, with leathery, hairless skin and thin, spiky limbs that seemed too frail to support the bulbous, ill-proportioned body. The face, with tiny bright eyes and a wet slit of a mouth, was like an evil monkey's. It saw him and moved in a crippled, spasmodic way. Reaching up, it made a clotted, strangled noise. The sound touched a nerve, like metal between the teeth, and the sight of it, mewling and choking and scrabbling, scaly claws flexing and wriggling, made him feel sick and terrified. He had no phobias, he found insects fascinating, not frightening, and regularly removed, unharmed, the spiders, wasps, and mayflies which made Jenny squeal or shudder helplessly.

But this was different. This wasn't some rare species of wingless bat escaped from a zoo, it wasn't something he would find pictured in any reference book. It was something that should not exist, a mistake, something alien. It did not belong in his world.

A little snarl escaped him and he took a step forward and brought his foot down hard.

The small, shrill scream lanced through him as he crushed it beneath his shoe and ground it into the road.

Afterwards, as he scraped the sole of his shoe against the curb to clean it, nausea overwhelmed him. He leaned over and vomited helplessly into a red-and-white-striped box of chicken bones and crumpled paper.

He straightened up, shaking, and wiped his mouth again and again with his pocket handkerchief. He wondered if anyone had seen, and had a furtive look around. Cars passed at a steady crawl. Across the road a cluster of schoolgirls dawdled near a man smoking in front of a newsagent's, but on this side of the road the fried chicken franchise and bathroom suppliers had yet to open for the day and the nearest pedestrians were more than a hundred yards away.

Until that moment, Stuart had never killed anything in his life. Mosquitoes and flies of course, other insects probably, a nest of hornets once, that was all. He had never liked the idea of hunting, never lived in the country. He remembered his father putting out poisoned bait for rats, and he remembered shying bricks at those same vermin on a bit of waste ground where he had played as a boy. But rats weren't like other animals; they elicited no sympathy. Some things had to be killed if they would not be driven away.

He made himself look to make sure the thing was not still alive. Nothing should be left to suffer. But his heel had crushed the thing's face out of recognition, and it was unmistakably dead. He felt a cool tide of relief and satisfaction, followed at once, as he walked away, by a nagging uncertainty, the imminence of guilt. Was he right to have killed it, to have acted on violent, irrational impulse? He didn't even know what it was. It might have been somebody's pet.

He went hot and cold with shame and self-disgust. At the corner he stopped with five or six others waiting to cross the road and because he didn't want to look at them he looked down.

And there it was, alive again.

He stifled a scream. No, of course it was not the same one, but another. His leg twitched; he felt frantic with the desire to kill it, and the terror of his desire. The thin wet mouth was moving as if it wanted to speak.

As the crossing signal began its nagging blare he tore his eyes away from the creature squirming at his feet. Everyone else had started to cross the street, their eyes, like their thoughts, directed ahead. All except one. A woman in a smart business suit was standing still on the pavement, looking down, a sick fascination on her face.

As he looked at her looking at it, the idea crossed his mind that he should kill it for her, as a chivalric, protective act. But she wouldn't see it that way. She would be repulsed by his violence. He didn't want her to think he was a monster. He didn't want to be the monster who had exulted in the crunch of fragile bones, the flesh and viscera merging pulpily beneath his shoe.

He forced himself to look away, to cross the road, to spare the alien life. But he wondered, as he did so, if he had been right to spare it.

*

he made himself a cup of tea, cursed, poured it down the sink, and had a stiff whiskey instead. He had just finished it and was feeling much better when he heard the street door open.

'Oh!' The look on her face reminded him unpleasantly of those women in the office this morning, making him feel like an intruder in his own place. Now Jenny smiled, but it was too late. 'I didn't expect you to be here so early.'

'Nor me. I tried to call you, but they said you'd left already. I wondered if you were feeling all right.'

'I'm fine!'

'You look fine.' The familiar sight of her melted away his irritation. He loved the way she looked: her slender, boyish figure, her close-cropped, curly hair, her pale complexion and bright blue eyes.

Her cheeks now had a slight hectic flush. She caught her bottom lip between her teeth and gave him an assessing look before coming straight out with it. 'How would you feel about keeping a pet?'

Stuart felt a horrible conviction that she was not talking about a dog or a cat. He wondered if it was the whiskey on an empty stomach which made him feel dizzy.

'It was under my car. If I hadn't happened to notice something moving down there I could have run over it.' She lifted her shoulders in a delicate shudder.

'Oh, God, Jenny, you haven't brought it home!'

She looked indignant. 'Well, of course I did! I couldn't just leave it in the street – somebody else might have run it over.'

Or stepped on it, he thought, realizing now that he could never tell Jenny what he had done. That made him feel even worse, but maybe he was wrong. Maybe it was just a cat she'd rescued. 'What is it?'

She gave a strange, excited laugh. 'I don't know. Something very rare, I think. Here, look.' She slipped the large, woven bag off her shoulder, opening it, holding it out to him. 'Look. Isn't it the sweetest thing?'

How could two people who were so close, so alike in so many ways, see something so differently? He only wanted to kill it, even now, while she had obviously fallen in love. He kept his face carefully neutral although he couldn't help flinching from her description. '*Sweet?*'

It gave him a pang to see how she pulled back, holding the bag protectively close as she said, 'Well, I know it's not pretty, but so what? I thought it was horrible, too, at first sight . . .' Her face clouded, as if she found her first impression difficult to remember, or to credit, and her voice faltered a little. 'But then, then I realized how *helpless* it was. It needed me. It can't help how it looks. Anyway, doesn't it kind of remind you of the Psammead?'

'The what?'

'Psammead. You know, *The Five Children and It*?'

He recognized the title but her passion for old-fashioned children's books was something he didn't share. He shook his head impatiently. 'That thing didn't come out of a book, Jen. You found it in the street and you don't know what it is or where it came from. It could be dangerous, it could be diseased.'

'Dangerous,' she said in a withering tone.

'You don't know.'

'I've been with him all day and he hasn't hurt me, or anybody else at the office, he's perfectly happy being held, and he likes being scratched behind the ears.'

He did not miss the pronoun shift. 'It might have rabies.'

'Don't be silly.'

'Don't *you* be silly; it's not exactly native, is it? It might be carrying all sorts of foul parasites from South America or Africa or wherever.'

'Now you're being racist. I'm not going to listen to you. *And* you've been drinking.' She flounced out of the room.

If he'd been holding his glass still he might have thrown it. He closed his eyes and concentrated on breathing in and out slowly. This was worse than any argument they'd ever had, the only crucial disagreement of their marriage. Jenny had stronger views about many things than he did, so her wishes usually prevailed. He didn't mind that. But this was different. He wasn't having that creature in his home. He had to make her agree.

Necessity cooled his blood. He had his temper under control when his wife returned. 'I'm sorry,' he said, although she was the one who should have apologized. Still looking prickly, she shrugged and would not meet his eyes. 'Want to go out to dinner tonight?'

She shook her head. 'I'd rather not. I've got some work to do.'

'Can I get you something to drink? I'm only one whiskey ahead of you, honest.'

Her shoulders relaxed. 'I'm sorry. Low blow. Yeah, pour me one. And one for yourself.' She sat down on the couch, her bag by her feet. Leaning over, reaching inside, she cooed, 'Who's my little sweetheart, then?'

Normally he would have taken a seat beside her. Now, though, he eyed the pale, misshapen bundle on her lap and, after handing her a glass, retreated across the room. 'Don't get mad, but isn't having a pet one of those things we discuss and agree on beforehand?'

He saw the tension come back into her shoulders, but she went on stroking the thing, keeping herself calm. 'Normally, yes. But this is special. I didn't plan it. It happened, and now I've got a responsibility to him. Or her.' She giggled. 'We don't even know what sex you are, do we, my precious?'

He said carefully, 'I can see that you had to do something when you found it, but keeping it might not be the best thing.'

'I'm not going to put it out in the street.'

'No, no, but . . . don't you think it would make sense to let a professional have a look at it? Take it to a vet, get it checked out . . . maybe it needs shots or something.'

She gave him a withering look and for a moment he faltered, but then he rallied. 'Come on, Jenny, be reasonable! You can't just drag some strange animal in off the street and keep it, just like that. You don't even know what it eats.'

'I gave it some fruit at lunch. It ate that. Well, it sucked out the juice. I don't think it can chew.'

'But you don't know, do you? Maybe the fruit juice was just an aperitif, maybe it needs half its weight in live insects every day, or a couple of small, live mammals. Do you really think you could cope with feeding it mice or rabbits fresh from the pet shop every week?'

'Oh, Stuart.'

'Well? Will you just take it to a vet? Make sure it's healthy? Will you do that much?'

'And then I can keep it? If the vet says there's nothing wrong with it, and it doesn't need to eat anything too impossible?'

'Then we can talk about it. Hey, don't pout at me; I'm not your father, I'm not telling you what to do. We're partners, and partners don't make unilateral decisions about things that affect them both; partners discuss things and reach compromises and . . .'

'There can't be any compromise about this.'

He felt as if she'd doused him with ice water. 'What?'

'Either I win and I keep him or you win and I give him up. Where's the compromise?'

This was why wars were fought, thought Stuart, but he didn't say it. He was the picture of sweet reason, explaining as if he meant it, 'The compromise is that we each try to see the other person's point. You get the animal checked out, make sure it's healthy and I, I'll keep an open mind about having a pet, and see if I might start liking . . . him. Does he have a name yet?'

Her eyes flickered. 'No . . . we can choose one later, together. If we keep him.'

He still felt cold and, although he could think of no reason for it, he was certain she was lying to him.

In bed that night as he groped for sleep Stuart kept seeing the tiny, hideous face of the thing screaming as his foot came down on it. That moment of blind, killing rage was not like him. He couldn't deny he had done it, or how he had felt, but now, as Jenny slept innocently beside him, as the creature she had rescued, a twin to his victim, crouched alive in the bathroom, he tried to remember it differently.

In fantasy, he stopped his foot, he controlled his rage and, staring at the memory of the alien animal, he struggled to see past his anger and his fear, to see through those fiercer masculine emotions and find his way to Jenny's feminine pity. Maybe his intuition had been wrong and hers was right. Maybe, if he had waited a little longer, instead of lashing out, he would have seen how unnecessary his fear was.

Poor little thing, poor little thing. It's helpless, it needs me, it's harmless so I won't harm it.

Slowly, in imagination, he worked toward that feeling, *her* feeling, and then, suddenly, he was there, through the anger, through the fear, through the hate to . . . not love, he couldn't say that, but compassion. Glowing and warm, compassion filled his heart and flooded his veins, melting the ice there and washing him out into the sea of sleep, and dreams where Jenny smiled and loved him and there was no space between them for misunderstanding.

He woke in the middle of the night with a desperate urge to pee. He was out of bed in the dark hallway when he remembered what was waiting in the bathroom. He couldn't go back to bed with the need unsatisfied, but he stood outside the bathroom door, hand hovering over the light switch on this side, afraid to turn it on, open the door, go in.

It wasn't, he realized, that he was afraid of a creature no bigger than a football and less likely to hurt him; rather, he was afraid that he might hurt it. It was a stronger variant of that reckless vertigo he had felt sometimes in high places, the fear, not of falling, but of throwing oneself off, of losing control and giving in to self-destructive urges. He didn't *want* to kill the thing – had his own feelings not undergone a sea change, Jenny's love for it would have been enough to stop him – but something, some dark urge stronger than himself, might make him.

Finally he went down to the end of the hall and outside to the weedy, muddy little area which passed for the communal front garden and in which the rubbish bins, of necessity, were kept, and, shivering in his thin cotton pyjamas in the damp, chilly air, he watered the sickly forsythia, or whatever it was, that Jenny had planted so optimistically last winter.

When he went back inside, more uncomfortable than when he had gone out, he saw the light was on in the bathroom, and as he approached the half-open door, he heard Jenny's voice, low and soothing. 'There, there. Nobody's going to hurt you, I promise. You're safe here. Go to sleep now. Go to sleep.'

He went past without pausing, knowing he would be viewed as an intruder, and got back into bed. He fell asleep, lulled by the meaningless murmur of her voice, still waiting for her to join him.

Stuart was not used to doubting Jenny, but when she told him she had visited a veterinarian who had given her new pet a clean bill of health, he did not believe her.

In a neutral tone he asked, 'Did he say what kind of animal it was?'

'He didn't know.'

'He didn't know what it was, but he was sure it was perfectly healthy.'

'God, Stuart, what do you want? It's obvious to everybody but you that my little friend is healthy and happy. What do you want, a birth certificate?'

He looked at her 'friend', held close against her side, looking squashed and miserable. 'What do you mean, "everybody"?'

She shrugged. 'Everybody at work. They're all jealous as anything.' She planted a kiss on the thing's pointy head. Then she looked at him, and he realized that she had not kissed him, as she usually did, when he came in. She'd been clutching that thing the whole time. 'I'm going to keep him,' she said quietly. 'If you don't like it, then . . .' Her pause seemed to pile up in solid, transparent blocks between them. 'Then, I'm sorry, but that's how it is.'

So much for an equal relationship, he thought. So much for sharing. Mortally wounded, he decided to pretend it hadn't happened.

'Want to go out for Indian tonight?'

She shook her head, turning away. 'I want to stay in. There's something on telly. You go on. You could bring me something back, if you wouldn't mind. A spinach bhaji and a couple of naans would do me.'

'And what about . . . something for your little friend?'

She smiled a private smile. 'He's all right. I've fed him already.'

Then she raised her eyes to his and acknowledged his effort. 'Thanks.'

He went out and got take-away for them both, and stopped at the off-license for the Mexican beer Jenny favoured. A radio in the off-license was playing a sentimental song about love that Stuart remembered from his earliest childhood: his mother used to sing it. He was shocked to realize he had tears in his eyes.

That night Jenny made up the sofa bed in the spare room, explaining, 'He can't stay in the bathroom; it's just not satisfactory, you know it's not.'

'He needs the bed?'

'I do. He's confused, everything is new and different, I'm the one thing he can count on. I have to stay with him. He needs me.'

'He needs you? What about me?'

'Oh, Stuart,' she said impatiently. 'You're a grown man. You can sleep by yourself for a night or two.'

'And that thing can't?'

'Don't call him a thing.'

'What am I supposed to call it? Look, you're not its mother – it doesn't need you as much as you'd like to think. It was perfectly all right in the bathroom last night – it'll be fine in here on its own.'

'Oh? And what do you know about it? You'd like to kill him, wouldn't you? Admit it.'

'No,' he said, terrified that she had guessed the truth. If she knew how he had killed one of those things she would never forgive him. 'It's not true, I don't – I couldn't hurt it any more than I could hurt you.'

Her face softened. She believed him. It didn't matter how he felt about the creature. Hurting it, knowing how she felt, would be like committing an act of violence against her, and they both knew he wouldn't do that. 'Just for a few nights, Stuart. Just until he settles in.'

He had to accept that. All he could do was hang on, hope that she still loved him and that this wouldn't be forever.

The days passed. Jenny no longer offered to drive him to work. When he asked her, she said it was out of her way and with traffic so bad a detour would make her late. She said it was silly to take him the short distance to the station, especially as there was nowhere she could safely stop to let him out, and anyway, the walk would do him good. They were all good reasons, which he had used in the old days himself, but her excuses struck him painfully when he remembered how eager she had once been for his company, how ready to make any detour for his sake. Her new pet accompanied her everywhere, even to work, snug in the little nest she had made for it in a woven carrier bag.

'Of course things are different now. But I haven't stopped loving you,' she said when he tried to talk to her about the breakdown of their marriage. 'It's not like I've found another man. This is something completely different. It doesn't threaten you; you're still my husband.'

But it was obvious to him that a husband was no longer something she particularly valued. He began to have fantasies about killing it. Not, this time, in a blind rage, but as part of a carefully thought-out plan. He might poison it, or spirit it away somehow and pretend it had run away. Once it was gone he hoped Jenny would forget it and be his again.

But he never had a chance. Jenny was quite obsessive about the thing, as if it were too valuable to be left unguarded for a single minute. Even when she took a bath, or went to the toilet, the creature was with her, behind the locked door of the bathroom. When he offered to look after it for her for a few minutes she just smiled, as if the idea was manifestly ridiculous, and he didn't dare insist.

So he went to work, and went out for drinks with colleagues, and spent what time he could with Jenny, although they were never alone. He didn't argue with her, although he wasn't above trying to move her to pity if he could. He made seemingly casual comments designed to convince her of his change of heart so that eventually, weeks or months from now, she would trust him and leave the creature with him – and then, later, perhaps, they could put their marriage back together.

One afternoon, after an extended lunch break, Stuart returned to the office to find one of the senior editors crouched on the floor beside his secretary's empty desk, whispering and chuckling to herself.

He cleared his throat nervously. 'Linda?'

She lurched back on her heels and got up awkwardly. She blushed and ducked her head as she turned, looking very unlike her usual high-powered self. 'Oh, uh, Stuart, I was just – '

Frankie came in with a pile of photocopying. 'Uh-huh,' she said loudly.

Linda's face got even redder. 'Just going,' she mumbled, and fled.

Before he could ask, Stuart saw the creature, another crippled bat-without-wings, on the floor beside the open bottom drawer of Frankie's desk. It looked up at him, opened its slit of a mouth and gave a sad little hiss. Around one matchstick-thin leg it wore a fine golden chain which was fastened at the other end to the drawer.

'Some people would steal anything that's not chained down,' said Frankie darkly. 'People you wouldn't suspect.'

He stared at her, letting her see his disapproval, his annoyance, disgust, even. 'Animals in the office aren't part of the contract, Frankie.'

'It's not an animal.'

'What is it, then?'

'I don't know. You tell me.'

'It doesn't matter what it is, you can't have it here.'

'I can't leave it at home.'

'Why not?'

She turned away from him, busying herself with her stacks of paper. 'I can't leave it alone. It might get hurt. It might escape.'

'Chance would be a fine thing.'

She shot him a look, and he was certain she knew he wasn't talking about *her* pet. He said, 'What does your boyfriend think about it?'

'I don't have a boyfriend.' She sounded angry but then, abruptly, the anger dissipated, and she smirked. 'I don't have to have one, do I?'

'You can't have that animal here. Whatever it is. You'll have to take it home.'

She raised her fuzzy eyebrows. 'Right now?'

He was tempted to say yes, but thought of the manuscripts that wouldn't be sent out, the letters that wouldn't be typed, the delays and confusions, and he sighed. 'Just don't bring it back again. All right?'

'Yowza.'

He felt very tired. He could tell her what to do but she would no more obey than would his wife. She would bring it back the next day and keep bringing it back, maybe keeping it hidden, maybe not, until he either gave in or was forced into firing her. He went into his office, closed the door, and put his head down on his desk.

That evening he walked in on his wife feeding the creature with her blood.

It was immediately obvious that it was that way round. The creature might be a vampire – it obviously was – but his wife was no helpless victim. She was wide awake and in control, holding the creature firmly, letting it feed from a vein in her arm.

She flinched as if anticipating a shout, but he couldn't speak. He watched what was happening without attempting to interfere and gradually she relaxed again, as if he wasn't there.

When the creature, sated, fell off, she kept it cradled on her lap and reached with her other hand for the surgical spirit and cotton wool on the table, moistened a piece of cotton wool and tamped it to the tiny wound. Then, finally, she met her husband's eyes.

'He has to eat,' she said reasonably. 'He can't chew. He needs blood. Not very much, but . . .'

'And he needs it from you? You can't . . . ?'

'I can't hold down some poor scared rabbit or dog for him, no.' She made a shuddering face. 'Well, really, think about it. You know how squeamish I am. This is so much easier. It doesn't hurt.'

It hurts me, he thought, but couldn't say it. 'Jenny . . .'

'Oh, don't start,' she said crossly. 'I'm not going to get any disease from it, and he doesn't take enough to make any difference. Actually, I like it. We both do.'

'Jenny, please don't. Please. For me. Give it up.'

'No.' She held the scraggy, ugly thing close and gazed at Stuart like a dispassionate executioner. 'I'm sorry, Stuart, I really am, but this is non-negotiable. If you can't accept that you'd better leave.'

This was the showdown he had been avoiding, the end of it all. He tried to rally his arguments and then he realized he had none. She had said it. She had made her choice, and it was non-negotiable. And he realized, looking at her now, that although she reminded him of the woman he loved, he didn't want to live with what she had become.

He could have refused to leave. After all, he had done nothing wrong. Why should he give up his home, this flat which was half his? But he could not force Jenny out onto the streets with nowhere to go; he still felt responsible for her.

'I'll pack a bag, and make a few phone calls,' he said quietly. He knew someone from work who was looking for a lodger, and if all else failed, his brother had a spare room. Already, in his thoughts, he had left.

He ended up, once they'd sorted out their finances and formally separated, in a flat just off the Holloway Road, near Archway. It was not too far to walk if Jenny cared to visit, which she never did. Sometimes he called on her, but it was painful to feel himself an unwelcome visitor in the home they once had shared.

He never had to fire Frankie; she handed in her notice a week later, telling him she'd been offered an editorial job at

The Women's Press. He wondered if pets in the office were part of the contract over there.

He never learned if the creatures had names. He never knew where they had come from, or how many there were. Had they fallen only in Islington? (Frankie had a flat somewhere off Upper Street.) He never saw anything on the news about them, or read any official confirmation of their existence, but he was aware of occasional oblique references to them in other contexts, occasional glimpses.

One evening, coming home on the tube, he found himself looking at the woman sitting opposite. She was about his own age, probably in her early thirties, with strawberry-blond hair, greenish eyes, and an almost translucent complexion. She was strikingly dressed in high, soft-leather boots, a long black woollen skirt, and an enveloping cashmere cloak of cranberry red. High on the cloak, below and to the right of the fastening at the neck, was a simple, gold circle brooch. Attached to it he noticed a very fine golden chain which vanished inside the cloak, like the end of a watch fob.

He looked at it idly, certain he had seen something like it before, on other women, knowing it reminded him of something. The train arrived at Archway, and as he rose to leave the train, so did the attractive woman. Her stride matched his. They might well leave the station together. He tried to think of something to say to her, some pretext for striking up a conversation. He was, after all, a single man again now, and she might be a single woman. He had forgotten how single people in London contrived to meet.

He looked at her again, sidelong, hoping she would turn her head and look at him. With one slender hand she toyed with her gold chain. Her cloak fell open slightly as she walked, and he caught a glimpse of the creature she carried beneath it, close to her body, attached by a slender golden chain.

He stopped walking and let her get away from him. He

had to rest for a little while before he felt able to climb the stairs to the street.

By then he was wondering if he had really seen what he thought he had seen. The glimpse had been so brief. But he had been deeply shaken by what he saw or imagined, and he turned the wrong way outside the station. When he finally realized, he was at the corner of Jenny's road, which had once also been his. Rather than retrace his steps, he decided to take the turning and walk past her house.

Lights were on in the front room, the curtains drawn against the early winter dark. His footsteps slowed as he drew nearer. He felt such a longing to be inside, back home, belonging. He wondered if she would be pleased at all to see him. He wondered if she ever felt lonely, as he did.

Then he saw the tiny, dark figure between the curtains and the window. It was spread-eagled against the glass, scrabbling uselessly; inside, longing to be out.

As he stared, feeling its pain as his own, the curtains swayed and opened slightly as a human figure moved between them. He saw the woman reach out and pull the creature away from the glass, back into the warm, lighted room with her, and the curtains fell again, shutting him out.

A Birthday

As with 'Born Dead', the origin of this story was a turn of phrase – actually, more than one. I was thinking about the way that perfectly natural, ordinary events in human life have long been shrouded in mystery, made into secrets to be passed down from mother to daughter at the right time, or shared among women but hidden from men. Phrases like 'the change of life', 'breakthrough bleeding', 'ordinary bleeding', as well as any number of euphemisms for menstruation are codes all women must learn, although men are allowed, sometimes even encouraged, to remain ignorant . . . and at what cost?

ALTHOUGH THEY BOTH LIVED IN LONDON, Peter Squyres did not see his mother very often. Once every few months, moved by a feeling of duty, he would phone her and a meeting would be arranged. Sometimes he took her out to dinner, and sometimes he went to her house in Holland Park. He was twenty-three, lived in a shared flat in Wood Green, had friends, hobbies, and a job in a bank. His mother, in her mid-forties, had a mysterious, busy life into which he did not enter. This seemed to suit them both.

One morning, unusually, she phoned him at work and invited him to come round that evening for a drink. While he hesitated, trying to think what to say, she went on, 'I know it's short notice, but I've only just remembered that it's my birthday, and I thought it would be nice . . .'

His eyes went to the calendar on the wall, and he felt guilty.

'Yes, of course,' he said. 'I'd love to. I was meaning to drop by, anyway, after work, to bring you a present.'

'Lovely,' she said. 'Shall we say sixish? Just a drink. You've probably made plans for dinner, so I won't keep you long.'

'Why don't you let me take you out to dinner?'

'No, Peter, I wasn't fishing for an invitation. Don't change your plans for me.'

'It's no problem.'

'Peter, don't fuss. I asked you for drinks. Just drinks,' she said. 'Sixish.'

He had to phone his girlfriend, then, and tell her about the change in plans.

'I didn't know you *had* a mother,' said Anna.

'What does that mean? Don't you believe me? It's her birthday, I really couldn't say no.'

'Yes, of course I believe you, don't get in a state. It doesn't matter. I understand about parents, believe me. Let's make it another night.'

'We can still have dinner tonight,' he said. 'I want to see you. How about the Malaysian place, at eight. I'll phone for a reservation, all right?'

'If you like.' He couldn't tell if she was annoyed or indifferent. She might even be smiling, pleased by his persistence. Only part of his difficulty was due to the fact that he couldn't see her expression. Peter and Anna had known each other for about three months, and had started sleeping together two weeks ago. He had thought that would make a difference, that sex would make things clear and definite between them, but it hadn't worked like that. He still didn't know what she thought, or how she felt about him, and it seemed he was always worrying, trying to please or placate her, as once, long ago, with his mother.

'I'll see you at the restaurant at eight,' he said. 'I miss you.'

On his lunch break he went out to buy a present for his mother. He bought red roses and then, at a loss, a bottle of Glenfiddich.

'Happy birthday, Liz,' he said when he opened the door.

He had stopped calling her 'Mummy' when he was five. He thought she looked smaller. He supposed most adults thought that about their parents, and he must have made that observation before, but it struck him with particular force as he bent down to her now.

She accepted his gifts with a gracious smile and conventional expressions of pleasure, as if he were any guest, any man she knew. There were always men in her life, but which of them were her lovers, or if one had ever meant more to her than the others, Peter never knew.

'What can I get you to drink?' she asked. 'G and T?'

'G and T, yes, please.' He sat down and watched as she fixed the drinks, his elegant, beautiful mother. Her hair was dark, without a trace of grey, cut short, and sleekly styled. She wore black silk trousers and a quilted Chinese jacket. Her shirt, also silk, was white with an odd, abstract pattern in red.

As she handed him his drink he frowned, seeing dirty fingerprints on the glass.

'This glass,' he said, rising. 'It seems to be – I'll get another.'

She reached out to take it from him, and then he saw that her hand was bleeding.

The whole hand was covered in blood.

'What?' she asked at his exclamation.

'Your hand,' he said, afraid to touch it, afraid of putting pressure on the wound and hurting her. 'You're bleeding.'

She looked down at her hand with a grimace of distaste, and put it behind her back. 'It's nothing,' she said. 'I didn't realize . . . I'll go wash it off.'

'Do you want me to help? Let me look. How did you hurt yourself?'

'It's nothing,' she said again. 'It happened earlier. It looks terrible, I know, but it doesn't hurt at all. It's nothing. Let me clean up . . .'

She seemed less concerned with her injury than with his reaction to it. When she had gone he stared down at the pale carpet, looking at two small, dark red spots. Her whole hand had been covered in blood. How could that be nothing?

She came back in, holding up a clean, unblemished hand. 'See? Nothing.'

She let him look, but when he tried to touch she pulled her hand away. 'I'm all right, Peter, honestly. Why don't you get yourself another glass?'

He did as she said. But when he came back he looked at her blouse and saw that the abstract pattern had altered. There were more red splotches on the white silk now, and they were larger.

'You're bleeding,' he said, shocked. 'Liz, what is it? What's wrong?'

She looked down and pulled the jacket closed, and fastened it, hiding the bloodstained blouse. He saw how blood sprang out on her fingertips as she used her hands. He saw a line of blood on her neck, seeping above the collar. Horrified, he saw that her feet were bleeding, too.

'I'm going to call a doctor,' he said. 'Or hospital . . . who's your doctor?'

'Peter, sit down and don't be silly. You don't know anything about it.'

Such was the force of habit – she was his mother, after all – that Peter sat down again. 'What is it?' he asked, trying to sound calm. 'Do you know what it means?'

'I'm not hurt,' she said. 'There's nothing wrong. No cuts or scratches. The blood . . . it's just coming from my pores, like perspiration. There's no injury. I'm not in pain. I don't feel any weakness for the blood I've lost, and this has been happening all day. There's nothing a doctor could do.'

Rivulets of blood were rolling down the smooth black leather of her shoes to be soaked up by the rough weave of the carpet.

'But it's not normal,' said Peter. 'Bleeding like that – there's something wrong! How do you know a doctor couldn't – '

'Hysterical bleeding,' she said calmly. 'Have you heard of that?'

He could not imagine anyone less hysterical than his mother. Even now, when anyone would be frightened, she was utterly rational. Her silk trousers stuck to her legs, dark and wet. 'I've heard of hysterical symptoms,' he said. 'A woman who thought she was pregnant, who showed all the signs of pregnancy, even fooled the doctors, but . . . it was an imaginary pregnancy, an hysterical pregnancy, not real. Do you mean this is like that? Do you mean it's not real blood?'

'I feel very well,' she said. 'If I had lost as much blood as I appear to have lost, I can't believe I would feel this well. On the other hand, if it's not blood, what is it?' She opened her hand, and they both stared at the blood that pooled to fill her cupped palm. After a moment she looked about, finally poured the red liquid into a crystal ashtray. 'It stains like real blood,' she said. 'I'm going to have to have these carpets done . . . I don't think I'll ever get it out of the mattress.'

'How long? How long has this been going on?'

'I suppose it must have started in the night. The early morning, really. It was the bed's being wet which woke me . . .' A flicker of emotion, then. 'It was a shock, I must admit. I have a strong stomach, and the sight of blood, my own blood, has never really bothered me. I remember how much blood there was when you were born, when the midwife put you in my arms, you were simply covered in it, every inch of you, and that didn't bother me at all – and yet, this morning, when I saw myself in so much blood . . . I had to think . . . it took me some time to realize there was nothing wrong – nothing *else* wrong – with me, and that I felt fine.' She shrugged. Blood began to seep from her cuffs, fat drops spattering the carpet.

'Just because you feel all right – look, you *must* see a doctor. No matter how you feel . . . you can't go on like this, just bleeding forever.'

'Yes, of course, I know that; I haven't lost my mind, Peter. And I haven't been alone – I've spoken to someone about it, to a nurse. She agrees with me. I'll see a doctor if I have to, if it doesn't stop naturally. But I'm sure it will stop . . . If it's still happening in the morning, I promise you I'll phone my doctor.'

'Morning!' Peter leaned forward, distressed, almost spilling his drink. 'You don't mean you're going to wait until tomorrow?'

'It's too late to phone now.'

'But you can't go on bleeding like this all night! Doctors have answering services – there'd be someone on call. What's the nearest hospital?'

'Peter, do calm down, please. I have been taking care of myself for years. This is not an emergency. I do have some knowledge of what doctors can and cannot do, and I am not going to go and sit in some hospital casualty ward for hours when I can be comfortable here at home. If I must see a doctor, I would like it to be my own doctor, someone who at least knows me. I can wait. It's not going to get any worse in the next few hours.' She raised her glass to her lips and drank while red from her fingers rolled down the side of the glass.

'That's crazy,' said Peter. 'You don't know it's not going to get worse – you don't know anything about it. You're not a doctor, you can't know. If something should happen – anything could happen. I won't let you stay here on your own all night.'

'I've already thought of that, and I'm not going to be on my own. I've asked Jean to come round just as soon as she gets the old lady settled for the night.'

'Who?'

'Jean Emery. She's a registered nurse. She looks after the old dear next door. Has done for the last few months. We've become quite good friends, and she often pops in for a cup of tea or a drink and a chat. In fact' – here Liz released a small, triumphant smile – 'in fact I've already seen her. She's seen me. Everything's under control. She agrees that there's no need for me to rush off to a doctor. She doesn't think there's anything a doctor could do. She's trained, Peter. She'll know if I need help, if anything starts to go wrong. She'll know what to do. She's agreed to stay the night. So you see, there's nothing for you to worry about.'

Peter drank the rest of his gin and tonic and went to pour himself another. 'I want to meet this woman before I leave you. I'd like to talk to her.'

'Well, of course. Nothing could be easier. Would you pour me another drink, too, darling?'

They had little enough to say to each other at the best of times. Now it was impossible. Her illness, or injury, made everything else sink into insignificance. Peter wished he could call a doctor and hand the problem over to someone else. Frightened and ill at ease, he drank too much. Liz left him after a quarter of an hour to shower and change. She returned wearing a black jersey dress for a much larger woman. It covered most of her body, voluminously, but left her lower legs bare. He couldn't stop staring at them. When the first bright drops of blood appeared he felt guilty, as if the pressure of his gaze had done it. Every few minutes she wiped her hands on a dark cloth that she then tucked into the chair cushions, out of sight.

'Your face isn't bleeding,' he said.

'No, not yet. But my scalp has started.'

He shuddered, finished what was in his glass, and looked at his watch. Nearly eight o'clock. He thought of Anna, waiting in the restaurant. He was about to ask if he could use the telephone when the doorbell chimed.

Jean Emery wore a crisp uniform and cap, and the very sight of her made him feel better. She was probably his mother's age, but her black hair was well-sprinkled with grey, and instead of Liz's elegance she had a kind of solidity and an air of practical efficiency that Peter instinctively trusted. He looked from her clear hazel eyes to her humorous mouth and liked her still more. He reminded himself that he was drunk. With a belligerence he didn't feel he demanded, 'You know what's happening to my mother?'

'You must be Peter,' said the nurse calmly. 'I'm glad to meet you at last. Liz has told me so much about you.'

'But what about her? Is she going to be all right?'

The women exchanged glances.

'He's worried about me,' said Liz.

'You didn't explain . . . ?'

Liz wrinkled her nose ever so slightly, pursing her lips in distaste, and Peter, staring at her, was assailed by a memory more than fourteen years old. She'd had that same expression when he asked her where babies came from, and she had given him a vague and unsatisfactory answer.

Jean gave a sigh that was half a laugh. 'How about a cup of tea, Peter? I could certainly use one.'

'I'm drinking gin,' he said.

'Perhaps you've had enough gin for now, eh?' She had a smile that stopped his anger. He nodded obediently.

'I'll put the kettle on,' said Liz, and left them alone.

'Sit down, Peter, do. I've been run off my feet today.' Jean settled herself on the couch.

'Look, I'm sorry if I seem a bit abrupt, but I'm very worried about my . . . about Liz. She won't let me call a doctor.'

'There's no need for a doctor.'

'But she's bleeding!'

Jean nodded. 'Yes, and I can see that's very worrying for you. Will you believe me when I tell you there's nothing to worry about? It's a change, and of course there are some risks; understandably, you're nervous. But you needn't be frightened. There is nothing wrong. Your mother is going to be fine.'

'But what's . . . what's happening?'

For just a moment Jean's steady gaze seemed to flicker, and Peter intuited reluctance to speak about female secrets to a man. 'She's my *mother*,' he said fiercely.

'Yes, of course, of course. That's why . . . Your mother is a very special woman, I don't know if you appreciate that, Peter.'

He nodded impatiently. 'Just tell me what's wrong.'

'Nothing is wrong. That's what I want you to understand. This is a normal . . . Have you heard of what they call the "change of life"?'

Peter frowned. 'Yes, of course. It means when women . . . when women can't . . . when women stop . . . at a certain age . . .' He felt hot and uncomfortable.

'Yes, I think you understand. You needn't spell it out.'

'But I thought that was when women *stopped* bleeding,' he blurted.

Jean smiled. 'You weren't wrong. But people aren't all exactly alike. It takes different women in different ways, the change of life.'

Liz came back into the room then, bearing a tray. 'Here we are,' she said.

Peter looked at his watch. He was sure he was blushing. He had blundered in where he was not wanted and he knew he wouldn't be able to question Jean further. Maybe it would be all right; she was, after all, a nurse, and Liz seemed comfortable with her. Nagging away at him was the awareness that even if he left now he would be almost an hour late to meet Anna.

'I can't stay,' he said. 'I'm supposed to meet someone for dinner.'

'Of course, I didn't mean to delay you,' Liz said. 'Run along. Really, Peter, you needn't worry about me.'

He looked at the blood pooling at her feet, and then he looked at Jean. 'Are you *sure* . . . ?'

'Quite sure,' said Jean.

'And you'll stay with her?'

'I will.'

'And call a doctor if there's anything . . .'

'Oh, Peter – '

'You have my word. Now run along. Come back in the morning and see how different everything will be then.'

'I will,' said Peter. 'I will be back in the morning. But if anything happens tonight, if anything changes or you're worried at all, please call me. It doesn't matter what time it is. Will you do that?'

'Everything is going to be all right,' said the nurse. 'I'll let you know as soon as there's anything to know.'

He was afraid that Anna would not be there, but she was in the Malaysian restaurant, eating. She looked up from her satay, unperturbed, as he rushed in.

'I went ahead and ordered, I didn't think you'd mind. You can start eating some of mine and then order whatever else you like.'

'I'm sorry I'm late, but – '

'Oh, that's all right. I know how parents can be.'

'It's not that – there was something wrong – I mean, something really odd, she was bleeding, you see, and it wouldn't stop.' He knocked over the chair in his first attempt to sit down. 'Sorry. Anyway, I tried to get her to phone a doctor, but she wouldn't; kept insisting she was fine, but of course I couldn't leave her, I didn't know – '

'Peter, have you been drinking?'

'A couple of gins. Well, maybe three or four. It was a shock. I mean, well, if you'd seen her, and all that blood . . .' he gestured helplessly.

'Blood? Your mother? Bleeding? What happened?'

'Oh, she wasn't hurt, it wasn't like that, but it had been going on all day. She said when she woke up the bed was soaked, but she didn't feel weak, there wasn't any pain, and her friend Jean, she's the nurse, when she came in she obviously wasn't bothered at all. Explained to me, calmed me down. Perfectly natural, change of life, she said. Well, of course I'd heard of that, and I guess my mother is getting to that sort of age, but I never imagined it would come on like that, with so much blood. I thought it was only when women, you know, stopped.'

Anna gazed at him sympathetically. 'Heavier bleeding than normal,' she murmured. 'Yes, I think I've read about that. There can be all sorts of different symptoms, I believe. Was your mother very upset?'

'Her! No, not at all. It was me who got upset. She kept telling me she felt fine and it didn't hurt and it was nothing to worry about, but I couldn't believe it.' Relief flowed through him, stronger than alcohol. It was all right. Anna's acceptance convinced him this was something women had to suffer but could cope with, and there was nothing he, as a man, either could or should do.

He was able to eat and enjoy his dinner, and afterwards they went to Anna's flat. Her flatmate was there with her bloke, and they invited Peter and Anna to watch a new video with them. It was just some low-budget slasher movie, and normally he would have found it as great a laugh as the others did, but now the sight of all that fake gore reminded him unpleasantly of his mother. He shifted uneasily on the couch. How much blood could someone lose and still survive? He excused himself – 'No, no, don't stop it on my account' – and went to the toilet. At the sink, watching clear water stream over his hands he recalled the redness flowing from his mother.

All at once he couldn't remember if he had left Anna's number with Jean Emery or only his own. He could call – but it was nearly midnight. He thought of his mother's icy annoyance if he should wake her. How many times over the years had he evoked her disapproval by being obtuse, by misunderstanding, by demanding attention she found it a bore to provide? He was a grown-up now, their lives were separate. That was how she wanted it. She hadn't asked for his help, and there was nothing he could do for her.

When he opened the bathroom door Anna was standing there in her dressing gown, smiling at him. 'Who cares how the stupid video ends. Let's go to bed.'

Yet even in bed with his love, happy and exhausted, he could not relax enough to sleep. Jean had told him to come back in the morning, but what was happening now? How much blood could a person lose and still survive?

'Peter?'

'Yes?'

'Are you worrying about your mother still?'

Love for her, gratitude for her empathy, coursed through him like a lesser orgasm. He rolled over and kissed her. 'You're a mind-reader.'

'Hardly.'

'You do think she's all right? I mean that it's normal and . . .'

'Peter, I'm not a doctor. I did a first-aid course last year, but that hardly qualifies me to make a diagnosis, especially sight unseen. If the bleeding was very heavy it could be a problem. But how heavy . . . I mean, I don't suppose she told you how often she had to change her – '

'Oh but she didn't have to say, I could see. Her clothes were soaked, absolutely soaked, in half an hour. Every time she touched anything, the slightest pressure, like handing me a glass, the blood would pour out. It poured out of her hands, it ran down her legs and arms, it was everywhere, she was bleeding from every pore, except on her face.'

While he was speaking, Anna had sat up and switched on the bedside lamp. 'You *are* awake.'

'What's the matter?'

'What's the matter? You're telling me your mother had blood streaming out of her, that she was bleeding from all over her body – '

'But you said it was normal.'

'Normal!'

'That it could be, you said . . .' he trailed off, unable to remember exactly what she had said, and realizing that it didn't matter because he had obviously misunderstood.

'There is no way that somebody bleeding from every pore, somebody soaked in blood, could be normal. Think about it.'

'But Jean said . . . and my mother . . . I thought it was the change of life. Even you said heavier bleeding could be normal.'

'Normal bleeding. Not like that.'

Peter hunched his shoulders, feeling resentful. What the hell was normal bleeding? If he bled, he knew he was injured. But women bled every month, and that was supposed to be normal, unless they bled too heavily, or on the wrong days, or when they were pregnant, at which point it became a cause for concern. How was he supposed to interpret such female mysteries? Women said one thing and then, using the same words, they said another. *They* knew what they meant, and the men who couldn't understand were the ones at fault. He wanted to wash his hands of the whole messy female business.

'Peter, get up. Get dressed.' She was already up, pulling on the dark sweater and skirt she had worn earlier. 'We've got to go over there.'

'They don't want me. They sent me away.'

'You can't leave your mother alone at a time like this.'

'She's with a nurse,' he said sullenly.

'A nurse who says it's normal.'

They made eye contact at last, and the frail structure of his childish resentment collapsed. Of course he would go if Liz needed him, even if she couldn't admit her need. Despite the emotional distance between them there was also an unbreakable bond. She would always be his mother.

Anna phoned for a cab, and then he tried to call his mother. There was no reply.

'Maybe they've gone. Maybe the nurse took your mother to hospital,' Anna suggested.

Or maybe Jean was so busy attempting to stanch the flow of blood that she simply couldn't be bothered to answer the phone. Horrific, chaotic, incomprehensible images, as from some particularly nasty video, crowded his brain. His heart raced and he broke out in a sweat. He should never have left. He should be there now. Liz had no one else. Jean was only a stranger.

Seeing his distress, Anna hugged him tightly. 'There, there. It'll be all right.'

All the way to Holland Park in the cab – a much swifter journey at this hour of the night than it would have been in heavier traffic – he clung to Anna's warm, strong hand, trying to control the fits of shivering that rocked his body. Her words, even when they lapsed into the almost meaningless baby talk of pure reassurance, were his lifeline to sanity. It would be all right because Anna said it would.

There was no reply when he rang the bell, and he froze in helpless panic.

'You said you had a key,' Anna reminded him.

'Oh, yes, of course . . .'

She took it from his trembling fingers and let them into the house.

The front room was empty. The blood on the carpet looked even more horrible now that it had dried. There were sounds from the back of the house. Anna put her arm around Peter and walked him through.

Jean was in the bedroom, but not Liz. He thought for a horrible moment that he glimpsed his mother's body, wet, collapsed, and impossibly shrunken, lying in a heap of blood-stained clothes at the foot of the bed, but before he could investigate his attention was caught by what lay on the bed: a tiny baby, newborn by the look of it, all red, as if covered in a glistening second skin of blood.

'You're just in time,' said Jean. She was beaming. Her once-fresh uniform was a bloody mess. 'I was going to give you a ring – it all happened a bit quicker than I thought, but I guess you sensed that, eh? Nothing like the bond between parent and child, I always say.'

The baby opened its mouth and began to squall.

'Hush, hush, Lizzie,' said Jean. 'Hush now, Peter's home.' She lifted the baby and held it out toward Peter. 'Congratulations,' she said. 'You have a lovely daughter.'

My Pathology

Thomas Tessier said of this story, 'It is some kind of diabolical masterpiece, straining credibility more and more with each passing page, yet utterly convincing and inescapable, a tale of obsessions and alchemy, babies, self-abasement, disease and the unbearable nightmare that love can become. "My Pathology" is a tour de force *and it ends with a stabbing last line that is one of the finest ever written in the literature of horror.' High praise, indeed, and I'm deeply thrilled to have written a story that made such an impact on a writer I admire for his own memorably chilling horror fiction.*

IT MAY NOT BE A TRUTH UNIVERSALLY ACKNOWLEDGED, but people value more that which is not easily won. Challenge and difficulty add to the appeal. As I once said to Saskia, unavailable men are always more attractive. I'd never known Saskia to fall for a man who wasn't already committed elsewhere – but she just said, '*If* that's your pathology.'

Certainly it was hers. The way she ignored perfectly nice men in favour of bastards belonging to someone else . . .

But love is a basic human need. Does it make sense to call it a disease?

Daniel and I were attracted to each other from the start, and there didn't seem to be anything difficult or inherently unavailable about him. The one slight little hitch – that the woman he described as his ex-girlfriend hadn't *quite* let him go – probably added to his attraction; I was touched by his tender concern for her feelings.

As he explained it: 'We were together for nearly three

years. At one time I thought we'd get married. But . . . We had a major disagreement, one of those things where there can be no compromise. I won't go into the details. Anyway, she knows it's over, knows we don't have a future together, and we're not . . . not sleeping together, you know, but she's afraid of being alone. She needs to know that I'm still her friend. I don't love her anymore, but I feel responsible. She's had a hard time lately.'

He told me about her (Michele, her name was) before we'd actually become lovers, on an evening when the possibility was quivering between us, so I knew his intentions toward me must be serious.

'Are you going to tell her about me?'

'I've already told her I've met someone.'

My heart leapt and I went to kiss him, this unknown woman's man who was now mine.

Daniel worked in an office in central London, as did I, but he lived out in Metroland – nearest station, Rayner's Lane – where the dear old London underground emerges above ground, transformed into a suburban commuter train. The rails ran behind his house, so we were treated to a view of his back garden a good quarter hour before we could expect to arrive at the front door, on foot, from the station. Once, on his way home, Daniel had seen someone entering by the back door, and even though he phoned the police immediately on his mobile, the burglars managed to get away with the TV and VCR.

These were easily replaced. Daniel kept little that he valued on the ground floor of his narrow, two-bedroomed turn-of-the-century terraced cottage. Practically everything that mattered to him was kept locked in his 'workroom', otherwise the spare bedroom.

Daniel was a chartered accountant in his ordinary life, but in his workroom he was an alchemist.

He told me this, as he'd told me about Michele, early in our relationship. It meant nothing to me then. If asked to define alchemy, I'd have said it was a sort of primitive, magical chemistry, bearing about the same relationship to modern chemistry as astrology did to astronomy. It seemed a very strange hobby for someone as sane and successful as Daniel, but I kept my mouth shut as he unlocked his workshop to show me the shelves filled with ancient, leather-bound volumes, sealed jars with Latin labels, beakers and retorts, a Bunsen burner, vessels of copper and of glass. The smells were what most struck me: half a dozen different odours lingering in the air. Sulphur, roses, hot metal, burnt sugar, tar, and something pricklingly acidic which made me cough.

'What do you do here, exactly?'

'Do you really want to know, "exactly"?'

'Generally, then.'

'Search. Explore. Study. Experiment. I'm looking for the Philosopher's Stone – does that mean anything to you?'

I shook my head apologetically. 'Afraid not.'

He kissed me. 'Never mind. If you are interested, I can help you learn, but it doesn't matter; we can't share everything.'

As I watched him lock the door to his workshop, I wondered if it would matter. Of course couples couldn't share all their interests, but this hobby seemed less like stamp collecting, more like a religion.

We didn't talk about alchemy and we didn't talk about Michele, and as the weeks and the months passed, and my love for Daniel became more deeply rooted, those two 'untouchable' areas of his life became irritants, and I wondered if there was a connection. I finally asked him if Michele had shared his interest in alchemy.

He tensed. 'She pretended that she did, for a while, but she didn't. It was my fault as much as hers. I let her know how important it was to me . . . but it's not as important as honesty.

If she'd just had faith in me, instead of pretending she understood . . . She lied to me.'

I held his hand. 'I won't lie to you. I won't pretend. But I would like to know more about something so important to you. You said you could teach me . . .'

But the shutters were down; I was trespassing. He shook his head firmly. 'No. I won't make that mistake again. It's better if you don't know, and you won't be put in an invidious position. If you don't know anything about The Work, we can't possibly argue about it.'

I wished I'd never mentioned Michele. I began to hate the invisible woman who still hovered on the periphery of my life, attached to my lover like a parasite, barring certain possibilities from me forever.

It was harder for me now to leave those two sore subjects alone, but at least I didn't speak to Daniel about them. I found a bookshop in Cecil Court which specialized in esoteric learning, and bought an armload of books about alchemy. On the evenings Daniel did his duty by his ex-girlfriend, I went back to my rented room and got into bed with his ancient philosophy.

The fact that I was still shelling out money for a room of my own, although I scarcely spent any time there, was a sore point. I wanted to live with Daniel and found his arguments against it pretty feeble. If he really felt that his two-bedroomed house wasn't big enough for the two of us, then he should sell it, and we could buy something else together. I'd been looking for something to buy when I met him, but I didn't want to commit myself to mortgage payments on some tiny flat if there was any future in our relationship.

We had been lovers for nearly nine months when I began to suspect I was pregnant.

I'd been careless about contraception. The truth was, I wanted to have a baby; I wanted to force the issue of our relationship to a crisis, even if I hadn't admitted it to myself.

When my period didn't arrive bang on time, my first response was an inward clutch of sheer joy. I was ready to change my life.

I didn't tell him straightaway. When I got on the train for Rayner's Lane one evening, two weeks later, I was still happy keeping my secret. I watched out the window for his house, as I always did. In the slanting, pre-dusk light and shade the view of row upon row of narrow back gardens was like the unspooling of a film, one I found inexhaustibly absorbing. Occasionally I saw people, either through windows or outside, children playing, men or women mowing their little carpet-strips of lawn or taking washing from a line, but more often there were no people to be seen, only the signs, ordinary and cryptic, of their invisible occupation.

The back of Daniel's house was normally almost exactly like its neighbours on either side, but not that evening.

That evening there was something growing out of it. It was a pale, whitish blister, a sort of bubble, or a cocoon, the size of a small room. I sensed it was organic, something which had grown rather than been added on. It was as if Daniel's house was a living organism, a body which could extrude a tissue-like substance.

I was astonished, and then it was out of sight. My mind immediately set to work revising and editing the memory of what I'd seen. It must have been something else, something ordinary, like a sheet of plastic or PVC. If there'd been an accident, fire, or explosion (my throat tightened with the memory of those smells, those volatile substances locked in his workroom) or even a break-in, it might have been necessary to shroud the back of the house in some protective material.

Alighting at the station, I ran practically the whole way back to his house, gulping and weeping in fearful suspense. If only Daniel were all right . . .

Daniel opened the door to my hysterical pounding and I

threw myself into his arms. 'Thank God! Oh, Daniel, what happened? When I saw the back of your house – '

'What are you talking about?'

I broke away and hurried through to the kitchen. The window offered me an unobstructed view of the fig tree at the very bottom of the garden. The back door was locked and bolted, but I got the keys from the top of the fridge and let myself out.

I could find nothing out of the ordinary. No protrusion, no growth, only the weathered grey paint beginning to peel away from the wall in a few places. Everything looked exactly as it always had. I touched it to be sure. I listened to a bird singing, and the distant wind-rush of traffic. Another train rattled by, and when I looked up a few pale faces gazed at me blankly over the fence. It was obvious that none of them saw anything to get excited about. I started to feel like an idiot.

Slowly I went back inside to offer Daniel some lame excuse for my excitement. 'I thought I saw something. I don't know what – a sort of hallucination, I guess it must have been. I don't know why . . .'

He laid a cool hand caressingly on my hot face and looked at me very tenderly. 'Excitement, maybe? Hormones?'

I realized then that he must have known, or at least started to suspect, about the pregnancy as soon as I did. Even though we didn't live together, we'd never spent more than a night or two apart.

I started crying. Daniel wrapped his arms around me and held me close. He murmured his love in my ear. 'When will you move in? This weekend?'

I gaped, sobs shuddering to a halt. 'But . . . if this place isn't big enough for the two of us . . .'

'But it's not just the two of us anymore. Everything's changed.' He smiled joyfully. 'My workroom can be the nursery.'

*

I don't like doctors, and I can't stand hospitals. I don't even like visiting people in them, and my one experience as a patient – after a burst appendix at the age of eight – was enough to put me off for life. I knew that even if I was to have a home birth (Daniel agreed that was best) I would still have to visit a doctor, but I kept putting it off, and somehow got through the whole of my first trimester, grimly putting up with the sickness and the pains, still avoiding the evil day.

Daniel, who had become very protective – ensuring that alcohol, caffeine, French cheeses, and shellfish did not pass my lips, constantly querying my emotional, mental, and physical health – accepted my fear of hospitals and didn't push. When I finally, with great reluctance, decided that I'd have to go register with the local GP, he shook his head. 'Really, that's not necessary. I know how you feel, Bess, so I've asked my mother to come round and have a look at you.'

'Your mother?' He'd never mentioned this personage before; from the way he shrugged off my questions about his background I'd gathered only that he and his parents were not close. 'Is she a doctor, then?'

He looked oddly embarrassed. 'Well, yes, of course. She's a specialist in, you know . . . in private practice, of course, but she won't charge us.'

And, for me, she would make house calls. I was relieved.

Her appearance surprised me. She had aquiline features very like Daniel's, but she looked far too young to be his mother. Except for her hair, which was coarse and heavily streaked with grey, I'd have thought her not much older than I was. She seemed uncomfortable with her own attractiveness, dressed in a frumpy, ill-fitting suit and wearing heavy, dark-framed spectacles.

She had a chilly, distant manner, never meeting my eyes, hardly even looking at me properly. Her examination of me seemed cursory; I didn't even have to undress. She prodded my barely-showing 'bump', took my blood pressure, which she pronounced excellent, got me to stand on the scales, asked me a few medical questions, and announced her pleasure at learning that I was 'giving Daniel a child'.

'Hang on,' I said. 'It's my baby. I'm not "giving" anybody anything!'

'It's only a manner of speaking,' said Daniel. He was standing behind me, stroking my hair, and I hoped he was shooting poison with his eyes at his mother.

'I'm sorry if I've disturbed you,' she said awkwardly. 'I didn't mean anything wrong by it. I'm sure you must understand how pleased I am that Daniel will be a father.'

Well, fair enough. After all, I thought, she hardly knew me; why should she feel pleased that I was to be a mother? And she might have preferred someone else as her son's partner. Yet I noticed she seemed almost as uncomfortable with Daniel as she was with me. Watching them as they stood, uneasily close, by the door, hesitating over whether and how to kiss goodbye, I wondered what had come between them.

Daniel's mother showed me how to take my own blood pressure, gave me some guidelines for monitoring my weight gain, and promised to send along a midwife in good time. Meanwhile, I read books about natural childbirth, drank herbal teas, and slept a lot. I was so tired all the time. Around about the sixth month I started suffering from backache in addition to everything else and decided to take my maternity leave earlier than planned.

One good thing about not going out to work anymore was that I didn't have to deal with seeing that thing on the back of the house so often. Because I hadn't stopped seeing it. Maybe it was hormonal – at any rate, whether it was a trick of the eye or of the brain, it bothered me.

I knew that Daniel didn't see it, but another time I took Saskia with me on the train. I didn't try to warn her or set her up; I just pointed out the house from the train window and waited, trembling with nerves, for her response. The thin, pale growth had become a huge bubble with the passage of time, inescapably strange, and I could hardly believe that I was the only person to see it.

'Which one?' asked Saskia, peering out at the monstrosity. 'Oh, there? With the red geranium in the kitchen window? My pot! Is that what you wanted me to see?'

Saskia had made me a lovely blue pot when I'd told her I was pregnant. I couldn't see it from the train; the whole of the kitchen window was blocked from my view by the sinister, gently bobbing growth.

I knew there was nothing 'really' there on the back of the house; what I saw came from within me.

It was in me.

I had nightmares about the baby.

Usually, in my dreams, I gave birth to a perfectly normal, sweet, much wanted little baby . . . then I'd lose it by doing something criminally insane: I put it in the oven to keep it warm, and only realized what I'd done hours later; I wrapped it in newspaper and absent-mindedly dropped it in a bin; I left it on a tube train.

But there were other dreams in which I gave birth to things which were not babies. Sometimes it was a deformed creature, armless and legless, or looking like a fetal pig; once it was a wizened, evil-looking old man who bit off my breast; another time it was an egg-shaped thing, glowing red-hot, the passage of which woke me screaming in pain.

One night I dreamed that I was inside the cocoon, Daniel and his mother on either side of me, holding down my arms and shouting at me to push. The struggle to give birth was inextricably bound with the struggle to breathe properly, and as I inhaled, gasping, I became aware that I'd used up nearly all the air in the room, and also that the soft, tissue-like walls were collapsing. They fell upon me (Daniel and his mother had vanished), enveloping me like vast sheets of cling film, incredibly strong, binding my limbs and closing off my mouth and nostrils, suffocating me.

With a snort and gasp I woke. Heart pounding, I sat up, breathing deeply in and out. I was alone in bed. The room felt horribly close and hot. I rolled out of bed and staggered across to the window with the idea of opening it, but then I looked out, and froze.

There below me, rising to just below the window ledge and ballooning out to fill nearly half the back garden, was that thing which before I had only seen from a distance, from the train window. Now, so close, I could appreciate its size and solidity. It gave off a glow; after a moment, I realized that the source of the glow was an inner light, and then I saw movement, like fish deep beneath murky water. I stared, concentrating so intensely that I forgot to breathe, until I was certain that the moving shapes I saw were human.

I screamed for Daniel. Below, the two figures stopped moving.

I stumbled across the room, calling his name, and out onto the landing. Light rose up from below, light from the kitchen, and as I started downstairs, leaning heavily on the rail, I saw the two of them: Daniel and a woman. She looked like his mother except for her hair, which was short, fair, and curly, and the fact that she was making no effort to hide the fact that she was young and attractive. All of a sudden I understood: I had never met Daniel's mother, only Michele in disguise.

The next thing I knew I was lying on the couch in the sitting room and Daniel was holding my hand.

'Where is she?'

'There's no one here.' He told me I'd been dreaming. According to him, he'd been asleep in bed beside me when I started screaming his name. He'd been unable to stop me from stumbling downstairs, although he had managed to catch me when I collapsed at the bottom.

I believed him. What I had seen had been 'only' a dream. But that didn't make it unimportant.

One of the strongest memories I have from my childhood is also the memory of a dream; more real to me than much that 'really' happened.

I was eight years old, asleep in my bed, when a strange, high, buzzing sound awoke me. I sat up and looked over at my sister, peacefully sleeping in her matching bed. The noise seemed to be coming from directly below us, from the kitchen. I got up to investigate.

As I came down the stairs I could hear my parents talking in the kitchen, but I couldn't make out their words. The hall was dark, and I arrived at the kitchen door unnoticed. There was a strong light on at one end of the kitchen which cast my parents' shadows on the wall. I had noticed the effect before, but this time it was different. This time the shadows on the wall did not correspond to the two familiar people. I could see my mother and father sitting at the table, but on the wall behind them were the shadows of monstrous insects.

Mum turned her head and saw me. She didn't seem surprised. She opened her arms. 'Come here, darling.'

I went to her, nervously watching the wall. Nightmares usually fled at the arrival of grown-ups, but the shadows didn't change as I'd expected. The one behind my Mum moved, becoming three-dimensional, an inky-black, gigantic insect which emerged from the pale wall and came for me. I began to scream and wriggle, trying to get away, but my mother held me tight, her face stiff, implacable. She held me fast as the shadow-creature's long, black proboscis snaked out and struck my pyjama-clad tummy. It pierced the cloth and then my skin, sinking deep into me. It hurt worse than anything I'd ever known. I screamed in agony before passing out.

The cocoon-thing on the outside of the house belonged to the same level of reality as the shadow insects of my childhood. Lying awake beside Daniel for what remained of that night, I let myself think, for the first time, about all the things which can go wrong with a pregnancy, let myself recall, clearly, those sections of my pregnancy-and-childbirth books which I'd skimmed so nervously. Because there had been signs that all was not well – signs which Daniel and his mother (if she was his mother) had dismissed as unimportant. The pains. The occasional show of blood. The fact that I had yet to feel my baby move.

I didn't tell Daniel what I had decided. For once, I didn't want him to soothe away my fears. In the morning, after he'd gone to work, I took the bus to Northwick Park Hospital.

At the maternity unit there I was scolded for not coming in sooner, my fears – both about hospitals and about the baby – reassuringly brushed away. I was given forms to fill out, and taken along for an ultrasound scan. Although I was dry-mouthed and twitchy with nerves, I thought the end of the nightmare was in sight, but in fact it was only the beginning.

There was no baby in my womb. It was a tumour.

In a state of shock, I was whisked from Maternity to Oncology where a grave-faced physician informed me that although many, perhaps most, ovarian cysts were benign, the size of this one did not incline him to be optimistic. It would have to be removed in either case; if it proved malignant, a complete hysterectomy would follow. He invited me to return three days later, perhaps with my partner or another family member, to discuss the prognosis further.

I had expected Daniel to be upset. What I did not expect was his rage.

'What have you done?' His voice was a vicious, strangled whisper. He looked as if he would have killed as soon as touched me. My tears dried up, misery overwhelmed by baffled fear. I wished it could have been a dream, like the one in which my mother held me still to receive the insect-man's terrifying attack.

'I didn't do anything, Daniel,' I said carefully. 'I'm telling you what they said at the hospital – '

He was in a fury. 'Why did you go to the hospital? Why? Why? Why couldn't you trust me? How could you do this to me?'

'What are you talking about? Are you crazy? This is happening to *me*, if you hadn't noticed! I had to go to the hospital – your bloody mother was no bloody use at all. She couldn't tell a baby from a tumour. That's what it is – a tumour, not a baby. And the doctor said it's so big that it's probably malignant, and if it is they'll have to take out my whole womb, my ovaries, everything!' I began to weep again.

'No they won't,' said Daniel, relaxing a little. He no longer looked so angry. 'I won't let them. We won't let them.'

'But they'll have to operate. Even if it's not malignant – '

'It's not malignant.'

'You can't know that.'

'I do know that.' His eyes drilled into mine with the intensity, the absolute certainty which I'd always found irresistibly sexy. 'I know what it is, and they don't. They think it's cancer. I know it's not.'

'What is it, then?'

'It's the Philosopher's Stone.'

I wanted so much to believe him. Who would choose cancer, surgery, a possibly fatal illness, over magic? Daniel, impassioned, was a convincing advocate. The so-called Philosopher's Stone, although sometimes identified with various gems or minerals, was also described as an elixir, a water, a dragon, and a 'divine child'. I'd thought it a symbol for the knowledge sought by alchemists, but Daniel told me that although symbolic, it was also very real. It was the stuff of creation, a kind of super-DNA, created, replicated, by life itself. By us. Our union was the rare and perfect Alchemical Marriage; my womb was the alembic in which the dragon, stone, or divine child was now growing. When perfect it would be born, and I would be transformed in the process.

'If you'll think about it, you'll realize your own transformation has already started,' he said. 'You can see things other people can't. The thing you saw on the back of the house – don't you realize what that is? It's an amniotic sac, indicating the impending mystical birth of knowledge.'

He'd been transformed himself by his wonder and joy; there was no doubt that he believed everything he told me. How I struggled to join him in his magical belief-system. For a little while, that evening, I managed to convince us both that I *did* believe – but the next day, alone in the house, the effort was too great, and I collapsed into dull despair. Daniel was the alchemist, not me. In my world, a lump in the womb couldn't be both child *and* stone; it was one or the other, and I knew which mine was.

As the days passed, I went on struggling to believe in Daniel's reality while the horror of mine threatened to overwhelm me. I was too frightened to go back to the hospital, anyway. Daniel believed that all was well. He shared his books, his notes, his experiments and fantasies with me: finally, every secret corner of his life was revealed to me. I was his partner now in what he called The Great Work.

I felt that I would burst with the secret and the stone inside me. Finally, I confessed all – or nearly all – to Saskia, who immediately arranged for me to see her own doctor.

'I had a cyst five years ago the size of a large grapefruit. It turned out to be benign. Lots of women get them. I lost one ovary . . . but I've still got the other *and* my womb, just in case.' She made a face. I knew already about the tipped cervix, the doctor who'd reckoned her chances of conceiving normally, without medical intervention, at less than ten percent, but the idea that she, too, had once carried a stone inside was new to me.

'I never knew that!'

'Sure you did. Remember, when I was in the hospital?'

'Oh.' Ancient guilt swept over me. I was her best friend, but I'd never visited her in the hospital.

'It's all right; it was always all right.' Telepathic, she patted my arm. 'I knew how you felt. I had enough visitors and enough chocolates – I was really grateful for the books you sent, a new one every day! Did I ever tell you what they found inside the cyst?'

I shook my head.

'Six tiny baby teeth, bits of bone and tissue, and a huge hairball. It was like a giant owl pellet!'

'Teeth?'

'It sounds creepy, but my doctor said it's not that unusual. The cyst is formed from ovarian cells gone wrong, and after all, that's where babies come from, teeth and bone and hair and all.'

I imagined our divine child a mass of skin and hair and bone and teeth all jumbled up together in the wrong order. What would Daniel say if he could see it?

'Could I keep it, do you think? I mean, after they take it out, would they save it for me?'

Saskia's face revealed no horror or dismay at my suggestion. 'I don't see why not. It's yours, after all.'

I told Daniel I was going to Lincolnshire to stay with my mother for a few days, and Saskia took me to hospital. She was with me nearly the whole time, comforting, advising, taking control when I couldn't cope.

'If I ever have a baby, Sask, I want you with me,' I said, gripping her hand just before I was wheeled into the operating room.

'Of course you'll have a baby. You'll have as many as you want, and I'll be godmother,' she promised.

But Saskia was wrong. There would be no babies for me. The surgeon removed both ovaries, my fallopian tubes, my entire womb. I was left with nothing except the cyst I had asked them to save.

It was a disgusting thing to have carried around inside me, to have imagined as a living child: a fleshy lump covered in hair. I cut it open with my Swiss army knife, balancing it on my bed tray.

A foul-smelling semi-solid liquid dripped out, and I gagged, but kept on sawing.

There was more hair inside, more disgusting pus, and soft baby flesh. No teeth, no bones, but, right at the centre, one hard, tiny nugget the size of a pea.

I picked it out with my bare fingers and wiped it on a tissue. It was a deep, reddish brown in colour and felt like stone. I rapped it against the bedside table and scraped at it with a fingernail. I felt a strong urge, which I resisted, to put it in my mouth and swallow it.

Holding it tightly between the thumb and forefinger of one hand, I rang for the nurse with the other, to ask her to please get rid of the grisly, oozing thing on my tray.

I felt much weaker than I'd anticipated, and I knew I would not be able to deceive Daniel, or to face him. He would be angry, I knew; he would be furious, at first, but then, I hoped, he would get over his disappointment and understand. Eager for his forgiveness, for the enveloping love which I needed to help me recover, I sent Saskia to break the news to him. I thought it would be easier for her, and that he would hide his true feelings from a relative stranger. I was wrong.

Afterwards, when she told me about it, she was shaking.

'He's grieving. He's like you've had an abortion. Didn't you tell him you weren't pregnant? Didn't you tell him what it was?'

'Of course I did!'

'Well, you didn't make him understand. The poor, sad man . . . I explained about the cancer, but he couldn't get the idea of a child out of his head, and the notion that you'd destroyed it. Oh, Bess!'

She looked at me with tears in her eyes and, horrified, I saw that she, like Daniel, blamed me. It was all my fault that I could only produce a malignant, hairy lump instead of a wanted child.

'But I didn't! I wanted a baby, too, as much as ever he did!'

Saskia put her arms around me and, not for the first time or the last, we cried together.

When it came time for me to leave hospital it turned out I had no home. Saskia took me by taxi to the house in Rayner's Lane where I found that Daniel had changed the locks. Saskia was furious, but it was so over-the-top that I had to laugh. She took me to Muswell Hill to stay in her flat until something else could be sorted.

Saskia went on being my intermediary with Daniel. He grudgingly agreed to meet me, to talk, and I spent hours hurling myself at his stony indifference. Saskia felt that as Daniel was so intransigent I should simply accept that the affair was over and get on with my own life. But I couldn't do that. I'd lost far more than he had, and it was his fault.

Guilt worked better on Daniel than reason; he could see what a state I was in, and he knew he owed me something. He tried to buy me off, but although I took his money I always let him know it wasn't enough. Given time, I felt I could win him back, until the day he told me, over the phone, that he was 'seeing' someone else.

In a panic, I played my last card and told him I had the Philosopher's Stone. 'I found it inside the, the thing they cut out of me. I kept it.'

'Why didn't you tell me before?'

For the first time since before the operation I felt the flutter of hope inside. 'Well, you know, Daniel, you haven't been very nice to me. If we're not partners anymore, then what business is it of yours what I have?'

'What does it look like?' When I described it, he said flatly, 'That's not very big.'

'When Helvetius complained that a piece the size of a mustard seed was too small to be of use he was given a piece only half that size, and used it to make several ounces of gold.'

'What do you know about Helvetius?'

He spoke as if he'd completely forgotten that he'd once shared the Great Work with me.

'Daniel, are you interested or not?'

No alchemist could have refused. I took the Metropolitan Line out to his house that very evening, for the first time since hospital.

Although it was still light and I was looking out for it, I didn't see his house on the journey. I realized why later: with the strange, shroud-like growth gone from the back of the house there was nothing to distinguish it from its neighbours. I wondered, had I dwindled back into the ordinary, too, now, my specialness cut out of me? Or would the tiny stone I kept clamped between finger and thumb redeem me?

The ancient texts advised a variety of methods for testing the Stone, each more lengthy than the last. We opted for the quickest. I managed to shave off a bit of the stone with a razor-knife and introduced it into a pan containing twelve ounces of lead, which we melted down over one of the gas burners on the kitchen cooker. Before morning dawned we had our result: two ounces of pure gold.

For a moment I saw euphoria and greed mingled undisguised on Daniel's face. 'We've done it!' I cried, thinking, *I've got you!*

But his face closed up at the sound of my voice. He shook his head. 'Big deal. Two ounces of gold. Worth about three hundred dollars per ounce on today's market.'

'We can make more.'

'Oh, yes. At *least* another six ounces.'

'I can't win, can I? The only reason you want me is to produce your precious Philosopher's Stone, and when I do – at huge cost to myself! – you turn me away.' In a withering tone I finished, 'It's not big enough!'

'You don't understand anything,' he said fiercely. 'It's not to do with size, or with gold. It's not the product, it's the process. Our child wasn't ready – and now we'll never know what might have been because you let them cut it out. You let them kill it.'

'It would have killed me!'

'Oh, you know that, do you? If you believe everything they tell you, you'd have to believe that's not real gold, that what we just did was impossible.' He sighed, becoming calmer. 'Pregnancy is a journey fraught with danger. Women do still die in childbirth, but is that a justification for abortion? You wouldn't have died, only changed, if you'd waited and let it be born.'

'Daniel, that was not a child. I saw it, remember?'

'You saw what they took out of you: the *magna mater*, the basic material of life, alive and growing until it was ripped from you. Oh, Bess.' He groaned. 'It's not about making gold – that's just one aspect. What you had inside you – it could have been all knowledge; it could have been eternal life, a transformation for both of us . . .' He looked stricken. 'It's my fault, isn't it? My fault, not yours. If I'd been a proper teacher, if I'd made you understand the risks and the rewards, you'd never have gone near that hospital.' He began to weep as nakedly and helplessly as a child, and I put my arms around him and tried to give him comfort.

Finally I realized that I was not the only victim in this. I recognized just how seriously I had hurt him.

'Poor, poor,' I murmured, and stroked his head and kissed away his tears. For the first time in ages I began to feel aroused, and when his tears were gone, I unfastened his trousers and snaked a hand inside.

He did nothing to encourage me. He stood very still, utterly passive, while in my hand he quickly grew hard. I pulled down his pants. Looking at his face I saw a familiar shy, boyish, slightly guilty smile quivering about his lips. In a rush of affection and desire I sank to my knees and sucked him, and when he came, I swallowed his semen. It was something I had never done before, but it felt right, a symbol of a new beginning, my new and utter commitment to him. I had let him down once, but would never do so again.

I went off to the bathroom for a wash, debating whether to take the day off. I wondered what Daniel planned to do, and thought what a warm and welcome relief it would be to spend the day in bed with him. When I came out, I found he'd made a pot of coffee.

I smiled at him as he poured me a cup, but lost the smile when he put the lump of gold into my saucer.

'Oh, no.'

'It's yours.'

'Ours.'

'Bess, it's over.'

'Oh, yeah? What was that just then?'

'That was sex. And it was your idea.'

I felt sick. 'You're saying you didn't enjoy it?'

'Enjoyment isn't the point. One sexual . . . spasm . . . can't revive a dead relationship.'

'Are you so sure it's dead?'

'You're the one who killed it.' He saw my face, and his own crumbled into grief. 'Oh, Bess! I'm not blaming you.'

'Like hell!'

'It was my fault, too, I see that now. Naturally, you were afraid, you didn't understand. How could you? The Work was still new to you. Never mind all that. Whatever happened, it's over now.'

'You hate me.'

'No, of course not.'

'Then why can't we forget the past and start over?'

'Because we can't.' He closed his eyes briefly, then looked straight into mine. 'Look, we can't even communicate. We live in different worlds. Where I see something wonderful, you see something terrible. A tumour instead of the Philosopher's Stone. It's not your fault; I was wrong to try to change you.'

'I *will* change.' I'd lost all shame, all sense of myself. I can't explain it. I would be whatever he wanted.

'It's too late for that.'

'Because you don't love me anymore.'

'No!' Tears rose to his eyes again; I felt I was looking through their clarity straight into his soul. He put out his hand and I gripped it. 'I love you, Bess. God help me, I do. Forever. But I can't give up The Work, not even for you. It would be like giving up my life.'

'I'm not asking you to. I'll help.'

'You can't.' He watched me warily as he pronounced my death sentence. 'I know you mean well, but you're no good to me without a womb. I must have a woman in my life, for The Work – a complete woman.'

Strangely enough, I did understand. And accepted what I know many would find unacceptable. I had entered into his alchemical world far enough for that. I saw the impasse before me, but still I refused to give up. I could not grow another womb, but there must be a way to keep him.

'We can still be friends,' I tried.

'If – if you can bear it.'

I would have to. 'I can if you'll be honest with me. You mustn't try to protect me, or control me, by keeping secrets. This woman you're seeing . . . ?'

'It might not work out,' he said swiftly.

'If it doesn't, there'll be someone else. You'll need your

other woman, for the physical side. She'll be your crucible. I can accept that as long as I know that I'm your *real* partner, spiritually and intellectually. As long as you still love me, ours will be the real sacred marriage.'

Was it love or hate that drove me down that road? My life seemed out of my own control. I was driven by a determination to cling to Daniel, for better or worse, to keep him as I had not been able to keep the fruit of my womb.

But if he was my weakness, I was also his. He did love me, I'm sure of it. He had not expected to have a second chance, but that's what I was offering, and he was grateful for it. When I said I must have my own key to his house he handed over the spare without a murmur, and I knew then that no new woman would be able to dislodge me from his life, no matter what.

My grandmother died that month, leaving me an inheritance which promised to change my life. Instead of the tiny flat I would have to scrimp and save to afford, I could look at houses. By great good fortune the house next door to Daniel's – the end of the terrace – was up for sale. I made an offer straightaway and had it accepted. The mortgage would mean large monthly payments, but it would be worth it to live so close to Daniel. I imagined how someday we would knock down walls to make our two houses one from within, just as our apparently separate lives were joined already.

While I waited for the survey and search to be completed, I divided my time between Saskia's flat and Daniel's house. We were still working out the boundaries of our new relationship; I knew I had to be careful not to push him too far, too fast, but to give him plenty of space. Things were a bit awkward with Saskia, too. Living together in her tiny flat had put a strain on our friendship. I sensed, too, that she disapproved of my clinging to Daniel after he'd treated me so badly, although she couldn't point the finger, having fallen for yet another inappropriate, unavailable man. By unspoken agreement, we didn't discuss our relationships. Sometimes, by prior arrangement, I spent the night at Daniel's when he was out with his new girlfriend, so Saskia and I could both have a break.

Daniel and I got together about twice a week. Usually, we would have a meal together, maybe go on to the pub, and I'd spend the night. We'd resumed a sexual relationship, although it was not as I would have liked. Frustratingly for me, Daniel found normal intercourse impossible. The thought of my missing womb, the idea that I was 'not whole', killed his sexual desire. He went limp every time. But I could usually arouse him with my mouth, so oral sex became usual for us.

One day as I was going 'home' to Saskia's flat – the exchange of contracts still hovering mysteriously just out of reach – I took a detour to search out a corner shop and came back a different way. Usually I approached Saskia's flat, which was on the second story of an old house, from the front, but this time my detour brought me out on the street immediately behind hers, and when I glanced up at the trees, which were just beginning to bud, I glimpsed through them a pale, translucent shimmering which was immediately and horrifyingly familiar to me.

Praying I was wrong, I began to dodge and shift about, desperate for a better view.

I saw it plain: a growth, like the puffed throat of a frog, projected from the back wall of Saskia's house. I knew at once what it meant, and only wondered how I could have been blind for so long. Daniel's nameless 'other' was Saskia, and Saskia's guilty secret was Daniel.

She didn't try to deny it when I confronted her; she actually felt relieved. 'He made me promise that I wouldn't hurt you by telling – I never wanted to hurt you! And I guess I kind of thought – well, it's so obvious that he loves you more than he cares about me, so I thought, what's the point of putting you through hell for a little sexual fling. He'd only find someone else – he's that sort, you know.'

'Yes, yes,' I said impatiently. 'I knew he had a girlfriend – I just didn't know it was you. I feel such a fool – '

'Oh, no, Bess, you mustn't! I'm sorry, I really am. I do love Daniel – I can't help how I feel – but you're my dearest friend; you're more important to me than he is. If you want me to, I'll break it off with him. I'll never see him again. All you have to do is ask.'

I hoped she was lying. I didn't like the idea that her feelings for him were so shallowly rooted. I shook my head, staring into her eyes. 'Of course not. You can't break it off with him now. You're carrying his child.'

Saskia knew nothing about it, and didn't believe me. She'd had her period only a week before, and besides . . . Yes, I knew about the single ovary, and the tipped cervix. But I had my own experience to go on, and I knew what I'd seen.

'Did Daniel tell you I was p.g.? He's got such a thing about wombs, and conception, and "proper" sex with simultaneous orgasms. He fantasizes . . .' She was concerned about me; I'd gone very pale because I'd just realized what I'd done with my thoughtless outburst. Saskia didn't know, and she *mustn't* know; not, at least, until I'd been able to make some plans.

'Bess, what is it? You're so pale. Is this all too horrible for you? I'm so sorry. But I'm not pregnant, I'm sure I'm not – you certainly don't have to worry that I'll take Daniel away. I'm not a very likely candidate to bear him a child . . .'

'No, I know that,' I said, thinking of her cyst. 'I got a bit hysterical, that's all. It was when I suddenly realized that you and Daniel . . . But now that I've had a chance to think about it, I'm glad it's you, Saskia, I really am.'

'I'll never take Daniel away from you, Bess. You do know that?'

'Yes. I do know that.'

*

I told Daniel the next day, and warned him to be careful. 'She's not like me. She trusts her doctor; she'll go for surgery at the first sign. You've got to *act* as soon as she tells you, or we'll lose it.'

'How? What can I do? I can't talk to her about alchemy. You're too right, she's not like you. Oh, Bess, this was a mistake, I should never have let it happen.'

His defeatism infuriated me. 'The past is past. Stop moaning about it. We've got another chance now, both of us, through her.'

'But how? She'll want to be rid of it as soon as she knows.'

'I thought the coal cellar. Yours, at a pinch, but mine would be better, if I get possession in time. It wouldn't be so hard to soundproof, we wouldn't have to worry about neighbours.'

Luckily, I was able to exchange contracts only a week later, with vacant possession following the week after that. I was able to invest a full month in getting my house ready before Saskia came to see me with her news.

She'd decided to tell me, but not Daniel.

'It's another cyst, and this one could be the big C. I just can't cope with Daniel's reactions. I'll have to tell him afterwards, of course. I know it'll be the end of us – he was so weird about your operation, and he really loved you. I know he doesn't really love me, not for myself. He's got such strange ideas about women's bodies! After the operation . . .'

Although I didn't expect to be successful, I had to try to talk her out of what she planned to do. 'Maybe you won't have to have an operation. Maybe, if you tell your doctor how important it is for you to be able to bear a child, he might suggest some alternative treatments first. You don't know it's malignant.'

'He's ahead of you on that,' Saskia said. 'He's done a biopsy *in situ*, and then, if it proves to be benign, we could leave it, while I tried to get pregnant: probably take some fertility drug, then *in vitro* fertilization, followed by a heavily monitored pregnancy – I could spend up to five or six months in the hospital, you know, even before the Caesarean. *Then* they'd do the hysterectomy. All that stuff just to make my body produce a baby. And I'm not even sure that I want one.'

'What? Of course you do!'

She shook her head.

'Come on, Sask, I can remember when you were trying to get pregnant.'

'That was long ago, and in another country, and besides, the wench is dead. Look, once upon a time I wanted to have a baby with a particular man. I don't want to have a baby with Daniel.'

'If you're worried about taking him away from me . . .'

She almost laughed. 'Oh, Bess, I know you love him, but he's not for me. I can see that now. I certainly don't want his baby.'

'Have you thought about what *he* might want?'

'Bess, I'm not pregnant, you know. And all this is hypothetical, dependent on the tumour being benign. If it's not . . .' She made a little cutting motion across her stomach, and I felt sick.

'What about Daniel?'

'Daniel's history. I thought you'd be pleased – I've finally come to my senses. I don't love him. I think probably I never did. All the time what I felt for him wasn't love, it was a kind of desperation. I was desperate to make him love me, value me for myself, and he just couldn't. That's my pathology, you know, to be hooked on men who are incapable of loving me, for whatever reason. Or at least it used to be. But now that I know . . . now I *am* sick, I'm going to get it cut out of me, the whole mess.'

'Let me make you a cup of tea,' I said.

She commented on the taste – it was very sweet – and I told her that it was a special herbal mixture with extra honey to help build up her immune system.

She smiled gratefully. 'Thanks, Bess. You're with me in this? I mean, I don't expect you to come to the hospital – '

'I'm with you all the way.'

The sedative took effect quickly, and I called Daniel to come over and help me carry her down to the cellar, afraid that I might do her an injury if I tried to haul her down on my own.

I'd decorated the low, windowless cellar to look as cosy and cheerful and as much to Saskia's taste as possible, although I knew she'd be bound to see it as a prison. It was just too bad that she didn't love Daniel, or me, enough to see things from our point of view.

I'll pass over the next months quickly. It should have been a happy time, and, of course, Daniel was anticipating the birth with joy, but Saskia couldn't. She was angry and fearful at first, and after the pain began, it was even worse.

My own pains began around the same time, about three months after the beginning of Saskia's confinement: strong, sickening pains deep in my stomach. I remembered what I'd read about the *couvade,* the sympathetic pregnancy suffered by men in some primitive societies. It occurred to me that since I no longer had a womb, this might be my way of sharing Saskia's mystical pregnancy.

Then I began to have trouble swallowing. What with one thing and another it became harder to function, to go out to work, even to take care of Saskia. I longed to give up and quit, to crawl into my bed and sleep, but I could not forget my responsibilities.

I received notice of an appointment with my oncologist. Normally I would have tossed the letter in the bin, but I wasn't feeling normal. I decided to go. It would mean a day off work and a chance to talk to someone who might be more sympathetic to my pain than either Daniel or Saskia.

I got more than sympathy. I learned that there were tumours growing in my throat and stomach.

What I was experiencing was not *couvade* but the real thing.

The cancer had spread so fast and so far that surgery wasn't an option. The doctor spoke hesitantly about radiation and chemotherapy, but I was firmly against.

'You can't kill them,' I said, and he agreed, not understanding that I was stating my firm objection to any attempt to try to kill what I welcomed. If I shook, it was not from fear, but with ecstatic joy. I couldn't wait to get home and share the news with Daniel.

According to the doctor, I have about two months, maybe three, before the end. I am not afraid. The end of this bodily life will be a new beginning, a great and previously unknown transformation. Out of our bodies will come treasures which will have made our lives worthwhile.

Food Man

This story from the mid-1990s made it onto the Tiptree Awards shortlist. The Tiptree is an award for 'works of science fiction that explore and expand gender roles'. I am all in favour of that, and happy for any of my work to be connected with such an aim, but I was a little surprised that it should be this *story, not merely because it is hardly science fiction, but also because although the main character suffers from an eating disorder, that's not something necessarily connected to gender. But, then, on second thought I realized that almost* anything *can be connected to gender; and, as plenty of writers have shown, food, sex, family relationships and body image are all feminist issues. 'Food Man' is not only about all of those things, but also, in a weird way, female empowerment . . .*

DINNER WAS THE REAL PROBLEM.

Mornings, it was easy to rush out of the house without eating; when it wasn't, when her mother made an issue of it, she'd eat an orange or half a grapefruit. At lunchtime she was either at school or out so there was no one to pressure her into eating anything she didn't want. But dinner was a problem. She had to sit there, surrounded by her family, and eat whatever her mother had prepared, and no matter how she pushed it around her plate it was obvious how little she was eating. She experimented with dropping bits on the floor and secreting other bits in her sleeves or in her pockets, but it wasn't easy, her mother's eyes were so sharp, and she'd rather eat than suffer a big embarrassing scene.

Her brother, the creep, provided the solution. He was always looking at her, staring at her, mimicking her, teasing, and while she didn't like it at any time, at mealtimes it was truly unbearable. She honestly could not bear to put a bite in her mouth with him staring at her in that disgusting way. Her parents warned him to leave her alone, and shifted their places so they weren't directly facing each other, but still it wasn't enough. He said she was paranoid. She knew that even paranoids have enemies. Even if he wasn't staring at her right now, he had stared before, and the prospect that he might stare again clogged her throat with fear. How could she be expected to eat under such circumstances? How could anyone? If she could have dinner on a tray in her room alone, she would be fine.

Her mother, relieved by the prospect of solving two family problems at once, agreed to this suggestion. 'But only for as long as you eat. If I don't see a clean plate coming out of your room you'll have to come back and sit with the rest of us.'

It was easy to send clean plates out of her room. After she'd eaten what she could stomach she simply shoved the rest of the food under her bed. Suspecting that the sound of a toilet flushing immediately after a meal would arouse her mother's suspicions, she planned to get rid of the food in the morning. Only by morning she'd forgotten, and by the time she remembered it was dinnertime again.

It went on like that. Of course the food began to smell, rotting away down there under her bed, but no one else was allowed into her bedroom, and she knew the smell didn't carry beyond her closed door. It was kind of disgusting, when she was lying in bed, because then there was no avoiding it, the odour simply rose up, pushed its way through the mattress and forced itself upon her. Yet even that had its good side; she thought of it as her penance for being so fat, and was grateful for the bad smell because it made her even more adamantly opposed to the whole idea of food. How could other people bear the constant, living stink of it? The cooking, the eating, the excreting, the rotting?

When she could no longer bear the enforced, nightly intimacy with the food she refused to eat, she decided it was time to get rid of it. Before looking at it, she decided she'd better arm herself with some heavy-duty cleaning tools, paper towels, rubber gloves, maybe even a small shovel. But when she opened the door of her room to go out, there was her mother, looking as if she'd been waiting awhile.

'Where are you going?'

'What is this, a police state?' Hastily, afraid the smell would get out, she pulled her door shut behind her. 'I want a glass of water.'

'From the bathroom?'

'No, I thought I'd go down to the kitchen and get a glass. Why, aren't I allowed to go to the bathroom?'

'Of course you are. I was just worried – Oh, darling, you're so thin!'

'Thin is good.'

'Within limits. But you're too thin, and you're getting thinner. It's not healthy. If you really are eating – '

'Of course I'm eating. You've seen my plates. I thought they'd be clean enough even for you.'

'If you've been flushing your good dinners down the toilet – '

'Oh, Mother, honestly! Of course I haven't! Is that why you're lurking around up here? Trying to catch me in the act?' She realized, with considerable irritation at herself, that she could've been flushing her dinner neatly and odourlessly away for a couple of weeks before arousing suspicion, but that it had now become impossible.

'Or throwing up after you eat – '

'Oh, yuck, you'll make me sick if you talk about it! Yuck! I hate vomiting; I'm not some weirdo who likes to do it! Really!'

'I'm sorry. But I'm worried about you. If you can eat regular meals and still lose weight there must be something wrong. I think you should see a doctor.'

She sighed wearily. 'All right. If it will make you happy, I'll see a doctor.'

She was just beginning to feel good about her body again. She didn't care what the doctor said, and when he insisted she look at herself in a full-length mirror, wearing only her underwear – something she had not dared to do for months – she was not grossed-out. The pendulous breasts, the thunder-thighs, all the fat, all the jiggling flesh, had gone, leaving someone lean, clean, and pristine. She felt proud of herself. The way the doctor looked at her was just right, too: with a certain distance, with respect. Not a trace of that horrible, furtive greed she'd seen in the eyes of her brother's friends just six months ago. The look of lust mixed with disgust which men had started giving her after her body had swelled into womanhood was something she hoped she'd never see again.

'How long since you had a period?' the doctor wanted to know.

'About four months.' She was pleased about that, too. You weren't supposed to be able to turn the clock back and reject the nasty parts of growing up, but she had done it. She was in control of herself.

In reality, of course, the control was in the hands of others. As a minor, she was totally dominated by adults, chief among them her parents. After the doctor's diagnosis that she was deliberately starving herself, she was forced to return to the dinner table.

Resentful and humiliated, she pushed food around on her plate and refused to eat it. Threats of punishment only strengthened her resolve.

'That's right,' she snarled. 'Make me a prisoner. Let everybody know. Keep me locked up, away from my friends, with no phone and no fun – that's really going to make me psychologically healthy. That's really going to make me eat!'

Bribes were more successful, but her parents either weren't willing or could not afford to come up with a decent bribe at every single mealtime, and she simply laughed to scorn the notion that she'd let someone else control every bit of food that passed her lips for an entire week just for a pair of shoes or the use of the car on Saturday. She didn't need new clothes, CDs, the car, or anything her parents could give her, and she wanted them to know it.

Now that the battle zone was marked out and war had been openly declared, food was a constant, oppressive preoccupation. She was reminded of food by everything she saw, by everything around her. Hunger, which had once been the pleasurably sharp edge that told her she was achieving something, was now a constant, miserable state. She no longer even controlled the amounts she ate; she ate even less than she wanted because she couldn't bear to let her mother feel that she was winning, that anything she put in her mouth was a concession to her. She couldn't back down now, she couldn't even appear to be backing down. If she did, she would never recover; her whole life would be lived out meekly under her mother's heavy thumb.

Lying in bed one night, trying to get her mind away from food, she realized that the smell which permeated her mattress and pillow and all her bedclothes had changed. A subtle change, yet distinctive. What had been a foul stench was now . . . not so foul. There was something *interesting* about it. She sniffed a little harder, savouring it. It was still far from being something you could describe as a *good* smell – it was a nasty smell, not something she'd want anyone else to suspect she could like, and yet there was something about it which made her want more. It was both deeply unpleasant and curiously exciting. She couldn't explain even to herself why the bad smell had become so pleasurable to her. It made her think of sex, which sounded so awful when it was described. No matter how they tried to make it glamorous in the movies, the act itself was clearly awkward and nasty. And yet it was obvious that the participants found that embarrassing, awkward nastiness deeply wonderful and were desperate for a chance to do it again. It was one of the great mysteries of life.

She wondered what the food under her bed looked like now. All the different foods, cooked and uncooked, pushed together into one great mass, breaking down, rotting, flowing together . . . Had it undergone a change into something rich and strange? Or would the sight of it make her puke? She had decided she was never going to clean under her bed – her refusal, although unknown by her mother, was another blow against her – but now, all of a sudden, she wished she could see it.

There was a movement under her bed.

Was it her imagination? She held very still, even holding her breath, and it came again, stronger and more certain. This time she felt as well as heard it. The bed was rocked by something moving underneath. Whatever was moving under there was coming out.

Although she'd turned out her lamp before going to bed, her room was not totally dark; it never was. The curtains were unlined and let in light from the street, so there was always a pale, yellowish glow. By this dim, constant light she saw the man who emerged from under her bed.

Her heart beat harder at the sight of him, but she was not frightened. There might not be light enough to read by, but there was enough to show her this man was no ordinary serial killer, burglar, or rapist from off the street. For one thing, he wore no clothes. For another, he was clearly not a normal human being. The smell of him was indescribable. It was the smell of rotting food; it was the smell of her own bed. And, she did not forget, she had wished to see what her food had become.

He made no menacing or seductive or self-willed motions but simply stood there, showing himself to her. When she had looked her fill she invited him into her bed, and he gave himself to her just as she wanted.

What took place in her bed thereafter was indescribable. She could not herself remember it very clearly the next day – certainly not the details of who did what to whom with what when and where. What she would never forget was the intense, sensory experience of it all: his smell, that dreadful stench with its subtle, enticing undercurrent, that addictive, arousing odour which he exuded in great gusts with every motion, and which, ultimately, seemed to wrap around her and absorb her like the great cloak of sleep; the exciting pressure of his body on hers, intimate and demanding and satisfying in a way she could never have imagined; and her own orgasms, more powerful than anything she'd previously experienced on her own.

She understood about sex now. To an outsider it looked ridiculous or even horrible, but it wasn't for looking at, and certainly not by outsiders – it was for feeling. It was about nothing but feeling, feeling things you'd never felt before, having feelings you couldn't have by yourself, being felt. It was wonderful.

In the morning she woke to daylight, alone in her deliciously smelly bed, and she felt transformed. She suspected she had not, in the technical sense, lost her virginity; far from losing anything, she had gained something. She felt different; she felt expanded and enriched; she felt powerful; she felt hungry. She went downstairs and, ignoring as usual her mother's pitiful breakfast offering, went to the counter and put two slices of bread in the toaster.

Wisely, her mother did not comment. Her brother did, when she sat down at the table with two slices of toast thickly spread with peanut butter.

'What's this, your new diet?'

'Shut up, pig-face,' she said calmly, and, yes, her mother let her get away with that, too. Oh, she was untouchable today; she had her secret, a new source of power.

At lunchtime the apple she'd intended to eat wasn't

enough, and she consumed the cheese sandwich her mother had made for her, and the carrot sticks, a bag of potato chips, and a pot of strawberry yogurt. Sex, she realized, took a lot of energy, burned a lot of calories. She had to replace them, and she had to build herself up. Now that she had a reason for wanting to be fit and strong she recognized how weak she had become by not eating. She wouldn't have to worry about getting fat, not for a long time, not as long as the nightly exercise continued.

It did continue, and grew more strenuous as her strength, her curiosity, her imagination, all her appetites increased. She no longer feared getting fat; on the contrary, she was eager to gain weight. She wanted to be stronger, and she needed more weight for muscle. More flesh was not to be sneered at, now that she knew how flesh could be caressed and aroused. She ate the meals that were prepared for her, and more. She no longer had to be obsessive about controlling her intake of food because it was no longer the one area of her life she felt she had some control over. Now she controlled the creature under her bed, and their passionate nights together were the secret which made the daytime rule of parents, teachers, and rules, bearable.

Her nights were much more important than her days, and during the night she was in complete control. Or so she thought, until the night her creature did something she didn't like.

It was no big deal, really; he just happened to trap her in an uncomfortable position when he got on top of her, and he didn't immediately respond to her attempts to get him to move. It was something anyone might have done, inadvertently, unaware of her feelings – but he was not 'anyone' and he'd never been less than totally aware of her every sensation and slightest desire. Either he'd been aware that he was hurting her because he'd intended it, or he'd been unaware because he was no longer so much hers as he'd been in the beginning, because he was becoming someone else. She wasn't sure which prospect she found the more frightening.

The rot had started in their relationship, and although each incremental change was tiny – hardly noticeable to someone less sensitive than she – they soon demolished her notion of being in control.

She was not in control. She had no power. She lived for her nights with him; she needed him. But what if he didn't need her? What if one night he no longer wanted her?

It could happen. He'd started to criticize, his fingers pinching the excess flesh which had grown back, with her greed, on her stomach and thighs, and she could tell by the gingerly way he handled her newly expanded breasts and ass that he didn't like the way they jiggled. When he broke off a kiss too quickly she knew it was because he didn't like the garlic or the onions on her breath. The unspoken threat was always there: one night he might not kiss her at all. One night he might just stay under the bed.

She didn't think she could bear that. Having known sex, she was now just like all those people she'd found so incomprehensible in books and movies: she had to keep on having it. And she knew no other partner would satisfy her. She'd been spoiled by her food man for anyone else.

She began to diet. But it was different this time. Once not eating had been pleasurable and easy; now it was impossibly difficult. She no longer liked being hungry; it made her feel weak and cranky, not powerful at all, not at all the way she'd used to feel. This time she wasn't starving to please herself and spite the world, but to please someone else. She went on doing it only because she decided she preferred sex to food; she could give up one if allowed to keep the other. And by promising herself sex, rewarding herself with explicit, graphic, sensual memories every time she said no to something to eat, she managed to continue starving herself back to desirability.

This suffering wouldn't be forever. Once she'd reached her – or his – ideal weight, she hoped to maintain it with sufficient exercise and ordinary meals.

But the sex that she was starving herself for was no longer all that great. She was so hungry it was hard to concentrate. His smell kept reminding her of food instead of the sex they were engaged in. Except when she was on the very brink of orgasm, she just couldn't seem to stop thinking about food.

And as time went on, and she still wasn't quite thin enough to please him, not quite thin enough to stop her killing diet, she began to wonder why she was doing it. What was so great about sex, anyway? She could give herself an orgasm any time she wanted, all by herself. Maybe they weren't so intense, maybe they were over quicker, but so what? When they were over she used to fall asleep contented, like someone with a full stomach, instead of lying awake, sated in one sense but just beginning to remember how hungry she still was for food. As for arousal – what was so great about arousal? It was too much like hunger. It was fine in retrospect, when it had been satisfied, but while it was going on it was just like hunger, an endless need, going on and painfully on.

She didn't know how much longer she could bear it. And then, one night, she went from not knowing to not being able. When her lover climbed into bed with her, swinging one leg across her, holding her down as he so often did now, keeping her in her place, the smell of him made her feel quite giddy with desire, and her mouth filled with saliva.

As his soft, warm, odorous face descended to hers she bit into it, and it was just like a dinner roll freshly baked. She even, as her teeth sank into his nose, tasted the salty tang of butter.

He did not cry out – he never had made a sound in all the nights she had known him – nor did he try to escape or fight back as she bit and tore away a great chunk of his face and greedily chewed and swallowed it. She felt a tension in him, a general stiffening, and then, as, unable to resist, she took a second bite, she recognized what he was feeling. It was sexual excitement. It was desire. He wanted to be eaten. This was what he had wanted from the very first night, when he had pressed himself, first his face and then all the other parts of his body in turn, against her mouth – only she had misunderstood. But this was what he was for.

She ate him.

It was the best ever, better by far than their first night together, which had seemed to her at that time so wonderful. That had been only sex. This was food and sex together, life and death.

When she had finished she felt enormous. Sprawling on the bed, she took up the whole of it and her arms and legs dangled off the sides. She was sure she must be at least twice her usual size. And the curious thing was that although she felt satisfied, she did not feel at all full. She was still hungry.

Well, maybe hungry wasn't exactly the right word. Of course she wasn't hungry. But she still had space for something more. She still wanted something more.

The springs groaned as she sat up, and her feet hit the floor much sooner than she'd expected. She was bigger than usual; not only fatter, but taller, too. She had to duck to get through her own bedroom door.

She stood for a moment in the hall, enjoying her enormous new size and the sense of power it gave her. This, not starving herself and not having secret sex, was true power. Food and eating and strength and size. She knew she wanted to eat something more, maybe a lot of something more before the night was over. There was a smell in the air which had her moist and salivating with desire. She licked her lips and looked around, her fingers flexing, but there wasn't much of interest in the hallway. A framed studio portrait of the family hung above the only piece of furniture, a small table with a wobbly leg. On the table was a telephone, a pad of yellow

Post-it notes, and a gnawed wooden pencil. The taste of the pencil was as immediately familiar to her as the salty tang of her own dandruff and sloughed skin cells beneath a nibbled fingernail, and did about as much to satisfy her hunger. The shiny, dark chocolate coloured telephone wasn't as easy to eat as the pencil had been, but she persevered, and had crunched her way through more than half of it before the unpleasant lack of taste, and the discomfort of eating shards of plastic, really registered. She finished it anyway – it was all fuel – and then sniffed the air.

From the bedrooms where her brother and her parents slept drifted the rich, strong, disturbing smells of sex and food. Aroused and ravenous, she followed the scent of her next meal.

Mr Elphinstone's Hands

I have a long-standing fascination with the history of spiritualism, especially nineteenth-century mediums and séances. The concept of ectoplasm intrigued me: what was *this stuff that was said to ooze from the body of the trance medium? Sometimes like a cloud that disappeared in the light, it could be light and airy like a luminous spiderweb, or solid, cold and sticky to the touch. Psychic investigators theorized it might be the basis of all psychic phenomena, the spiritual equivalent of protoplasm, allowing insubstantial spirits to take on physical form. This interest came together with a true story I read about an old New England family (coincidentally named Tuttle) whose unmarried daughter became pregnant. They did not throw her out to starve, but kept her (I don't remember what happened to the baby) at home for the rest of her days. Although they provided food and shelter, they made her a pariah in their midst, refusing to look at her or speak to her ever again, as if she was a sort of living ghost they suffered to share their house.*

MR ELPHINSTONE'S HANDS were cold and slightly damp. This unpleasant physical detail was Eustacia Wallace's first impression of the medium, and even after she had a good look at him in the light – the large, deep-set eyes, the greying beard, the high forehead – even after she had heard him speak in a well-modulated, educated voice, Eustacia could think only of how much she had disliked the touch of his hands.

She glanced at her sister and saw that, like the others in the stuffy, overcrowded parlour, Lydia Wallace Steen was completely enraptured. She found herself rubbing the palms of her hands on her skirt, and forced herself to stop. If she had been wearing gloves, like any properly brought up young lady – if she hadn't been such a hoyden as to lose her last pair and too careless to borrow from her sister – if she had been dressed as the other ladies, dressed as she should be, she would have known nothing of the condition of Mr Elphinstone's flesh.

Lydia would be horrified – quite rightly – if she knew her younger sister's thoughts. Eustacia struggled, as she had struggled so often before, to lift them to a higher plane. Mr Elphinstone was talking about Heavenly Rapture, Life Eternal, and the Love Which Passeth All Understanding. Eustacia found it hard to concentrate. It wasn't that she preferred to think about Mr Elphinstone's hands, or about the unpleasant warmth of the room, or about the fact that she hadn't had enough to eat at dinner, only . . . all these things, things that belonged to the real world, had a power that abstract ideas, for all their beauty, lacked. What chance had Perfect Love against a joint of beef or a cold, moist, human hand?

'We imagine the dead, our loved dead, as being like us; as being, still, the people we knew – our children, parents, siblings, friends, sweethearts. We think of them wearing the same bodies, with no difference, only passed beyond our ken. But, my dear, dear, brothers and sisters,' Mr Elphinstone went on, lowering his voice dramatically, 'this is *not so*. Death is a transformation much greater than the birth to which it is sometimes compared. The soul leaves the body at death, achieving a new and wonderful existence. Mortality is burnt away with the flesh. There are no bodies in the afterlife, no flesh in heaven. Do you understand me?'

Heads nodded around the room. Eustacia nodded, too, wondering if there would be refreshments later.

'They are different, the dead. We cannot comprehend how different; we will know that only when we join them. The wisest course is to accept our ignorance, to accept that they are gone from us, God's will has been done, and all is well . . . But, of course, it is the nature of the living to question and to mourn . . . *not* to accept, but to want, always, to know more. Isn't that why you're here?'

He stopped, apparently expecting an answer. There were uneasy shiftings from his listeners, and Eustacia took advantage of this to scoot her chair a little farther away from the fire. A thin, elderly woman in rusty black silks cleared her throat gently, and Mr Elphinstone let his dark eyes rest on her. 'Yes, Mrs Marcus? Tell us why you have come.'

'You know.'

'Yes, I know, but tell us.'

'It's my son, Nathanael. He died at Bull Run. He was only eighteen. My only boy . . . I never knew the moment of his passing; I waited a long time before I heard of his death, and even then I couldn't be certain . . . For years I— But finally . . . I thought I had accepted it. Two years ago my husband passed on. And since then I have thought more and more about our Nathanael . . . worrying about him. Waking up nights fearing he was cold, or hungry, or hurting. Mr Marcus could always take care of himself, and I was beside him at the end. But Nathanael was only a boy, and he died on a battlefield – I'll never really know *how* he died. I keep thinking, if only I could have been with him at the end, to mop his brow or hold his hand – to give him some little comfort . . . If only I could see him once more, to know that he's not in pain, and he's not unhappy . . . Just to see him once more . . . just to have a message from him, would make such a difference.'

'Ah, yes,' said Mr Elphinstone softly. 'Yes, of course. Touch and sight and hearing are all so important to us, the living. We cannot communicate without our senses; without them we cannot even *believe*. And the dead, who have passed beyond that, still feel our needs and attempt to give us what we want . . . they attempt to touch us, speak to us, communicate. Yet how can they communicate without a body? How can they speak, how can they touch without flesh?'

Mr Elphinstone's burning eyes fixed upon Eustacia. She went hot and cold. What did he want from her? Everyone was waiting for her to answer. There was no escape. She opened her mouth and out popped: 'Ghosts.'

'Ghosts?' He smiled gravely. 'But what are ghosts? Of what are they formed? The dead have no material substance. They do not block the light. *They cannot be seen*. And if they are to communicate with us in some way, in any way, physical substance is required. Where is it to come from? Nothing comes from nothing, as the poet said. And they must have something if we are to know them. From whence does it come? Why, dear people; dear, dear friends: it comes from me.' His smile became positively beatific; his face seemed to shine. 'I am uniquely gifted to give our dearly departed a brief, a transitory, yet not entirely unsatisfactory, semblance of life. Certain mediums are gifted in this way with the ability to produce a substance known as *ectoplasm*, an emanation from my very flesh which clothes the fleshless spirits and allows them, however briefly, to live and speak to their loved ones. It is not God's will that they should be returned to *this* life, when he has lifted them to a greater one, but neither is it God's will that those they have left behind should suffer unduly, or doubt His promise of eternal life. It has been said, truly, 'Seek and ye shall find; Ask and it shall be given.' So now, dear friends, dear seekers, I ask you to watch and wait as I offer myself unselfishly for the use of any spirits hovering near.'

The lamps were extinguished as he spoke, and the room was lit only by firelight. Lydia touched her arm and whispered: 'Watch *him*.'

Mr Elphinstone's eyes were closed. He sat like a statue. The others, having been here before, knew what to look for, so they were aware of what was happening before Eustacia noticed anything unusual. It was only by their rustlings and murmurings, and by Lydia's clutching hand that she understood it was not a trick of her eyes in the dim light: there was a whitish vapour issuing forth from the region of Mr Elphinstone's knees, upon which his hands rested.

But it wasn't only a vapour. It seemed to have more mass and solidity than that. Now he raised his hands to chest-level and it was obvious that this amorphous, shifting, cloudy-white stuff adhered in some way to his hands, grew out of them, perhaps. To the sound of gasps and moans and sighs from the assembly, the shining cloud between Mr Elphinstone's unmoving hands began to shape itself, to take on form. A human form, although small. A head, a neck, shoulders, arms . . . That was a face, surely? Eustacia wasn't sure if there were facial features to be discerned in the flickering light, or if she was unconsciously making pictures, as one did when watching clouds.

Suddenly Lydia cried out. 'That's my baby! Oh, sweet George!'

Then she tumbled off her chair in a dead faint.

The séance was brought to an abrupt halt by the need to help Lydia. In all the turmoil of fetching smelling salts and water and relighting the lamps, Eustacia did not see what happened to the ghostly baby, but it was gone. Mr Elphinstone, pale and worn-looking, remained aloof and said nothing as the women fussed about poor Lydia.

But poor Lydia was ecstatic. A trifle shaky, but, she assured everyone, the shock had been a joyful one, and she had not felt so well, so uplifted, in years.

'He was smiling,' said Lydia. 'I never thought I'd see my baby smile again! Taken from me at three months, but he's happy in Heaven. He'll always be happy now, smiling forever. Such a comfort, to see him again and know he's happy.'

It was for this Lydia had come to see Mr Elphinstone, of

course. Eustacia felt ashamed of herself for not realizing. She had thought at first this evening's outing one of Lydia's ways of introducing her younger sister to society and, therefore, to more eligible young men. Then she had thought the séance simply another of Lydia's larks, like going to hear the speakers for women's suffrage. She hadn't realized it was personal . . . Indeed, she tended to forget that her sister had ever known the brief, bitter blessing of motherhood. The babe had not lived long; had died three years ago, and in that time there had not come another to fill his cradle. And yet it had not occurred to her that Lydia might still be mourning. Usually Eustacia envied her sister the freedom granted her by marriage, but now she felt only pity.

For days afterwards, back at home on the farm, the excitements of visiting her sister left behind, Eustacia was plagued by something wrong with her hands. She couldn't seem to get them warm, not even by chafing them in front of the fire, which she was seldom allowed to do. For there was work to be done – there was always work to be done – and the best way to keep warm, said her sister Mildred, was to keep busy: it wasn't worth arguing. And it wasn't really the temperature of her fingers which bothered her but something else that seemed at odds with it: although they felt chilly, her hands perspired profusely and constantly. She wiped them whenever she could, on her apron or a towel, but it did no good. Her hands were always cold and damp.

Just like Mr Elphinstone's hands.

She tried not to think of it. It was too silly. What could his hands possibly have to do with hers? Was there such a thing as a cold in the hands that she might have caught from him? She had never heard of such a thing – a cold in the head, a cold in the chest, but not the hands – but that didn't mean it wasn't possible. A doctor would know . . . but doctors were expensive. Her father, seeing her perfectly healthy, would not countenance a visit to a doctor. If she tried to explain to her father she was certain his idea of a 'cure' would be the same as Mildred's: more hard work, less idle dreaming. She didn't try to tell him, or anyone. Embarrassed by this odd problem, she washed her hands often, and kept a supply of pocket handkerchiefs.

One afternoon as she helped her sister shake out and fold clean linen from the drying line, Mildred suddenly screwed up her face and said sharply, 'Eustacia! Have you a runny nose?'

'No, sister.' She felt her face get hot.

'Where do you suppose this came from?' There on the stiff, freshly washed whiteness of the sheet glistened four little blobs of mucus. On the other side, Eustacia had no doubt, would be found a fifth, the imprint left by her thumb. She stood mute, blushing.

'Have you lost your pocket handkerchief? 'Tis a filthy, childish habit, Eustacia, to blow your nose into your fingers; something I would not have expected from you, careless though you often are in your personal habits. And so unhealthy! You should think of others.'

'I didn't! My nose isn't – ! I didn't, Mildred, honestly!'

Mildred might have believed her since Eustacia, for all her faults, was no liar, but she couldn't stop, was scarcely aware of, the little furtive gestures by which she attempted to dry and hide her hands.

Mildred's eyes narrowed. 'Show me your hands.'

There was a kind of relief in being caught, in being forced, at last, to share her dirty secret. Despite her having just wiped them, her hands were already moist again. Welling up from the ball of each finger, pooling in the palms, was something thicker, stickier, and less liquid than the perspiration she had, for several days, believed – or wished – it to be.

Face twisting in disgust, Mildred held her sister's hands and examined them. Something nasty. But it had to be as obvious to Mildred as it was to Eustacia herself that the substance had not been blown or wiped onto the hands but was being produced – excreted – through the skin of the hands themselves.

'I don't know what it is,' Eustacia said. 'It's been happening . . . several days now. I told you my hands were cold. You can feel that. At first it was only the cold . . . then, they seemed to be wet – and now . . . this. I don't know what it is; I don't know how to make it stop.' She burst into tears.

Tears were always the wrong tactic with Mildred. Scowling, she flung Eustacia's hands back at her, and wiped her own harshly in her apron. 'Stop bawling, girl, it doesn't pain you, does it?'

Still sobbing, Eustacia shook her head.

'Well, then. It's nothing. No more'n a runny nose. Go wash yourself. Wash your hands well, mind. And keep them warm and dry. Maybe you should rest. That's it. Lie down and keep warm. You can have a fire in your room. Rest and keep warm and you'll be as right as rain by tomorrow.'

Eustacia stopped crying, pleased to know she would have the luxury of a fire in her room, and the still greater luxury of being allowed to do nothing at all.

In a family of hard workers, Eustacia was the lazy one. Lydia, too, had disliked the labour required of daughters in a house without servants, but Lydia was never idle. She enjoyed sewing, particularly embroidery and fine needlework, loved music, and was often to be found reading improving books. Whatever time she could steal from chores she invested in her own artistic and intellectual pursuits. Eustacia, on the other hand, enjoyed conversation and reading novels, but was happiest doing nothing. She liked to sleep, she liked to dream, she liked to muse and build castles in the air, sitting by the fire in the winter, or beneath a shady tree in the summer.

Although Mildred and Constance often castigated Eustacia for laziness, Lydia had formed an alliance with her, believing her younger sister was, like herself, of an artistic temperament. She encouraged Eustacia to forget her present woes by thinking of the happiness that would be hers in a few years, once she was married and the mistress of her own household. She, after all, had married well: a man who gave her a piano as a birthday present, and paid for private lessons. Their house in town was staffed by a cook, two maids, and a manservant, and there was a boy who came to do the garden twice a week. Lydia's husband was not rich, but he was, as they said, 'comfortable,' as well as being very much in love with his wife. Lydia was not so vulgar as to propose that Eustacia 'marry money,' but her husband knew a number of young men who were up and coming in the business world; men who would soon be able to afford a wife. It was to give Eustacia a chance of meeting an appropriate mate that Lydia often invited her to stay and took her out to concerts, soirées, balls, and other social gatherings.

Eustacia went along with Lydia wherever and whenever she was asked, but wasn't sure she believed marriage was the answer. She was not beautiful; more fatally, she lacked the personal charm that made men dote on Lydia. She might find a husband, but surely not romance. And even if she managed to marry a man who loved her, who was not a farmer, not poor, and not a petty tyrant like her father, her fate might still be that of her mother: to bear ten live children in twelve years, and die of exhaustion. She was not eager to exchange one form of servitude for another.

In the bedroom she had once shared with Lydia and Constance but now had to herself, Eustacia laid a fire in the hearth. The clear, sticky muck on her hands transferred itself to logs and paper but they burned with no apparent ill effect. When the fire was drawing nicely, she undressed and put on her nightgown. By that time she was yawning mightily, and as soon as she had crawled into bed she felt herself slipping deliciously into sleep.

When she woke the next morning her eyes were sticky,

the lashes so gummed together that it was a struggle to open them; and it was not only her eyes which were affected. All over her face, her head, her hands, her upper body, she could feel the tight, sticky pull of dried mucus. It was there like spiderwebs, or a welter of snail tracks, criss-crossing her face, looping around her neck, her arms, and dried stiffly in her hair. She felt a myriad cracks open as her face convulsed in disgust. A tortured moan escaped her lips as she scrambled out of bed. The water in the pitcher was icy cold, but for once she didn't mind, scarcely even noticed, as she splashed it onto hands and face and neck and chest, splashing it everywhere in a panic to get the slimy stuff off. It was not cold but revulsion which made her shiver.

Eustacia was not the excessively sensitive, refined creature contemporary manners held women should be. The daughter of a working farmer could not afford a weak stomach, but Eustacia knew that she was not so fastidious, not so 'nice', as her sisters, and this was a matter of some shame to her. Sometimes it made her angry. It wasn't fair. Men didn't have to pretend they were made of porcelain, so why should women? Perfection was unnatural. The body was a messy thing.

But not like *this*. This mess was not natural. Thank God, it proved to be easily washed away. Calming now that face and neck and hands were clean, Eustacia poured the last of the water into the bowl and tried to judge if there was enough to wash her hair.

There was a knock at the door and before she could say anything to stop her, Mildred had entered.

'Are you feeling better this morning? Ah!' Her sharp eyes saw something and the hidden worry on her face was transformed in an instant to something else, to understanding. 'It's your sick time, of course.'

'No – ' But before she could protest, Eustacia realized what she had been too preoccupied and frightened to notice earlier. She felt the wetness between her legs, twisted around and saw what Mildred had seen: the bloodstain on her gown, the unmistakable badge of her condition.

'But what are you doing up? You'll only make yourself ill. You want to keep warm. I'll fetch some clean towels. Now, into bed with you. I'll tell Pa you're feeling poorly and won't be down today. I'll bring you up some toast and tea, and build up the fire in here. Well? What are you waiting for?'

She made a gesture below her waist. 'I . . . have to clean myself.'

'All right. But be quick about it, don't be standing about in the cold . . . you know a woman's constitution is at its weakest at these times.'

Left alone, Eustacia realized that Mildred had decided there was nothing seriously wrong with her. The strangeness of hands exuding mucus had been redefined as a side effect of menstruation. No matter how odd and unpleasant, because it was happening now, when she was bleeding, it was to be accepted as yet another symptom of the female sickness.

She fashioned a towelling diaper for herself, put on a fresh nightgown, and got into bed. There was blood on the sheets, but it had dried. Why change them now, when she would surely soil them again? With five sisters she had seen how differently Eve's Curse afflicted different women, even women with the same parents and upbringing. She wondered: could Mildred be right?

But Mildred didn't know what she knew – that her hands had been cold and damp, sweating this strange substance not for just a day or two, but for more than a week.

A hand went to her head as she remembered. Tentative at first, then, frowning with surprise, she combed her fingers through clean hair: not clotted, not matted, not sticky, not stiff. Clean.

She got up to find the hand-mirror, to let her eyes confirm what her fingers told her. She picked her dress off the chair where she had hung it the previous night and examined the skirt. But although she remembered how often she had wiped her wet, sticky hands there, now she could neither see nor feel any trace of foreign matter. Her pocket handkerchief, too, was clean, although she could remember quite vividly the horrid slimy ball she'd made of it.

All gone now. Gone to nothing. Was it over?

She pressed her fingertips against her cheeks and brushed them against her lips. They felt cold and ever so slightly damp.

So quickly it had become a habit to wipe her hands whenever she felt them becoming wet. Now, half-reclining in bed, propped up on pillows, she decided to do nothing and see what happened.

Her hands rested on top of the blanket at chest-level. She felt a tingling sensation in the fingertips, and then she saw the stuff oozing out in faint, wispy tendrils.

Her skin crawled at the sight, and a horrible thought occurred to her. What if those slimy tendrils were now emerging not only from her fingertips, but all over her body? Those prickling feelings . . . She gasped for breath and held herself rigidly still, fighting down the urge to leap up and rip off her gown. She would wait and see.

The shining tendrils thickened and grew more solid. They took on the appearance of ghostly fingers. They *were* fingers. They were hands.

She thought of Mr Elphinstone's hands, and of the ghostly form which had appeared between them, had appeared to grow out of them. Meanwhile, the hands attached to her hands grew larger still, and then began to elongate, to grow away from her into arms. She stared in wonder. So she could do it, too! Mr Elphinstone wasn't so special, after all.

But these hands and arms were not those of a baby. They were much too big for any baby. And there was something unpleasantly familiar about them as they grew into the chest and shoulders of a man. The head was still unformed, but Eustacia suddenly knew who it was.

It was Mr Elphinstone, of course. He had done this to her. It was his wicked plan to come to her secretly in this nasty, ghost-like manner. In a moment his head would grow out of that neck, his face would form, and eyes would open, and he would look down on her and smile in triumph, his hands closing firmly over hers, his lips . . .

No. It was impossible. She would not have it. She refused.

Growling incoherently, she rubbed her hands fiercely against the blanket. The half-finished, cloudy likeness of a man still hung in the air, a face beginning to form. Once it had formed, once his eyes had opened and looked down at her, it might be too late. She might never escape his clutches. Feeling sick and furious, concentrating all her mind on denying his power, she swung both hands at it. She had imagined dispersing it, but although its appearance was cloudy, it was not made of smoke. Her hands sank into something horribly cold and slimy. It was thick and soupy, not entirely liquid, but not solid, either; something like clotted milk or half-set cheese, but worse; indescribably worse. It was something that should have been dead but was alive; something that looked alive and yet was dead. And it was cold – she'd never felt such a cold. Not a clean cold like ice or snow. This cold had the quality of a bad smell.

The feel of it made her gag. It made her head swim. But she persisted. Her fingers grasped and tore until she had pulled it to pieces, until she had completely destroyed the unnatural, unwanted effigy.

Then she got out of bed and tottered across the floor on weak legs and threw up in the washbowl. Her head ached fiercely. She rested a moment, and then opened the window. It was a cold and windy day, and she was grateful for that. The wind would rush into the room and sweep out the nasty smells of sickness: the smells of blood, and vomit, and something much worse.

I've won, she thought, weary but triumphant. *You haven't got me. I'm* free.

Mildred came in and found her leaning on the windowsill, head half out the window, shivering with the cold but still sucking in deep, invigorating breaths of the pure winter air.

'What on earth are you doing? Do you want to catch your death?' Mildred's hands, firm and controlling, on her arms. Eustacia resisted, refusing to be steered back to bed, afraid of the horrible remains she had left quivering and clotted on the blanket. 'I felt sick . . .'

'Yes, I see. You must get back into bed, you must keep warm.'

Every muscle, every bone, every ounce of flesh still resisted – until she saw the bed, clean and dry and empty, not a trace of the horror left.

She collapsed with relief and let Mildred tuck her into bed where, utterly exhausted, she fell asleep immediately.

When she woke, her hands were warm and dry.

Her body's only discharge came from between her legs, and that would pass after a few days. She was back to normal. She had won. She made a face at the Mr Elphinstone in her mind, his image fading fast, and almost laughed out loud. She was happy, with four days ahead of her in which she would not be expected to work at all, time in which she could sleep and dream and read and think. Despite the mess and bother of it, Eustacia never minded her monthly visitor; on the contrary, she was grateful for the regular holiday it brought. She knew she was quite capable of working throughout her sick time, but she certainly wasn't going to argue with Mildred about it. Mildred thought permanent damage could be done to a woman who overstrained her constitution at such times. And a menstruating woman (not that such a word ever passed her lips) could do harm to others as well: milk would turn and bread not rise in her presence, and the scent of her would drive domestic animals wild. Modesty forbade a woman displaying herself when the Curse was upon her, which meant she must keep to herself and the company of women. Eustacia thought Mildred was over-nice in regard to their father – after all, he had been married and shared a bed with his wife for years – but she was happy enough to avoid her brothers, and even more men to whom she was not related. The thought that they might notice something wrong with her was humiliating. She was happy to keep to her room and rest.

It was not until late that evening, after Mildred had taken away her supper dishes and left her an empty chamber pot and a bundle of clean towels, that she felt the tingling in her fingers again. She realized then that they were cold, and, as she tucked them into her armpits to warm them, she felt the dampness.

She stared at her hands and saw the mucus blobs swelling and stretching from her fingertips, elongating and thickening as she watched into fingers –

'No!'

Long fingers, hands, bony wrists – hands she recognized.

'No!'

Denial was of no use. It was in her, and it had to come out. She thought she could feel it seeping out of the flesh beneath her breasts and behind her knees, and there was a tickling sensation on the soles of her feet. She couldn't keep it in. It had to come out.

It had to, but *he* didn't. She stared at the hands and willed them to break off at the wrists. Two disembodied hands floated free, but more of the whitish matter gushed out, forming new hands.

Ectoplasm, Mr Elphinstone had called it. The stuff produced by the bodies of the living to provide the dead with temporary flesh.

There were his hands, his arms . . . But why his? Dead or alive, she had no wish to communicate with him. If she was to provide a habitation for spirits they should at least be shapes of her own choosing.

She thought about her mother. Her mother had had lovely hands, even though roughened by toil: slender fingers, graceful, shapely hands. As she thought of them, creating them in her mind, they were recreated before her. Cloudy, milky shapes, but recognizably *not* Mr Elphinstone's hands. They were a woman's hands. Her mother's hands.

She gazed at them with feelings of awe and accomplishment, unsure whether this was her own work, or if she had her mother's spirit to thank for routing Mr Elphinstone. She tried to join arms onto the hands, wanting to see more of her mother, but, as she struggled, she fell asleep.

Her hands stayed dry through the night, but this time she did not expect that condition to last. Indeed, her fingers were dripping like infected sores before midday.

She knew that meant Mr Elphinstone was trying to get out. She didn't know exactly why, but she could guess: she had read enough novels. This was not the usual way that men attempted to overpower young women, but that didn't mean it was any less dangerous. Probably, she thought, he had been planning this from the start, from the very first moment when his damp, chilly flesh had pressed hers. She didn't know how his ghost could harm her, or even if it could, but she would certainly not give it the chance to try.

During the next four days Eustacia successfully fought off his every attempt to return. She couldn't stop the ectoplasm, but she could control the forms it took. It was hard work, but she enjoyed it. She came to think of it as a new kind of art, a sort of mental modelling, as if the ectoplasm had been clay, and she was using the fingers of her mind to push and smooth and mould it into the shapes of her choice.

At first, it was her mother she concentrated on, for her mother was the only person who had 'passed over' whom Eustacia knew well or had any real desire to see again. But it was difficult, and not really very satisfying. Whole bodies were out of the question, requiring more ectoplasm than her body could produce at one time, so she concentrated either on hands (which were easiest) or on heads. Her mother's head was never quite right, and the more often she tried to produce it, the harder she found it to recall what her mother had really looked like. She was not limited to the dead, so she also created likenesses of Lydia and Mildred. But even the form of Mildred, whom she saw every day, was not really very like. The faces she made were just as clumsy and unfinished as they might have been if she had been working, untutored, in clay or stone. She knew who they were because she knew what she intended. She was not sure anyone else would have recognized them.

Unsatisfying as it was, it was also the most amazingly tiring work. More exhausting than milking the cows or laundry day. After less than an hour working on another ghost of Lydia, sleep would catch her up, inescapable, and she would slumber heavily for several hours.

Yet the energy spent was worth it. Not only did her efforts ward off Mr Elphinstone, but they temporarily exhausted her supply of ectoplasm, winning sometimes a whole day of normal life and dry hands.

If she would do that every evening, if she would spend an hour willing ectoplasmic shapes into existence before falling to sleep, Eustacia figured she could keep her peculiar condition secret and under control. But it wasn't so easy. Perhaps it was laziness – she imagined Mildred would think so – but there were many nights when she was simply too tired to do anything at the end of the day but put herself to bed. She enjoyed playing with the ectoplasm, making faces and hands, but it was hard work all the same. It took reserves of energy she did not always have, especially by the time she was ready for bed.

Fortunately, she didn't have to share her bed with anyone.

She didn't mind – now that she knew the stuff could be washed off, or, if left, would soon dry to nothing – the morning stickiness of the sheets or the mess on her body. Her hands were not the only source, if they had ever been. Like perspiration, the slime oozed from all the pores of her skin: from her legs, her feet, under her arms, her chest and back, even (and most horribly, because most visible) her face. Afraid that someone might notice, Eustacia took more care, forcing herself to stay awake past her usual bedtime, or waking early, or escaping to the privacy of her room on one pretence or another for long enough to do something with the excess ectoplasm.

But despite her best intentions, her body leaked, and, one suppertime, Mildred noticed. When everyone had left the table, she stopped her sister with a look and said: 'You must be more careful.'

'I wiped my hands – and I did wash them before I came to table – '

'It's not only your hands, now, is it? You've left a trail – no, don't look, I cleaned it up. Father didn't notice, nor did Conrad, but what if they should? Next time, I think you'd best take supper in your room.'

'What? But why? How can I? Every night? Never eat with the family?'

'Of course not every night. But while you're – during your – ' she nodded her head meaningfully, unable to pronounce the euphemism.

'But it's not like that. I'm not – '

'Your *face*,' Mildred muttered with a look of revulsion. She made small brushing gestures at her own forehead, and Eustacia became aware of the by-now familiar, chilly, tingling sensation from three different spots along her hairline. Both her handkerchiefs were already saturated, but she raised one, balled in her hand, to her head and wiped away the offensive trickles.

'Go to your room,' Mildred said. 'Clean yourself. I'll tell the others you're feeling poorly – '

'But I'm not! I'm not feeling poorly. This is something else. I don't know what it is, but it's not connected to – to *that* – at all. And it's not like a cold, something that clears up or goes away after a few days . . . It's never gone away at all, not wholly, not since it started. It's a part of me now. Sometimes I can control it a bit, but I can't make it stop – I can't make it go away.' Mildred had never been her favourite sister; indeed, had they not been related, Eustacia was not certain she could have loved her. But that look on her face, even had it been the face of a stranger – a look of horror, of loathing, barely controlled – for that look to have been caused by her – it was unbearable.

Eustacia burst into tears.

'Oh, stop that! Stop that at once. Crying never helps.'

'Why are you so angry?'

'Because you're being silly.'

'But why do you look at me like that? As if . . . as if it's *my fault*. You can't blame me – I didn't make this happen – I never wanted it. If I were bleeding you wouldn't tell me to stop; you couldn't expect me just to stop; you'd clean my wound and bind it and perhaps send for the doctor – '

'I shall send for the doctor. Not now, but in the morning. I would have done so sooner if I had realized – but I can't think there's any urgency, if this has been going on all month, and you still walking around as if it were nothing . . . Now will you go to your room, before you make any more mess? You're dripping.'

'It's not my fault.' Her tone was belligerent, but what she wanted was reassurance. Acceptance.

'We don't choose our afflictions,' Mildred said coldly, looking away. 'But we shouldn't be proud of them.'

Alone in her room, Eustacia wept again. She had been very young when her mother died, and was seldom aware of missing her. But she missed her now. Mildred might have taken Mother's role as the female head of the family, but Mildred was not her mother. Her real mother would not have been horrified by the changes taking place in Eustacia, no matter what they were. Her real mother now would have embraced and comforted her, wept with her, not kept Mildred's chilly distance.

A pale, semi-opaque tendril was snaking out of her wrist when a fat teardrop fell, disintegrating it. Saltwater – or maybe it was only tears? – seemed to work more efficiently than plain water. Eustacia was so fascinated by this discovery that she forgot to cry.

After some time, she lit the lamp and sat down to write to Lydia. Downstairs, she suspected, Mildred would be writing a letter to be dispatched to Dr Purves in the morning. Well, she would send a letter, too, on the same topic but from a different perspective, and to someone who would probably be of more use than a doctor. Lydia, after all, had seen for herself what Mr Elphinstone could do. Lydia would be in sympathy, and she might know someone who could help. Not Mr Elphinstone, but there must be other mediums – perhaps even a lady medium? Lydia, with her wide social circle, was bound to know someone who knew someone . . . If absolutely necessary, some third party might even approach Mr Elphinstone in a roundabout way. He must have realized by now that his plan to take control of her had not worked, so perhaps he could be persuaded to lift his curse.

Composing the letter was difficult. When put into words, what had happened to her sounded horrible, and Eustacia didn't want Lydia thinking that. She didn't want her favourite sister horrified or revulsed, as Mildred was. She had to choose her words carefully. She couldn't say too much. She was mysterious. She evoked the spirit of the séance. Lydia must come and see for herself. When she was here, Eustacia would be able to make her understand.

*

Until the doctor arrived, Eustacia was made to keep to her room as if she were contagious. She usually never minded solitude, and was grateful for any excuse to avoid work, but what once would have felt like freedom was now an imposition. She was being punished for something which was not her fault.

Alone in her room, cut off from her family, she concentrated on extruding ectoplasm and forming it into shapes. She created shaky likenesses of Mildred and Lydia. She worked herself to exhaustion and beyond, determined to clear her system of the ghost-matter, to give the doctor, when he came, nothing to find. Let him think he had been called all the way out here for some fantasy of Mildred's.

But it was no use. Perhaps she had been overconfident about the laws of cause and effect and in believing she had some control over what her body produced and when, for despite her labours, she woke the next morning lying in a puddle of something half liquid, half matter. And when Dr Purves arrived in the afternoon, mucus dripped from her fingertips, her clothes clung stickily to damp flesh, and she felt trails of drool beside her mouth, on her brow, and beneath her ears.

'Hmmm!' said Dr Purves, and, 'Well, well!' and, 'What's this?' He didn't look revolted, horrified, or even astonished. There was, on his face, a carefully schooled, non-judgmental look of mild interest. 'Feeling a bit hot, are we?'

He thought it was perspiration. 'No,' said Eustacia hopelessly.

'Ah, do you mind if I . . . ?'

She gave him her hand, and felt the surprise he did not allow to register on his face. He looked at her hand, touched the stuff, waited, watching it well up again. 'Hmmm. And how long has this been going on?'

She told him. He asked questions and she answered them truthfully. He did not ask her what she thought was happening to her or why, so she did not tell him about Mr Elphinstone or the matter produced by the bodies of mediums for the use of those who had passed over. She didn't tell him that she could, with her thoughts, increase the flow and cause it to shape itself into images. Dr Purves was a man of science; she knew he would not believe her, and she didn't believe he could help her. Undoubtedly, Mildred hoped the doctor would be able to give a name to Eustacia's disease and also provide the cure, but she knew otherwise. She knew, now, watching him watch her, that he had never seen the like of this before, and that he didn't like it.

He asked her to undress. He examined her. He told her he was taking a sample for testing. She watched him scoop a tendril of ectoplasm from her armpit into a small glass bottle and cap it firmly. The piece he had captured was the size of a garden snail without the shell. She watched him put the bottle safely away in his bag. By the time he got home, perhaps even by the time he left this house, that bottle would be empty. Would he come back for more, or would he decide it had never existed, preferring not to know anything that might contradict his rational view of the universe?

While she was dressing, he washed his hands very thoroughly. She wondered if soap and water were a protection, or if she had now infected him. But perhaps the doctor, sceptical of spiritualism, would be protected by science and his own unbelief. She wondered how he would explain it, and what he would do, if his body began leaking ectoplasm.

'Now, you're not to worry,' he said. 'Rest, don't exert yourself. Keep yourself warm. And clean. Wash and, er, change your sheets as often as you feel the need.'

'What's wrong with me?'

'There's nothing wrong. You mustn't think that. Didn't I say you weren't to worry? Just keep warm and rest and you'll soon be as right as rain. I'll have a word with your sister before I go, about your diet. I'll tell her everything she needs to know.' He made his escape before she could ask again.

She slumped back in her bed with a grim smile. She hadn't expected an intelligent reply. She knew he didn't know what was wrong with her, and no amount of thinking, no amount of study, no amount of second opinions from his learned colleagues, would change that. Even if he locked her up in a hospital somewhere and watched her day and night, he'd be none the wiser, because what had happened to her belonged to another realm, not of scientific medicine, but of mysticism.

She could suddenly see herself in a hospital somewhere, locked in an underfurnished room in a building where lunatics screamed and raged, watched by men in white coats through a hole in the door, and she went cold with dread. She burrowed under the sheets and pulled the blankets up to her nose with hands that were cold but, for once, miraculously dry. That must not happen – surely Mildred wouldn't let that happen to her? But of course Mildred didn't understand, and she might well trust a doctor who promised a cure. She wished the doctor had never come. She knew he would never cure her, no matter what he tried, and she did not want to be studied by him. If he decided she was an interesting case . . . Eustacia clenched her teeth to stop them chattering. She wouldn't let it happen. Mildred wouldn't let it happen. Lydia wouldn't let it happen. Lydia was coming soon. Lydia would understand; Lydia would save her.

Lydia arrived four days later. Sitting in her chair by the window, well wrapped in shawls and blankets, with nothing to do but watch and wait, Eustacia thought she'd never been so glad to see another person. It was life Lydia brought into her room – the sickroom, her prison – life and a taste of the world she had grown hungry for.

'Whatever is the matter with Mildred?' Lydia asked as she swept in. 'A face as long as a wet Sunday when she said you were poorly but – oh!' The cheerful prattle ended, the exclamation shocked out of her, when, as she bent to kiss her sister, her lips encountered not the familiar warm, soft texture of her check, but flesh slippery with a chill and slimy coating.

'I'm not ill,' Eustacia said looking urgently into her sister's eyes. To her relief, she saw neither horror nor disgust reflected there, only a puzzled concern. 'No matter what Mildred thinks, or the doctor. It is odd, though . . . hard to understand . . . hard to write about in a letter. That's why I wanted to see you. I wanted you to see me. Because I am all right . . . I am still *me*.'

'Of course you are! Still my own dear sister. Is this some new ploy to escape doing chores? Or is that what Mildred thinks? I had thought, from the way she spoke, that it was your time.'

She shook her head. 'Do sit down, Lydia. I'll have to show you.' She was excited and scared. There was a tingling inside, a nervous reaction to match the purely physical, localized tingle in her hands. The feeling of something that had to come out. And, now, a new excitement because there was meaning and new purpose to what she was about to do. For the first time she had an audience. Was she good enough for her audience? Lydia's response was all-important.

'You remember . . . Mr Elphinstone?'

'Yes, of course.'

'And what he did that evening, and what he showed us? The ectoplasm? He did something else that same evening, to me. When he touched me. I don't understand how or why, but he gave it to me somehow.' She paused, aware of gathering her power, of concentrating it all in her hands, which she held now before her, just above her lap. Lydia said nothing, and there was nothing in her look but waiting and wonder.

'Watch,' said Eustacia, and stared at her own hands as the thick, wavering white steam poured out of them, her fingers become fountains. Ten separate streams merged and grew into one almost-solid form: head, neck, shoulders, chest . . .

until it was a baby floating there, its features somewhat vague and undefined but still and undeniably a baby. *There.*

Eustacia felt a little dizzy, and had the familiar sensation of having been drained. But she also felt triumphant, and as she looked up from her creation she was smiling happily. 'There – see? It's your baby.'

Lydia's face had gone an unhealthy yellowish colour. She shook her head slowly. 'No,' she said, sounding tortured. 'That's not my baby – it's not!' She clapped her hands to her mouth, retching, and staggered to her feet, knocking the chair over with the heavy sideways sweep of her skirts. She managed to get to the basin before she threw up.

Eustacia closed her eyes, but the noise and smell made her stomach churn in terrible sympathy. She kept her gorge down with great effort. 'I'm sorry,' she said, when Lydia's crisis seemed to have passed. 'I know it must be a shock to see your baby – '

'No! That's not my baby! How can you?'

Eustacia struggled to rise, reaching for her sister.

Lydia shrieked. 'Don't touch me! You monster!'

'But – but you were so happy when Mr Elphinstone did it – this is the same – don't you see? I can do the same thing – '

'It's not the same! It's not the same!' Lydia glared at her, and this look was much worse than the look Mildred had given her, for there was not merely horror in it, but hate. 'How could you . . . what are you trying to do, make me miscarry?'

Eustacia's mouth hung open. 'I didn't know . . .'

'Monster! Monster!'

The door opened then – Mildred, attracted by the noise. Weeping, Lydia rushed to the safety of her older sister's embrace. They went out of the room together and the door closed, shutting Eustacia in alone with the thing she had made.

She looked at her creation, the baby bobbing and floating in the air like something unborn. Like something dead. But it had never been alive. It wasn't real, not a real baby. But neither was the thing Mr Elphinstone had made, although, in the dim and flickering firelight, it had seemed real enough to eyes that wanted it to be. She understood that the situation was different here and now. But she hadn't meant any harm. She thought of getting up and going downstairs, going after Lydia and explaining, making her understand. But she had not the energy for it. It was impossible. She could scarcely even think. All she could do was fall back in her chair and fall asleep.

When she woke, with a throbbing head competing for attention against a painfully empty stomach, it was much later in the day and the room was thick with shadows. The baby had vanished back into the nothing from which it had been conjured. She rose from her chair and stretched aching muscles, feeling as if she had become an old woman while she slept. Certainly she felt like a different person from the hopeful girl who had waited impatiently for her sister that morning. She hoped that the passing of the hours had calmed Lydia. Maybe she would be ready to listen now, and surely if she listened she would understand. She still felt Lydia was the one person in the world who *could* understand.

But when she reached the door she could not open it. She thought at first it was her own weakness, and continued twisting the handle to no avail. Her wits were still so slow after her sleep that it took her some time to realize that the door to her room had been locked from the outside.

They had locked her in.

It had to be a mistake. She went back to her chair, turned it so she could look out the window, and sat down. She did not want to find out that it had not been a mistake, so she would not pound on the door and make demands that could be refused. Mildred would come up and unlock it later. It must have been locked on account of Lydia's fright. Once she was allowed to explain there would be no more need for locked doors.

By the time Mildred came up with her dinner on a tray Eustacia was almost ready to weep with hunger and worry.

'Mildred, I have to see Lydia, I have to explain – '

'She's gone home.'

'I didn't mean to upset her; I have to tell her – '

'Oh, I know. It's not your fault.' A sneer was not Mildred's usual expression. She would not meet her sister's eye as she spoke.

'It's *not* my fault – I can't help it – I didn't mean it – oh, please – '

'*I* know. You're ill.' She snorted. 'I saw the doctor. I rode with Lydia into town, and I had a consultation with him. Do you know what he said? There's nothing wrong with you at all. Not physically. He says it's all in your head. You know what I say? I say it's evil. Not sickness – evil. Not in your head, but your heart, Evil in your heart. And that *is* your fault. You'd better admit it, missy. And pray to God to take it away. There's your dinner.'

'Please!'

But Mildred was already out of the room without a backward look. And then came the sound of the key turning in the lock.

Eustacia ate her dinner. What else was there to do? After she had eaten she could think more clearly, but the thoughts were not pleasant ones. It was obvious Lydia would be of no help; she had been too badly frightened. If only she had been more cautious . . . if only she had led Lydia on a bit more carefully . . . She thought of Mr Elphinstone's pompous speech; the way he had elicited responses from his audience; the extinguishing of the lamps. By firelight, my baby would have looked more real, she thought. But it was too late to think of that now. Lydia would not help her. The doctor had, literally, washed his hands of her, declaring her either a fake or mad. And Mildred was of no use, either, having decided she was bad. Worse than that, Mildred was her jailor, and represented her whole family.

Who was there who could help her?

She remembered the cold, damp touch of Mr Elphinstone's hands, and the way his eyes had pierced into hers. He had marked her then, that evening; he had made her his, although she had tried to deny it. To give in now, to go to him despite her revulsion . . . she would be trading one sort of imprisonment for another. But at least it would be different. Not the life she would have chosen freely, but still a life. And she would learn to use her talent: it would *be* a talent then, and not a loathsome illness.

But how could she go to him when she couldn't leave this room? She might write a letter, but anything she sent out would have to go through Mildred. She imagined Mildred reading it and throwing it on the fire. And even if she managed to bypass Mildred she realized with despair that she had no address for Mr Elphinstone.

Hopeless.

There was a tingling in her fingertips.

No, not hopeless.

She remembered how the form of Mr Elphinstone had first emerged from her body – the struggle, and how terrified she had been. He was still there, still waiting to come out. She no longer feared him, at least not in the same way. There were other, greater fears. She was ready now to welcome him and his plans for her.

She put out her hands and let the solid smoky stuff stream out; watched as it formed into fingers touching her own at the tips. A man's fingers, a man's large hands, bony wrists lengthening into skinny arms, naked shoulders and naked chest. She was trembling now and starting to feel faint, but she held her hands as steady as she could and let it go on happening, thinking all the while of Mr Elphinstone, remembering him as he had been, and as he was. Now the neck and head. The shifting clouds of his face roiled and finally solidified into bearded chin and mouth, long thin nose, high brow, and the eyes – the eyes were closed.

She stared and waited for them to open; waited to have those blazing orbs fixed on her, and see the lips move, and hear him speak. He was finished now, at least, as much of him as she could make. She could do no more. It was up to him to take over. But Mr Elphinstone looked dead, like the baby, hanging motionless in the air.

Lydia had said that at most séances when ghosts appeared they spoke, answering questions and making cryptic remarks. Her baby of course had been too young.

'Talk to me,' said Eustacia. 'Tell me what to do.'

Her breath disturbed the figure, making it bob slightly. A bit of one arm disintegrated, leaving a hole the size of a baby's fist just above the right elbow. She cried out again, and her fingers closed on cold, dead matter. When she pulled away, sickened, she saw she had destroyed parts of both lower arms, and the hands floated free, detached from the arms. One of the hands floated up toward the ceiling, becoming more insubstantial as it rose.

Mr Elphinstone could not speak to her, for Mr Elphinstone was not here. She had created something that looked like Mr Elphinstone – or like her memory of Mr Elphinstone – and that was all. It did not live. It never had and never would. It was inhabited by no ghosts. There were no ghosts. She could not blame Mr Elphinstone for that, nor for the fact that he could neither enslave nor save her.

She was alone in her room as she watched her dream disintegrate. She was alone with her disease, her curse, her madness – her strange, useless talent.

The Dream Detective

I've always been interested in dreams, and not just my own. The connection between dream and story, between dream-life and waking life, the unconscious and conscious mind are all fascinating, and still little understood. I was attracted by the title of Sax Rohmer's The Dream Detective, *but found the stories far less memorable. So I decided to write my own take on the subject. There is more than one way to interpret the meaning of a dream detective. (Although I had forgotten it until recently, Gene Wolfe's 'The Detective of Dreams' was published in 1980 in* Dark Forces.)

IN THE BEGINNING, I was not attracted to her at all. Quite the opposite.

I don't know if it was intentional on her part, and honestly, I'm not the sort of dick who always judges women on how hot they are, but if there's *any* situation in which a person's attractiveness matters, I think everybody would agree it's a blind date.

Hannes and Mardi, my so-called friends, so worried about my single state, had once more stepped into the breach and invited me to dinner to meet someone 'very special'. They had introduced me to several very nice, lovely, smart, sexy women in the past, and all had been good company even though there'd never been the necessary, mutual spark that would ignite a love affair – but not this time.

My first sight of Mardi's old housemate Grace was of a lumpy little figure in drab, ill-fitting clothes. Her hair probably hadn't been brushed since she'd rolled out of bed, her eyebrows looked like hairy caterpillars, and apart from a slash of bright red lipstick, she hadn't bothered with makeup. 'Couldn't be bothered' was a good description of her in general, and from her sullen look, she was equally unimpressed by me.

As it was only the four of us for dinner, I couldn't ignore her without being rude. But my first few attempts to engage her attention fell flat.

Hannes kept the ball rolling with some stories I hadn't heard before – he's very funny, especially considering English isn't his first language – until Mardi shrieked for his help in the kitchen, and we were left alone together.

'So what do you do?' I asked.

I could have kicked myself as soon as the words were out. I didn't want to talk about my own tedious job, so why put her on the spot?

She stared at me for a long moment while I tried to figure out a way of withdrawing the question that wouldn't make things worse, and finally she said, 'I'm a dream detective.'

I thought I'd heard wrong. 'Dream?'

She nodded. 'Detective,' she added, helpfully.

If it was a joke I didn't get it. 'You mean you solve dreams?'

'What does that mean?'

'I don't know. You said it.'

'I didn't say I solved *dreams*. I solve *crimes*, and other mysteries, in dreams.'

'What's your success rate?'

'Quite good, actually.' She made a modest face. 'Although, I shouldn't brag; I have to admit I haven't done much of anything lately . . .'

She was playing it straight, so I had to do the same. 'But you've solved a few, over the years?'

'Oh, yes.'

'How long have you been helping the police with their enquiries?'

She looked as if she was about to laugh, but stopped herself, and simply shook her head. 'The police aren't interested in dreams.'

'But – I mean, if you are solving crimes – '

'Dream crimes.'

'What's a dream crime?'

She sighed, as if I were deliberately obtuse. 'A crime committed in a dream.'

'In a dream.'

'That's what I said.'

This fey game of hers was really getting up my nose. It wasn't funny, and it wasn't clever – if it *was* a game. Just checking, I said, 'But not in the real world.'

I was reminded of one of my least favourite teachers by the snooty look she gave me and her retort: 'In your opinion, dreams aren't part of the real world?'

'I don't know. *You're* the one who – '

'You don't dream?'

'Everybody dreams.'

'You'd be surprised how many people say they don't. Or that they can't remember. It's not for me to say they're lying, but forgetfulness can be a cover for things people find too painful to think about.'

'I dream a lot.' Since childhood, I'd enjoyed my dreams and enjoyed thinking about them; if I rarely told them to anyone, it was out of the fear that my descriptions would be inadequate, and they'd sound boring or nonsensical, instead of the fascinating adventures they were to me.

She leaned across the table, fixing me with eyes that were larger, darker and more eloquent than I'd realized. 'Have you committed a crime? In your dreams?'

I felt a sudden surge of adrenaline, as if she'd come too close to a deeply guarded secret. My heart was racing, and I felt a powerful urge to run, the need to hide – and what an admission that would be!

I faced her down, smiling, although maybe it looked more

like a snarl. 'Is that how you solve your mysteries? You ask everyone you meet to confess to an imaginary crime? No wonder if your success rate is high! Who would dare to say no?'

'I'll take that as a yes,' she said, staring at me so hard her twin caterpillars became one. Her eyes no longer held the slightest allure; they were like laser beams, science-fictional weapons able to bore right through the bones of my skull, into my brain, where her unnatural vision would find the image of something I had done that was so shameful, so deeply buried, that even *I* couldn't remember it.

Hannes came through the door then, thank God, carrying a platter, announcing dinner was served, followed by his wife carrying a covered bowl.

Over the meal, conversation was general, on the subjects of food, travel, movies and then food again when Mardi brought out cheesecake and fruit salad for dessert. It was not the most scintillating conversation; in fact, it was one of the most restrained and boring I could remember ever having around that table, as if we were four random strangers forced to share in a crowded restaurant.

When Hannes left the room to make coffee there was a silence until Mardi turned to speak to Grace as if I wasn't there: 'How's the job-hunting? Any luck?'

Grace shook her head.

'Still at the charity shop?'

'Two days. They'd have me for more hours, which would be great if I was getting paid, but, you know, I need to make some money.'

'So your dream detecting doesn't pay?' I don't know what possessed me to jump in with that.

Mardi stared hard at the other woman. 'You *told* him?'

The chair creaked as Grace leaned back and crossed her arms. Her face was flushed. She spoke flatly. 'I had a feeling he might need my help.'

'What?' Mardi's voice rose almost to a wail. 'You're still doing that? You never told me!'

Hannes poked his head through the door. 'Stop it; no fair having fun without me.'

Mardi's hair was messy, her lipstick eaten away, her face as red as Grace's – but on her it looked good. 'Oh, honey, you won't believe it, but Gracie – she's still – you know, remember that dream thing she did?' She groped with her hand in the air above her head.

Grace looked at me and said earnestly, 'I don't do it for money. I would never, it would be wrong, it's a *gift*. It would be wrong for me to try to exploit it.'

'Exactly!' Mardi exclaimed. 'Like me and the tarot. I'll read the cards if someone asks, but I'd never, ever charge money.'

'I'm astonished,' said Hannes, deadpan. 'I thought they only talked about these things in private, when all three witches got together.'

'We're not witches.'

'Who's the third?' I asked.

'Remember little Holly?'

'From your wedding? Ah, yes.' I recalled the tiny yet perfectly formed maid of honour everyone had wanted to dance with.

He nodded. 'The three weird sisters. Or former flat-sharers – but that doesn't sound so good, does it?'

I wondered if Grace had been at the wedding, too, and sneaked a look at her. I saw a frumpy, shapeless lump who didn't know how to make herself interesting. I wondered if the idea of the dream-investigation had been her own, or borrowed from one of her smarter roommates. She did not notice me looking, just went on staring at nothing, seemingly undisturbed by the queasy excitement roiling around the room even when Mardi shouted:

'We're not *witches*.'

'Sorry, darling, how silly of me. You predict the future, and Holly heals people by stroking their auras, and Grace goes into people's minds to affect their dreams, and all that is completely ordinary and normal and not at all witch-like or weird.'

'You're horrible.'

'Horribly irresistible.' She scowled at him, then giggled; he invited me to help him get the coffee, and I jumped up, happy for any excuse to leave.

In the kitchen, I asked: 'Fortune-telling?'

'I'm surprised she's never dealt the cards for you. She still has them in a velvet bag. True, she doesn't often get them out these days, hardly ever since we were married, but back then, when she was living with Holly and Grace . . . they scared me sometimes, I don't mind telling you, those three women in the same room together, looking like they could read your mind and tell your future from the way you sipped your coffee.' He shuddered melodramatically. 'But each girl on her own . . . a different proposition.'

'I wouldn't want to proposition Grace,' I said sourly. 'Is that what you thought? She's *really* my type.'

He gave me a sheepish smile and pressed the plunger down on the cafetiere. 'Sorry, man. It wasn't supposed to be like this. We had invited two other people, and at the last minute they couldn't make it.'

'Two? A couple?'

'Sister and brother. Both single. One for each of you. I swear.'

'Well, better luck next time,' I sighed, and lifting the tray of mugs, followed him out of the room.

After I went home that night I did not give Grace a second thought, but she wasn't done with me.

I was a turkey-farmer, somewhere in the country, rounding up my herd and then driving them, on foot, down a dirt road until I reached London, which was like the set for a low-budget TV version of Dickens' *A Christmas Carol*. I sold the big birds to an East Ender in a patched coat and shabby top hat ('Aow! God bless you, Guvnor!') and took my little velvet bag of gold coins to buy myself a drink, but at this point wintry London morphed into Paris in the spring, so I walked into a sidewalk cafe and ordered *un café, s'il vous plaît*. It was as I was sitting there, waiting for my coffee, that I realized, from the nervous clenching in my gut, that I'd been followed.

She was sitting at another table, pretending to read a newspaper, and although she looked nothing like the woman I'd met over dinner – she looked like Edith Piaf, or, rather, like Marion Cotillard playing Piaf in *La Vie en Rose* – I knew her. I knew she was on to me. But she couldn't follow me into the men's toilet, so I was able to get away from her quite easily, although there was still some running and dodging down narrow alleys and in and out of shops before I woke up, heart pounding, feeling I'd had a narrow escape, but with no idea why. Was she police, or a foreign agent? Was I the good-guy spy, or an innocent who knew too much? Dreams feel like stories, but they leave out a lot of the information we'd need to make sense of a movie or a book.

Another night, another dream: I was in a theatre, up in the gods, where the rows of seats kept morphing into chutes and ladders, and every time I tried to get out, I ran into a little blonde girl in a blue dress, blocking the exit. She looked like Disney's Alice, but when she trained her eyes on me like a twin-bore shotgun, I knew who she really was, and knew I was in trouble.

Another time, in the midst of a ripping yarn featuring neo-Nazi conspirators and a fabled treasure hidden at the heart of an Egyptian pyramid, I became aware of her again. I never saw her, but felt the disturbing presence of an outsider;

someone female who did not belong, an uninvited visitor who was spying on me. Only afterwards, awake, thinking it over as I showered and dressed for work, I became convinced that it was Grace; and I began to wonder what she was after, and how to get rid of her.

On my way home that night – I'd been working late, required to be on hand for a conference call with partners in other time zones – I stopped to buy a few things. It wasn't the store where I usually shopped, but I'd just remembered there was almost nothing in my fridge when I spotted a sign for Morrison's, and nipped in.

I found Grace in the wine aisle, inspecting the bottles. At the sight of her I felt disorientated, almost dizzy; that may have been the first time in my life when I genuinely wondered if I was really awake or only dreaming.

But maybe it wasn't her. The woman shopping for wine was dressed up and looked quite sexy. Had I become obsessed, was I starting to see the detective of dreams everywhere I went?

She turned her head and the recognition on her face told me I wasn't fantasizing. 'Oh, hi! How are you? Do you live around here?'

'Sort of, not too far – but I don't usually shop here; how about you?'

She shook her head. 'I'm on my way to ... a party. Thought I'd better bring a bottle.'

She wore a snug, scoop-necked top and short skirt, clothes that revealed that she wasn't fat at all, perhaps a little thick-waisted, but she did have a pair of enormous breasts. Maybe she hadn't wanted to show them off to me, but, clearly, she didn't feel obliged to keep them hidden all the time; I wondered what made the party she was on her way to now so very different from the dinner at Mardi and Hannes'. She was still far from beautiful, but just then she had a glow about her that made up for any small deficiencies in her appearance.

I saw her look in my basket, recognize the pathetic shopping of the single man (frozen chips, pizza, bacon, eggs, and a loaf of bread) and felt suddenly defensive, almost angry at her presumption in judging me, spying on me.

Without pausing to think, I asked her, 'How do you do it?'

She looked honestly bewildered.

'The dreams . . .' Before I got it out, I'd realized how utterly idiotic my question was. She hadn't done anything. This meeting was coincidence; my dreams were my own. I stalled and fumbled and finally managed: 'I was just wondering . . . You said you were a dream detective . . . I guess you were joking?'

'Oh. No, it wasn't a joke.' She looked apprehensive. 'It was true, but . . . I really don't know why I said it. I don't usually tell people. Mardi knows, because I used to do it when we lived together. But not anymore.'

I know that's not true. I kept my accusation to myself, though, and only said, 'Yeah? It's odd. I'd never heard of a dream detective before.'

She cleared her throat and glanced around at the ranks of wine bottles. 'No . . . that's not surprising. Neither had I. I guess I made it up. I was sharing a house with two friends, one read cards and the other read auras; they did it to help people and it was kind of cool and I wanted something I could do, so . . .' She shrugged and moved away from me to read a price label.

'But how did it work? Did people invite you into their dreams, or did you just kind of dream your way inside their heads, or – '

'What?' Now she was staring at me.

'How – how did you do it? The dream-detecting?'

'People told me about their dreams and I interpreted them. What did you think?' Her eyes had widened, and I could see that she knew perfectly well what I had thought, and I realized how crazy it was. Why had I imagined for a moment that this less-than-ordinary woman could see inside my brain, even enter my dreams to spy on me?

To distract her from my idiocy, I asked another question. 'And it worked?'

She shrugged. 'People seemed to think so. They liked it, anyway. It was something I could do, it seemed vaguely useful, I had a lot of free time and no money – '

'So why did you stop? I mean, you must still have a lot of free time and no money, and since you're looking for a job – why not create your own employment? You'd have it to yourself, you'd be the expert, the only dream detective in England – '

'Oh, shut up. What did I ever do to you?'

I was surprised to realize she was angry. I hadn't meant to offend her, but she wouldn't let me explain.

'You don't know anything about it! You think it's a joke, but it's *not*.'

'No, I don't think that – I really do take you seriously, that's why – '

'I *told* you, I couldn't charge money for using this gift – it would be wrong. It's not a job, it's a calling. Have you ever seen a rich and famous so-called psychic? What they're like? Do you think I'd ever be one of those media whores?'

'Sorry,' I said, holding up my hands as if her shiny eyes were loaded guns. 'Sorry, I didn't understand; I didn't mean anything . . .'

She grabbed a bottle off the shelf without looking. 'Forget it.'

My dream that night began like a road trip, a pleasurable sort of dream I've enjoyed for years. As usual, it was set in the American west, a place I've never seen except in movies, out on a flat, open highway, Route 66, maybe. I was in one of those big old-fashioned sedan cars from the 1950s, white and shiny, with fins. Inside, the front seat was like a big leather couch, and the gearshift was stuck out the side of the steering wheel. No seat belts, no airbags, just a cigarette lighter and an AM radio tuned to a station belting out songs by Buddy Holly, the Everley Brothers, Elvis Presley.

I myself had more than a touch of Elvis about me, my hair in a quiff with long sideboards, wearing tight jeans, cowboy boots, and a black shirt with pearl-covered snaps, a packet of Camels squashed into the breast pocket. Sitting behind the wheel of that automotive behemoth, singing along to 'Jailhouse Rock', driving through the desert towards somewhere unknown, I was free, and as purely happy as I've ever been. Everything was fine, better than fine it was *perfect* until, glancing in the rearview mirror, I spotted a little black dot in the distance. Just in case, I checked my speed.

I was right; it was a cop. As the motorcycle drew closer, I told myself not to worry. I was going just under the speed limit, my tax disc was valid, the exhaust and tires were good, there was absolutely no reason for him to pull me over . . . but he did.

Even as I was slowing to obey his peremptory command I was no more than annoyed. It was only when I was stopped, watching the cop dismount, that I remembered there was a dead body in the trunk of the car.

I knew I must not panic, that I had to stay calm and convince the cop I was a good, law-abiding citizen he could have no interest in detaining. He came over to my window, asked to see my driver's licence, told me to get out of the car and step away, keeping my hands where he could see them. I obeyed, but perhaps not quickly enough, or maybe there was something in my attitude he didn't like, because he became more aggressively authoritarian with every passing second. He sneered at my hairstyle, asked where I went to church, and about my political affiliations, and when I reminded him that this was America, the land of the free, he said I sounded like a limey bastard, and demanded my passport.

The tedious, threatening argument went on and on, and I was relieved to wake up before my guilty secret was revealed.

I found that dream unusually disturbing. I had no idea whose body was in the boot, or how it had come to be there. I didn't even know if I was a killer. In the dream there had been no guilt or shame attached to the knowledge that I was driving around with a dead body, only anxiety about the consequences if it was found. Did that mean I wasn't a murderer? Or did it indicate the opposite, that my dream persona was a cold-blooded psychopath?

Over the next few weeks, the dream continued to haunt me. I'd had recurring dreams before, anxiety dreams in which I was forever doomed to miss my flight, getting lost on my way to take an exam, or finding I had to give a speech wearing nothing but a skimpy bathrobe. Now, my pleasurable dream of driving across America had been spoiled, turned to another variant of angst.

After the first time, as soon as it began I was obsessed with the problem of how to dispose of the body. My every attempt to find a hiding place was foiled: there were fishermen on the lake, a family having a picnic in the woodland glade, kids playing in the old quarry, people with their prying eyes everywhere I went.

Gradually I came to understand that the body was that of my former girlfriend, but what had actually happened, and why I was burdened with her corpse remained unclear. I knew that my past connection with her would make me the prime suspect if her body was discovered, but I didn't actually know how she had died, and I didn't feel guilty.

In my waking hours I thought more and more about this dream, although I wished I could forget it. I wondered if talking to someone might help, and I thought of Grace.

Another coincidental meeting would have been perfect, but of course that wasn't going to happen. If I knew where she lived, though, I could make it happen, so in the end I phoned Mardi.

'Her *address?*' She made my simple request sound outrageous.

'I thought I might send her a card.'

'Oh, really.' Her scepticism was palpable.

'All right, then, phone number.'

'I don't think so.'

'Why not? You try to match us up, and then – '

'I did *not*. Anyway, that was a month ago, and you clearly didn't get on. In fact – '

'That's not fair. She was quite interesting, actually. Not my type, but – I'd like to talk to her again. I've been thinking about her.'

'Well, don't.'

I wished we were speaking face to face instead of on the phone. 'Why do you say that? Did she say something about me?'

'Of course not.'

But there had been a pause before she answered. 'Did she tell you we ran into each other about a week after dinner at yours?'

She made a noise and I winced, remembering how Grace had suddenly taken flight. What had she said about me to Mardi? How bad was it?

'I want to apologize. Please, Mardi.'

'I'll tell her.' When I said nothing more, she sighed. 'I promise. I'll call her tonight and give her your number, and then, if she wants, she can call you.'

Grace did not phone me, but about a week later, she returned to me in a dream.

I was on the road again, and had pulled into a service station to fill the tank. When I came back from paying, there she was, in the front seat. She was a prettier, idealized version of Grace in a tight-fitting cashmere sweater beneath a trench-coat. Her hairstyle was long, old-fashioned, hanging down in waves, one dipping across an eye like Veronica Lake's in an old black and white movie. I think the dream was in black and white, too.

'Drive,' she said.

It was night now, and raining, but there was enough traffic on the road for the passing headlights to reveal her to me in occasional, strobe-like glimpses.

'I hear you've got a case for me,' she said.

An enormous wave of relief washed over me, and between the pulsing beats of the windshield wipers I told her my story: brief, laconic, just the facts, ma'am. When I had finished, she continued to gaze straight ahead for awhile before saying, her voice low, 'Pull over.'

'Where?'

'Doesn't matter. Wherever you can.'

There was an exit just ahead, sign-posting a roadside picnic area, so I pulled off the highway and drove even deeper into darkness, away from the lights and the traffic, to a secluded spot, utterly deserted on this dark and rainy night.

When I had parked, I turned to face the detective. Light from an unknown source gently illuminated her features. She looked wise and gentle and I was suddenly certain she was the one person who could save me from this nightmare.

'Do you know who killed her?' I asked.

'Of course.'

'Will you help me?'

'Yes.' She touched my hand. 'I'll take you in.'

'What?'

'To the police. You have to turn yourself in.'

'No.'

'It's the only way.'

'I can't. I won't. They'll think I'm the killer.'

'You *are* the killer.'

I looked into her eyes (one half-obscured by a silky fall of hair) and knew she told the truth.

'Give me the keys,' she said. 'I'll drive. They may not go so hard on you if you confess, if you can explain . . .'

But how could I explain something I could not remember?

As in a montage of scenes from an old black and white movie I saw my future: the grim faces of the jury, the old judge banging his gavel, the bleak and lonely cell, the walk – shuffling in ankle chains – to the electric chair, the hood coming down over my face, the soft voice of the priest exhorting me to confess and repent before I died . . .

It wasn't fair! I wanted to live!

Driven by desperate need, I reached for Grace. My hands closed around her slender neck and squeezed. My reaction took her by surprise, and my thumbs must have been in just the right spot to inflict maximum damage, for she scarcely even struggled; when she could not draw another breath she went limp. I continued to squeeze, making sure, venting my terror and rage on her frail and vulnerable neck, and by the time I let go, she was dead.

There was no one around to see, but I did not want to take the risk that some tired motorist might decide to drive in next to me, and considered simply pushing the detective's body out of the car and driving away. Then I had an idea: why not get rid of both bodies at once? I discovered a shovel in the trunk, and with it I dug a single grave, deep enough to hold them both. I drove away feeling satisfied, certain the evidence of both my crimes was now hidden so well they would never be found. Even if in future years someone found the bones, there would be nothing to link them to me.

I woke filled with regret and sorrow and a sense of terrible loss, but also with the cooler, steadying awareness that I'd done what I had to do, and it was over. I never had that dream again. Case closed. I would have liked to see Grace's reaction if I told her about it – but not enough to make any effort to find her. More than a year went by, actually closer to two, before I found out what had happened to her.

Hannes had asked me to meet him in Waterstone's at around six – I thought we were going for a drink, and had no idea why he'd suggested the bookshop rather than the pub across the street, not even when I saw him standing, grinning, beside the sign announcing a book signing. He pointed at the author's photograph, and still I didn't twig, didn't recognize her until the title of the book – *Dream Detective* – gave me a clue.

'Grace Kearney – that's your Grace?'

'Not mine, mate!'

The woman in the photo looked ordinary: was blandly pretty, smiling, heavily made-up, the eyebrows plucked into anorexia. 'Really? That's her? Mardi's old friend? She wrote a book?'

'And sold it for a bundle, and that's the least of it. Have you never seen her on TV? First it was guest appearances, but now I've heard she's going to have her own show.'

I looked at the picture again, trying to summon up a mental image of the woman I'd met to compare it to, and failing. All I could think of was Veronica Lake struggling feebly in my murderous grasp.

'Are we meeting Mardi?' I hadn't seen her in months; although I tried to keep in touch, the two of them no longer entertained the way they'd used to, and rarely went out, since their baby had been born.

'No way! She doesn't approve.'

'Of what, the book?'

'The book, the TV show, the celebrity clients, the publicity, glitz, bling, dosh . . .'

I recalled how badly Mardi had responded to Grace's telling me what she did. 'Grace charges people money to investigate their dreams?'

'You sound like Mardi! Yeah, well, everybody's got to make a living. But my dear, idealistic wife does not approve. She thinks her old friend has gone over to the dark side. They don't speak anymore.'

The long-ago dinner party conversation came back to me. 'Grace said she didn't believe in taking money for her gift.'

'That was the *old* Grace. She changed. Even before all this – ' he gestured at the sign and the bookstore beyond. 'Something happened. I have no idea what it was, but it changed her, like, overnight.'

I felt a chill, an unwanted memory intruding, and repressed it.

'Does Mardi know what happened?'

He shook his head. 'I told you, they don't talk. "She's dead to me," says my lovely wife. Or was it "She's dead inside" – maybe both those things.' He shrugged it off. 'Want to go for a drink?'

'Maybe I'll just get a book signed, first. Since we're here.' I felt no nervousness about seeing her again, and I was curious. That mousey little girl, a celebrity! Recalling her vehemence about how wrong it would be to take money for using her gift, I realized I had met her at a moment of crisis, sounding out other people and arguing with herself over the decision she had to make. What I found harder to understand was how her imaginary profession could be taken seriously by so many. A TV show!

Picking up a book, taking it to the counter to pay, I reflected that people were eager to believe in all sorts of nonsense. And there was the 'entertainment' argument – that justified the regular publication of horoscopes in newspapers, and psychics making their predictions on television. Just a bit of slightly spooky fun. Grace had simply tapped into that. Why not? It might upset someone like Mardi, who believed she could see the future in her special deck of cards, but a realist like me ought to applaud her initiative.

There was a small, orderly queue near the back of the shop. I joined the end of it by myself – Hannes said he'd meet me in the pub across the road – and while I waited my turn I wondered if Grace would recognize me, and decided she would not.

But I was wrong. When I reached the front of the queue and put the book down, open, before her, she raised her eyes to mine, and at once, although there was no change in her mild, professionally pleasant smile, greeted me by name.

I looked into her eyes and saw nothing there. The emptiness was unsettling. 'I'm surprised – I didn't think you'd remember me,' I said, stammering a little.

'How could I forget? After what you did . . . If not for you, I wouldn't be here now. In a way, I owe my whole career to you.'

A woman standing near the wall behind her took notice and stepped forward. 'Really? That's *very* interesting! I don't recall this from your book . . . Will you introduce us, Grace?'

Grace went on smiling mildly at me and staring at me with her dead eyes; without turning she said, 'Not now' – and although there was nothing threatening or even unpleasant in her tone, it was enough to make the other woman fall back.

'I don't know what you mean,' I said.

'I think you do.'

If I said Grace was dead, that the woman signing books was only a simulacrum, or some kind of zombie, who would believe me? Yet I knew, and so did she, that it was true. Mardi had sensed it as well. She was physically still alive, but dead inside – and it was my fault.

'Thank you for coming,' she said. While I had stood there speechless, she had finished writing in my book and now she handed it back to me. 'Thank you. Next!'

At her command, I stumbled away. I'd forgotten everything else in the horror of my discovery, forgot I was supposed to meet Hannes, and made my way home, alone, across the city. There was no one I could talk to about it, and I could think of nothing else. What had I done to that poor girl?

Poor? I could just imagine what Hannes might have said: 'Are you kidding? She used to be poor, and now she's not. She's a success! I can't see how it's anything to do with you, but she thanked you, right? She's changed, sure, and maybe her old friends don't like it, but that's life.'

Mardi alone might have understood – but if I told her what I'd done to the dream-Grace, she would have hated me, and however much I deserved it, I couldn't bear the thought.

When I got home, I took a cursory look at *Dream Detective,* reading a few pages, wondering if it would give me any answers, but there was something smug and flat and false about the paragraphs I skimmed that killed that hope. I turned back to the title page where I found what I later learned to be the author's standard inscription: My name, and *Dream well! Sincerely yours, Grace Kearney.*

Her signature was a florid scribble which I imagined she had worked up as an impressively individual, if nearly illegible, autograph. Yet there seemed to be something wrong with it. A closer look revealed that something had been written in the same space *before* she signed; two words in tiny letters, hand-printed, almost obliterated by the signature. I knew they had not been there when I bought the book, were not on the page when I opened it before her, and they were written with the same pen – Grace herself was the only possible author. Had she started to write a more personal message, then changed her mind?

Under the brightest light I had, with the aid of a magnifying glass, I examined the page until the half-hidden words became clear:

save me

Those words have changed my life. I've been asked to do

something, and although I don't know how, I will find a way.

Some things, once broken, can never be mended. Murder, no matter how deeply the killer repents, can't be undone – except, of course, in dreams.

Where the Stones Grow

In 1979, Kirby McCauley invited me to submit a story to an ambitious new anthology he was editing. I realized even more what an honour this was when Dark Forces *was published the following year and I found myself in the company of such great writers as Robert Aickman, Theodore Sturgeon, Ray Bradbury, Stephen King, Isaac Bashevis Singer, and Joyce Carol Oates. I was one of only two women, and, at twenty-eight, one of the youngest of the newer writers. Looking at it now, my contribution strikes me as oddly old-fashioned, more traditional, without my usual focus on problematic relationships, gender issues, or weird sex. Yet it is obviously mine, and close to my heart, revealing as it does a continuing, long-held obsession with stone circles and ancient legends, and drawing the first connecting line between Great Britain (where I went to live at the end of 1980) and my old home in Texas.*

HE SAW THE STONE MOVE. Smoothly as a door falling shut, it swung slightly around and settled back into the place where it had stood for centuries.

They'll kill anyone who sees them.

Terrified, Paul backed away, ready to run, when he saw something that didn't belong in that high, empty field which smelled of the sea. Lying half-in, half-out of the triangle formed by the three tall stones called the Sisters was Paul's father, his face bloody and his body permanently stilled.

When he was twenty-six, his company offered to send Paul Staunton to England for a special training course, the offer a token of better things to come. In a panic, Paul refused, much too vehemently. His only reason – that his father had died violently in England eighteen years before – was not considered a reason at all. Before the end of the year, Paul had been transferred away from the main office in Houston to the branch in San Antonio.

He knew he should be unhappy, but, oddly enough, the move suited him. He was still being paid well for work he enjoyed, and he found the climate and pace of life in San Antonio more congenial than that of Houston. He decided to buy a house and settle down.

The house he chose was about forty years old, built of native white limestone and set in a bucolic neighbourhood on the west side of the city. It was a simple rectangle, long and low to the ground, like a railway car. The roof was flat and the gutters and window frames peeled green paint. The four rooms offered him no more space than the average mobile home, but it was enough for him.

A yard of impressive size surrounded the house with thick green grass shaded by mimosas, pecans, a magnolia, and two massive, spreading fig trees. A chain-link fence defined the boundaries of the property, although one section at the back was torn and sagging and would have to be repaired. There were neighbouring houses on either side, also set in large yards, but beyond the fence at the back of the house was a wild mass of bushes and high weeds, ten or more undeveloped acres separating his house from a state highway.

Paul Staunton moved into his house on a day in June, a few days shy of the nineteenth anniversary of his father's death. The problems and sheer physical labour involved in moving had kept him from brooding about the past until something unexpected happened. As he was unrolling a new rug to cover the ugly checkerboard linoleum in the living room, something spilled softly out: less than a handful of grey grit, the pieces too small even to be called pebbles. Just rock-shards.

Paul broke into a sweat and let go of the rug as if it were

contaminated. He was breathing quickly and shallowly as he stared at the debris.

His reaction was absurd, out of all proportion. He forced himself to take hold of the rug again and finish unrolling it. Then – he could not make himself pick them up – he took the carpet sweeper and rolled it over the rug, back and forth, until all the hard grey crumbs were gone.

It was time for a break. Paul got himself a beer from the refrigerator, and a folding chair from the kitchen, and went out to sit in the back yard. He stationed himself beneath one of the mimosa trees and stared out at the lush green profusion. He wouldn't even mind mowing it, he thought as he drank the beer. It was his property, the first he'd ever owned. Soon the figs would be ripe. He'd never had a fig before, except inside a cookie.

When the beer was all gone, and he was calmer, he let himself think about his father.

Paul's father, Edward Staunton, had always been lured by the thought of England. It was a place of magic and history, the land his ancestors had come from. From childhood he had dreamed of going there, but it was not until he was twenty-seven, with a wife and an eight-year-old son, that a trip to England had been possible.

Paul had a few dim memories of London, of the smell of the streets, and riding on top of a bus, and drinking sweet, milky tea – but most of these earlier memories had been obliterated by the horror that followed.

It began in a seaside village in Devon. It was a picturesque little place, but famous for nothing. Paul never knew why they had gone there.

They arrived in the late afternoon and walked through cobbled streets, dappled with slanting sun rays. The smell of the sea was strong on the wind, and the cry of gulls carried even into the centre of town. One street had looked like a mountain to Paul, a straight drop down to the grey, shining ocean, with neatly kept stone cottages staggered on both sides. At the sight of it, Paul's mother had laughed and gasped and exclaimed that she didn't dare, not in her shoes, but the three of them had held hands and, calling out warnings to each other like intrepid mountaineers, the Stauntons had, at last, descended.

At the bottom was a narrow pebble beach, and steep, pale cliffs rose up on either side of the town, curving around like protecting wings.

'It's magnificent,' said Charlotte Staunton, looking from the cliffs to the grey-and-white movement of the water, and then back up at the town.

Paul bent down to pick up a pebble. It was smooth and dark brown, more like a piece of wood or a nut than a stone. Then another: smaller, nearly round, milky. And then a flat black one that looked like a drop of ink. He put them in his pocket and continued to search hunched over, his eyes on the ground.

He heard his father say, 'I wonder if there's another way up?' And then another voice, a stranger's, responded, 'Oh, aye, there is. There is the Sisters' Way.'

Paul looked up in surprise and saw an elderly man with a stick and a pipe and a little black dog who stood on the beach with them as if he'd grown there, and regarded the three Americans with a mild, benevolent interest.

'The Sisters' Way?' said Paul's father.

The old man gestured with his knobby walking stick towards the cliffs to their right. 'I was headed that way myself,' he said. 'Would you care to walk along with me? It's an easier path than the High Street.'

'I think we'd like that,' said Staunton. 'Thank you. But who are the Sisters?'

'You'll see them soon enough,' said the man as they all began to walk together. 'They're at the top.'

At first sight, the cliffs had looked dauntingly steep. But as they drew closer they appeared accessible. Paul thought it would be fun to climb straight up, taking advantage of footholds and ledges he could now see, but that was not necessary. The old man led them to a narrow pathway which led gently up the cliffs in a circuitous way, turning and winding, so that it was not a difficult ascent at all. The way was not quite wide enough to walk two abreast, so the Stauntons fell into a single file after the old man, with the dog bringing up the rear.

'Now,' said their guide when they reached the top. 'Here we are! And there stand the Sisters.'

They stood in a weedy, empty meadow just outside town – rooftops could be seen just beyond a stand of trees about a half a mile away. And the Sisters, to judge from the old man's gesture, could be nothing more than some rough grey boulders.

'Standing stones,' said Edward Staunton in a tone of great interest. He walked towards the boulders and his wife and son followed.

They were massive pieces of grey granite, each one perhaps eight feet tall, rearing out of the porous soil in a roughly triangular formation. The elder Staunton walked among them, touching them, a reverent look on his face. 'These must be incredibly old,' he said. He looked back at their guide and raised his voice slightly. 'Why are they called the 'Sisters'?'

The old man shrugged. 'That's what they be.'

'But what's the story?' Staunton asked. 'There must be some legend – a tradition – maybe a ritual the local people perform.'

'We're good Christians here,' the old man said, sounding indignant. 'No rituals here. We leave them stones alone!' As he spoke, the little dog trotted forward, seemingly headed for the stones, but a hand gesture from the man froze it, and it sat obediently at his side.

'But surely there's a story about how they came to be here? Why is that path we came up named after them?'

'Ah, that,' said the man. 'That is called the Sisters' Way because on certain nights of the year the Sisters go down that path to bathe in the sea.'

Paul felt his stomach jump uneasily at those words, and he stepped back a little, not wanting to be too close to the stones. He had never heard of stones that could move by themselves, and he was fairly certain such a thing was not possible, but the idea still frightened him.

'They move!' exclaimed Staunton. He sounded pleased. 'Have you ever seen them do it?'

'Oh, no. Not I, or any man alive. The Sisters don't like to be spied on. They'll kill anyone who sees them.'

'Mama,' said Paul, urgently. 'Let's go back. I'm hungry.'

She patted his shoulder absently. 'Soon, dear.'

'I wonder if anyone has tried,' said Staunton. 'I wonder where such a story comes from. When exactly are they supposed to travel?'

'Certain nights,' said the old man. He sounded uneasy.

'Sacred times? Like All Hallows maybe?'

The old man looked away towards the trees and the village and he said: 'My wife will have my tea waiting for me. She worries if I'm late. I'll just say good day to you, then.' He slapped his hip, the dog sprang up, and they walked away together, moving quickly.

'He believes it,' Staunton said. 'It's not just a story to him. I wonder what made him so nervous? Did he think the stones would take offence at his talking about them?'

'Maybe tonight is one of those nights,' his wife said thoughtfully. 'Isn't Midsummer Night supposed to be magical?'

'Let's go,' said Paul again. He was afraid even to look at the stones. From the corner of his eye he could catch a glimpse of them, and it seemed to him that they were leaning towards his parents threateningly, listening.

'Paul's got a good idea,' his mother said cheerfully. 'I could do with something to eat myself. Shall we go?'

The Stauntons found lodging for the night in a green-shuttered cottage with a Bed and Breakfast sign hanging over the gate. It was the home of Mr and Mrs Winkle, a weathered-looking couple, who raised cats and rose bushes and treated their visitors like old friends. After the light had faded from the sky, the Stauntons sat with the Winkles in their cosy parlour and talked. Paul was given a jigsaw puzzle to work, and he sat with it in a corner, listening to the adults and hoping he would not be noticed and sent to bed.

'One thing I like about this country is the way the old legends live on,' Staunton said. 'We met an old man this afternoon on the beach, and he led us up a path called the Sisters' Way, and showed us the stones at the top. But I couldn't get much out of him about why the stones should be called the Sisters – I got the idea that he was afraid of them.'

'Many are,' said Mr Winkle equably. 'Better safe than sorry.'

'What's the story about those stones? Do you know it?'

'When I was a girl,' Mrs Winkle offered, 'people said that they were three sisters who long ago had been turned to stone for sea-bathing on the Sabbath. And so wicked were they that, instead of repenting their sin, they continue to climb down the cliff to bathe whenever they get the chance.'

Mr Winkle shook his head. 'That's just the sort of tale you might expect from a minister's daughter,' he said. 'Bathing on the Sabbath indeed! That's not the story at all. I don't know all the details of it – different folks say it different ways – but there were once three girls who made the mistake of staying overnight in that field, long before there was a town here. And when morning came; the girls had turned to stone.

'But even as stones they had the power to move at certain times of the year, and so they did. They wore away a path down the cliff by going to the sea and trying to wash away the stone that covered them. But even though the beach now is littered with little bits of the stone that the sea has worn away, it will take them till doomsday to be rid of it all.' Mr Winkle picked up his pipe and began to clean it.

Staunton leaned forward in his chair. 'But why should spending the night in that field cause them to turn to stone?'

'Didn't I say? Oh, well, the name of that place is the place where the stones grow. And that's what it is. Those girls just picked the wrong time and the wrong place to rest, and when the stones came up from the ground the girls were covered by them.'

'But that doesn't make sense,' Staunton said. 'There are standing stones all over England – I've read a lot about them. And I've never heard a story like that. People don't just turn to stone for no reason.'

'Of course not, Mr Staunton. I didn't say it was for no reason. It was the place they were in, and the time. I don't say that sort of thing – people turning into stones – happens in this day, but I don't say it doesn't. People avoid that place where the stones grow, even though it lies so close upon the town. The cows don't graze there, and no one would build there.'

'You mean there's some sort of a curse on it?'

'No, Mr Staunton. No more than an apple orchard or an oyster bed is cursed. It's just a place where stones grow.'

'But stones don't grow.'

'Edward,' murmured his wife warningly.

But Mr Winkle did not seem to be offended by Staunton's bluntness. He smiled. 'You're a city man, aren't you, Mr Staunton? You know, I heard a tale once about a little boy in London who believed the greengrocer made vegetables out of a greenish paste and baked them, just the way his mother made biscuits. He'd never seen them growing – he'd never seen anything growing, except flowers in window boxes, and grass in the parks – and grass and flowers aren't good to eat, so how should he know?

'But the countryman knows that everything that lives grows, following its own rhythm, whether it is a tree, a stone, a beast, or a man.'

'But a stone's not alive. Its not like a plant or an animal.' Staunton cast about for an effective argument. 'You could prove it for yourself. Take a rock, from that field or anywhere else, and put it on your windowsill and watch it for ten years, and it wouldn't grow a bit!'

'You could try that same experiment with a potato, Mr Staunton,' Mr Winkle responded. 'And would you then tell me that a potato, because it didn't grow in ten years on my windowsill, never grew and never grows? There's a place and a time for everything. To everything there is a season,' he said, reaching over to pat his wife's hand. 'As my wife's late father was fond of reminding us.'

As a child, Paul Staunton had been convinced that the stones had killed his father. He had been afraid when his mother had sent him out into the chilly, dark morning to find his father and bring him back to have breakfast, and when he had seen the stone, still moving, he had known. Had known, and been afraid that the stones would pursue him, to punish him for his knowledge, the old man's warning echoing in his mind: *they'll kill anyone who sees them*.

But as he had grown older, Paul had sought other, more rational, explanations for his father's death. An accident. A mugging. An escaped lunatic. A coven of witches, surprised at their rites. An unknown enemy who had trailed his father for years. But nothing, to Paul, carried the conviction of his first answer. That the stones themselves had killed his father, horribly and unnaturally moving, crushing his father when he stood in their way.

It had grown nearly dark as he brooded, and the mosquitoes were beginning to bite. He still had work to do inside. He stood up and folded the chair, carrying it in one hand,

and walked towards the door. As he reached it, his glance fell on the window ledge beside him. On it were three light-coloured pebbles.

He stopped breathing for a moment. He remembered the pebbles he had picked up on that beach in England, and how they had come back to haunt him more than a week later, back at home in the United States, when they fell out of the pocket where he had put them so carelessly. Nasty reminders of his father's death, then, and he had stared at them, trembling violently, afraid to pick them up. Finally he had called his mother, and she had got rid of them for him somehow. Or perhaps she had kept them – Paul had never asked.

But that had nothing to do with these stones. He scooped them off the ledge with one hand, half-turned, and flung them away as far as he could. He thought they went over the sagging back fence, but he could not see where, amid the shadows and the weeds, they fell.

He had done a lot in two days, and Paul Staunton was pleased with himself. All his possessions were inside and in their place, the house was clean, the telephone had been installed, and he had fixed the broken latch on the bathroom window. Some things remained to be done – he needed a dining room table, he didn't like the wallpaper in the bathroom, and the back yard would have to be mowed very soon – but all in all he thought he had a right to be proud of what he had done. There was still some light left in the day, which made it worthwhile to relax outside and enjoy the cooler evening air.

He took a chair out, thinking about the need for some lawn furniture, and put it in the same spot where he had sat before, beneath the gentle mimosa. But this time, before sitting down, he began to walk around the yard, pacing off his property and luxuriating in the feeling of being a landowner.

Something pale, glimmering in the twilight, caught his eye, and Paul stood still, frowning. It was entirely the wrong colour for anything that should be on the other side of the fence, amid that tumbled blur of greens and browns. He began to walk towards the back fence, trying to make out what it was, but was able only to catch maddeningly incomplete glimpses. Probably just trash, paper blown in from the road, he thought, but still . . . He didn't trust his weight to the sagging portion of the fence, but climbed another section. He paused at the top, not entirely willing to climb over, and strained his eyes for whatever it was and, seeing it at last, nearly fell off the fence.

He caught himself in time to make it a jump, rather than an undignified tumble, but at the end of it he was on the other side of the fence, and his heart was pounding wildly.

Standing stones. Three rocks in a roughly triangular formation.

He wished he had not seen them. He wanted to be back in his own yard. But it was too late for that. And now he wanted to be sure of what he had seen. He pressed on through the high weeds and thick plants, burrs catching on his jeans, his socks, and his T-shirt.

There they were.

His throat was tight and his muscles unwilling, but Paul made himself approach and walk around them. Yes, there were three standing stones, but beyond the formation, and the idea of them, there was no real resemblance to the rocks in England. These stones were no more than four feet high, and less than two across. Unlike the standing stones of the Old World, these had not been shaped and set in their places – they were just masses of native white limestone jutting out of the thin soil. San Antonio lies on the Edwards Plateau, a big slab of limestone laid down as ocean sediment during the Cretaceous, covered now with seldom more than a few inches of soil. There was nothing unusual about these stones, and they had nothing to do with the legends of growing, walking stones in another country.

Paul knew that. But, as he turned away from the stones and made his way back through the underbrush to his own yard, one question nagged him, a problem he could not answer to his own satisfaction, and that was: why didn't I see them before?

Although he had not been over the fence before, he had often enough walked around the yard – even before buying the house – and once had climbed the fence and gazed out at the land on the other side.

Why hadn't he seen the stones then? They were visible from the fence, so why hadn't he seen them more than a week earlier? He should have seen them. If they were there.

But they must have been there. They couldn't have popped up out of the ground overnight; and why should anyone transport stones to such an unlikely place? They must have been there. So why hadn't he seen them before?

The place where the stones grow, he thought.

Going into the house, he locked the back door behind him.

The next night was Midsummer Eve, the anniversary of his father's death, and Paul did not want to spend it alone.

He had drinks with a pretty young woman named Alice Croy after work – she had been working as a temporary secretary in his office – and then took her out to dinner, and then for more drinks, and then, after a minor altercation about efficiency, saving gas, and who was not too drunk to drive, she followed him in her own car to his house where they had a mutually satisfying, if not terribly meaningful, encounter.

Paul was drifting off to sleep when he realized that Alice had got up and was moving about the room.

He looked at the clock: it was almost two.

'What're you doing?' he asked drowsily.

'You don't have to get up.' She patted his shoulder kindly, as if he were a dog or a very old man.

He sat up and saw that she was dressed except for her shoes. 'What are you doing?' he repeated.

She sighed. 'Look, don't take this wrong, okay? I like you. I think what we had was really great, and I hope we can get together again. But I just don't feel comfortable in a strange bed. I don't know you well enough to— It would be awkward in the morning for both of us. So I'm just going on home.'

'So that's why you brought your own car.'

'Go back to sleep. I didn't mean to disturb you.'

'Your leaving disturbs me.'

She made a face.

Paul sighed and rubbed his eyes. It would be pointless to argue with her. And, he realized, he didn't like her very much – on any other night he might have been relieved to see her go.

'All right,' he said. 'If you change your mind, you know where I live.'

She kissed him lightly. 'I'll find my way out. You go back to sleep, now.'

But he was wide awake, and he didn't think he would sleep again that night. He was safe in his own bed, in his own house, surely. If his father had been content to stay inside, instead of going out alone, in the grey, pre-dawn light, to look at three stones in a field, he might be alive now.

It's over, thought Paul. Whatever happened, happened long ago, and to my father, not me. (But he had seen the stone move.)

He sat up and turned on the light before that old childhood nightmare could appear before him: the towering rocks lumbering across the grassy field to crush his father. He wished he knew someone in San Antonio well enough to call at this hour. Someone to visit. Another presence to keep away the nightmares. Since there was no one, Paul knew that he would settle for lots of Jack Daniel's over ice, with Bach on the stereo – supreme products of civilization to keep the ghosts away.

But he didn't expect it to work.

In the living room, sipping his drink, the uncurtained glass of the windows disturbed him. He couldn't see out, but the light in the room cast his reflection onto the glass, so that he was continually being startled by his own movements. He settled that by turning out the lights. There was a full moon, and he could see well enough by the light that it cast, and the faint glow from the stereo console. The windows were tightly shut and the air-conditioning unit was labouring steadily: the cool, laundered air and the steady hum shut out the night even more effectively than the Brandenburg Concertos.

Not for the first time, he thought of seeing a psychiatrist. In the morning he would get the name of a good one. Tough on a young boy to lose his father, he thought, killing his third drink. So much worse for the boy who finds his father's dead body in mysterious circumstances. But one had to move beyond that. There was so much more to life than the details of an early trauma.

As he rose and crossed the room for another drink (*silly to have left the bottle all the way over there*, he thought), a motion from the yard outside caught his eye, and he slowly turned his head to look.

It wasn't just his reflection that time. There had been something moving in the far corner of the yard, near the broken-down fence. But now that he looked for it, he could see nothing. Unless, perhaps, was that something there in the shadows near one of the fig trees? Something about four feet high, pale-coloured, and now very still?

Paul had a sudden urge, which he killed almost at once, to take a flashlight and go outside, to climb the fence and make sure those three rocks were still there. *They want me to come out*, he thought – and stifled that thought, too.

He realized he was sweating. The air conditioner didn't seem to be doing much good. He poured himself another drink and pulled his chair around to face the window. Then he sat there in the dark, sipping his whiskey and staring out into the night. He didn't bother to replace the record when the stereo clicked itself off, and he didn't get up for another drink when his glass was empty. He waited and watched for nearly an hour, and he saw nothing in the dark yard move. Still he waited, thinking, *They have their own time, and it isn't ours. They grow at their own pace, in their own place, like everything else alive.*

Something was happening, he knew. He would soon see the stones move, just as his father had. But he wouldn't make his father's mistake and get in their way. He wouldn't let himself be killed.

Then, at last – he had no idea of the time now – the white mass in the shadows rippled, and the stone moved, emerging onto the moonlit grass. Another stone was behind it, and another. Three white rocks moving across the grass.

They were flowing. The solid white rock rippled and lost its solid contours and reformed again in another place, slightly closer to the house. Flowing – not like water, like rock.

Paul thought of molten rock and of lava flows. But molten rock did not start and stop like that, and it did not keep its original form intact, forming and re-forming like that. He tried to comprehend what he was seeing. He knew he was no longer drunk. How could a rock move? Under great heat or intense pressure, perhaps. What were rocks? Inorganic material, but made of atoms like everything else. And atoms could change, could be changed – forms could change –

But the simple fact was that rocks did not move. Not by themselves. They did not wear paths down cliffs to the sea. They did not give birth. They did not grow. They did not commit murder. They did not seek revenge.

Everyone knew this, he thought, as he watched the rocks move in his back yard. No one had ever seen a rock move.

Because they kill anyone who sees them.

They had killed his father, and now they had come to kill him.

Paul sprang up from his chair, overturning it, thinking of escape. Then he remembered. He was safe. Safe inside his own home. His hand came down on the windowsill and he stroked it. Solid walls between him and those things out there: walls built of sturdy, comforting stone.

Staring down at his hand on the white rock ledge, a half-smile of relief still on his lips, he saw it change. The stone beneath his hand rippled and crawled. It felt to his fingertips like warm putty. It was living. It flowed up to embrace his hand, to engulf it, and then solidified. He screamed and tried to pull his hand free. He felt no physical pain, but his hand was buried firmly in the solid rock, and he could not move it.

He looked around in terror and saw that the walls were now molten and throbbing. They began to flow together. A stream of living rock surged across the window glass. Dimly, he heard the glass shatter. The walls were merging, streaming across floor and ceiling, greedily filling all the empty space. The living, liquid rock lapped about his ankles, closing about him, absorbing him, turning him to stone.

Vegetable Love

In the early nineteenth century, Japanese knotweed was introduced from East Asia to Britain and then to the United States. It was considered an attractive addition to many gardens until it began spreading more widely in the wild, where it became reclassified as a dangerous invasive plant that could quickly overwhelm native plant life and watercourses, and even damage roads and buildings. Residents in England and Wales are still allowed to have it in their gardens, but if it ever escapes they could face a fine of £5,000 or two years in prison. Reading government guidelines on how to keep it under control, the plant comes across as some sort of undead vampire or concrete-eating zombie that is practically impossible to defeat. A flamethrower might do the trick, or regular treatment with herbicides over several years, but even then the dead, leftover remains must be wrapped in a growth-resistant material and buried at least five metres deep. Is it any wonder, then, that when I was invited to contribute a new story to an anthology about 'weird plants' I chose to write about Japanese knotweed, considering any made-up plant of my own could not compete in the beautiful-but-deadly stakes?

One moment you've never seen it, never heard anything about it, have no idea what it might be. Then you hear the name, someone leads you into the presence, and from that moment the world is changed.

Hannah went to the local community meeting on an impulse. She was restless, tired of staying in, unable to think of anything better to do, something that wouldn't be another expense, when she saw the notice on a lamppost near her house.

Memories of a chilly church hall and heated discussions about dog-fouling and the need to save the local play-park came rushing back, recollections of an earlier time, when the children were small, and it had been so important to make common cause with other mums and dads. She'd been drifting, lately, or coasting, both at work and at home. They had their routines. The children – now hardly 'children' – made fewer demands. She would not say she was unhappy, but she was just a little bit bored.

She wanted Neil to come with her, but he gave her a look that said she was mad. Clearly, he did not share her vague dissatisfaction, or he could not imagine sitting through a discussion about the new one-way system would do anything but make it worse.

She didn't argue. Of course he didn't share her feelings, how could he? His experiences of life as a parent, of their early years here, had been so very different from hers. She didn't expect the meeting to be exciting, but it might offer some practical way of reconnecting with her neighbours. It was through those gatherings in the church hall a decade ago that she'd made two of her best friends, women she still felt close to, although since they had moved away she did not see them very often.

So she went on her own to the church hall, walking through the familiar south London streets, the evening air as balmy as if summer would never end. As she passed by the houses she looked over hedges or through fences and admired the gardens of strangers, feeling the imaginative pull of other lives. She wished Neil was beside her, to take her hand or put his arm around her as they strolled, to see the same things she saw. They might at least have talked about something different, for a change.

The moment she stepped through the door she caught a whiff of the old building's familiar, distinctive smell, like a combination of mushrooms and feathers, and it was as if time had turned back, she was a young mother again, frazzled and spent after a day of balancing work and childcare, invigorated yet nervous about the unknown experience ahead, and she entered with a tentative smile, hoping for a welcome.

But there were no familiar faces among those turned briefly towards her and then away again; the only one she recognized was Mr Patel, who owned the corner shop where she often bought a newspaper and bottle of water, and he looked away again quickly as if she was not who he had been expecting. She had an urge to turn around and go home; maybe she could tempt Neil away from the internet long enough to watch another episode of 'Homeland'. Too late. She'd been spotted by a silver-haired woman who now bore down, brandishing a clipboard, and Hannah must add her name and address to the list and then find a seat.

Perched on one of the hard metal chairs, she felt a not-unpleasant glaze of bored acceptance settle over her. What else had she expected? Why had she come? If she wanted company, friendship, support, she'd have done better to pick up her phone, or go on the computer – Bella in New York, Mary in Wales, were only a few clicks away. She had no friends *here,* and if she wanted new ones she had better find something that really mattered to her, or something more congenial – an evening class in Tai Chi or conversational Italian.

The end was near; the chairwoman made a perfunctory request for 'any other business?' and then, out of the sea of shaken heads, one clear, female voice rang out:

'Japanese Knotweed.'

The phrase meant nothing to Hannah, and she was startled by the immediate reaction from others, as people shifted and muttered angrily. She craned her neck and peered around curiously, seeking the source. The words, to her, seemed mysterious and lovely. She imagined long, supple strands of grass knotted into artistic origami shapes by a pair of slender hands emerging from the wide, silken sleeves of a kimono. Yet it was clear that they inspired a very different response in others.

'Bloody disgrace!'

'I call it criminal.'

'Surely they realize ... the amount of money we've spent ...'

'Must be fly-tipping.'

'Saw it on the verge ...'

'What can you do? ... empty properties ...'

'In the bin! Cuttings actually *in the bin*.'

'*Two* gardens on my way here!'

'... in the garage!'

'... facing a fine and can't possibly sell and it's not my fault!'

'Outrageous!'

A storm, a positive tsunami was building, all because of a plant that grew where it was not wanted. Hannah felt bemused by so much passion directed at a weed. Was everyone here such a keen gardener? She felt little interest in the subject, except as a passive observer. It was nice to be able to sit outside on a pleasant evening, or grill some meat on the barbecue in the open air, but neither she nor Neil had the time or inclination to indulge in all the care a proper garden required, so they'd put in decking, and placed a few shrubs and miniature trees in pots, leaving a bit of rather scruffy lawn at the end, where the children used to play. The odd weed peeked through now and then, tolerated if it was small and pretty, plucked out if it wasn't, and while she agreed dandelions could be a nuisance, she wasn't that bothered.

The chairwoman restored order, reminding everyone that the subject had been quite thoroughly discussed at previous meetings, and saying there was nothing to be gained by repeating the same complaints. If someone found knotweed growing on their property they had a legal obligation to have it disposed of by a properly licensed firm. If they believed it had been introduced to their property deliberately, or through carelessness, by another, they must report this to the proper authority (information could be found on the council's website) and might wish to pursue a civil action. After all, a patch of knotweed on a property adjacent to one you wished to buy could mean you'd be refused a mortgage.

'As everyone knew . . .'

Hannah was astonished. She found herself a resident of a veritable plague-zone, and she'd never suspected. The session concluded with the chairwoman inviting everyone to stay for tea and biscuits.

This was really what she had come for, the time when people chatted and agreed to help one another, when new ideas were hatched, volunteers enlisted, committees and friendships were formed. Waiting patiently in the queue for tea, she listened to the conversations going on around her, and they were all about the same thing, the latest sightings, the threat the invader posed to their homes, worries about insurance, bills for disposal, the fear that it was already too late . . . No one seemed able to talk about anything else, as if they were in a war zone.

It seemed absurd that people could be so terrified of something she had not heard of before this evening, but she could hardly say so. She wanted to ask questions, but hesitated to expose the extent of her ignorance. If she could find just one sympathetic soul, someone who would tell her it was all right, six months ago *she'd* never heard of it, either, and quickly bring her up to speed . . .

Accepting her cup of tea, she slowly turned away from the table, and, as she did, another woman caught her eye and, like a reflection, smiled across the room at her. She was rather pretty, but not startlingly so; her face was heart-shaped, her hair glossy and smartly cut, her expression somehow clever, amused and sympathetic all at the same time. Hannah was drawn to her.

When she was close enough, she said brightly, 'You'll think me a complete ignoramus, but before this evening I'd never heard of Japanese knotweed!'

'*Fallopia japonica*.'

It was the same, bell-like voice that had raised the subject after the chairwoman had asked about any other business. Hannah blinked in surprise. 'That was you!'

She gave a modest nod, and a somewhat Oriental bow. '*Itadori*.'

'I'm sorry?'

'That is the Japanese name: *itadori*. I believe it translates as "takes away pain", or "heals the sick".'

'Really! I suppose it's used in Japanese traditional medicine?'

The woman gave a small shrug. Close to, in the unflattering glare of the overhead lights, she looked somewhat older than Hannah had thought. 'I don't really know. I understand it can be eaten, if the young shoots are gathered in the spring.'

'But you haven't tried it?'

'I'm not very adventurous. I shop at Tesco.'

Hannah laughed. 'I guess it's not likely to turn up on supermarket shelves. So it isn't poisonous. I thought, from the way people spoke, it must be toxic.'

'No.'

'Why are they so afraid of it?'

Her faint smile was unreadable. 'Because it is different? And powerful – but not in an obvious way. Some people find that attractive, but others – frightening.'

Their eyes met again, and Hannah felt a *frisson*. Fear? Or desire? '*You* aren't afraid.'

The woman made a weaving motion with her hand. 'Do you know the expression – I saw it on a T-shirt during the marathon – "Feel the fear and do it anyway"?'

Do what? She wondered. 'What does it look like? Knotweed. Itadori. I've never seen it.'

'Oh, you must have! It is well established in these parts –

the hysteria of the others, it's not without reason. It spreads very rapidly and is hard to destroy. But it is a most strikingly beautiful plant, not likely to have escaped your notice.'

There was something charmingly odd, attractively old-fashioned in the way she spoke. 'Well, I don't know. I'm not very clever, when it comes to plants. Can you describe it?'

The other woman gazed at her for a long moment in silence. 'It would be easier for me to show you.'

Hannah glanced around.

She laughed. 'Not inside! But if you're ready to leave? I can take you there. I see you've finished your tea. Let me.' She took Hannah's cup and saucer, still holding her gaze, and their fingers touched.

Hannah felt a little shock. What was going on? Was she being flirted with? She watched her walk away, noticing her slender legs, the sway of her hips, the way the light gleamed off her dark hair, and had to admit she was flattered, even somewhat aroused by the thought. She'd never had a sexual relationship with another woman, but had always enjoyed the physical element in her friendships – the hugs and the back rubs and the occasional foot massage – and had wondered sometimes, when she was young and single, what it would be like to go further. To live in a world of women. She was married now, and she loved Neil, and would never do anything to risk her marriage – but even though she would not act on it, the mutual attraction was undeniable, and the mere fact of it sent a pulse of energy through her; she felt more alive than she had in months.

From the doorway, the woman looked back with a smile of invitation, and Hannah went to join her.

'We never introduced ourselves. I'm Hannah.'

Any reply was lost in the terrible, grating screech the door made in opening.

Waiting until the booming thud of the closing door was well behind them, she tried again. 'I'm sorry, I – '

'Don't apologize!' She tossed that teasingly over her shoulder, striding so briskly Hannah almost had to run after her down the narrow lane, and when she abruptly stopped, there was a collision.

'Oh! Sorry!' She bit her lip, flustered, and backed away. The other woman had not flinched, and now caught hold of Hannah's arm, pulling her gently in beside her.

'Don't run away. Look. This is what I want to show you. Look, there. Now, tell me, don't you recognize her?'

In order not to think about the touch of those firm, strong yet gentle fingers locked around her forearm, she fastened onto the grammatical oddity. *Her?* Not a native speaker of English. She felt relieved by this. Women in other countries often went about arm-in-arm, she thought, and so she relaxed and regarded the lush cluster of leaf and flower pushing through a bit of wire fence by the side of the footpath. Although the yellow glare of the streetlamp above made it hard to be sure of the colours, the large, heart-shaped leaves must be green, the thick pale sprays of blossom white, yellow or cream.

'I don't know, it doesn't look familiar, but I don't pay much attention to plants,' she said apologetically. 'I'm not a gardener. But it is quite pretty.'

'*She.*'

'No, we don't say "she".'

Her new friend laughed at her. 'Oh, but we do! Even a non-gardener should know that much. It's not only animals – plants, too, are male and female.'

Hannah felt a swoop of embarrassment. Now the woman's formal way of speaking and lack of identifiable accent seemed not foreign, but the sign of someone educated at some posh, old-fashioned school. Rather than apologize yet again, she managed to call on some reserve of *sang froid* and said, 'I was always a bit rubbish at botany. I'm amazed that you can tell a girl-plant from a boy-plant, especially in this light.'

'Ah, but there is no trick to that, because every single one of *these* in *this* country is a clone of the original mother. All are sister-plants.'

They stood a moment longer, gazing at the knotweed. She was aware of an elusive, faint, attractive scent, but did not know if it came from the plant or the woman. From away up the lane, she heard the sound of the heavy hall doors banging open, and then voices, footsteps approaching, and was spurred to make a move.

'I say . . . shall we go somewhere for a drink? It's still early.'

'No.' She let go Hannah's arm and stepped back. 'My turn to apologize. I have to go now.' A group of women had drawn near, and as Hannah stepped aside to let them pass, the other woman stepped into the group and managed to merge with the flow. 'So lovely to meet you!' As she spoke, she'd already linked arms with another woman, who looked slightly startled, but not displeased.

Hannah felt as if she'd been given a sharp push. What was that all about? Had she simply imagined the attraction between them? Or was that the problem? Maybe it meant nothing, or maybe the nameless woman was now hurrying home to her own husband, wife, or lover and a night of guilty second thoughts . . .

To settle her own turbulent mind, she returned her attention to the flourishing weed. Even after hearing it described in terms of fear and outrage, an enemy of the city and destroyer of all life that was not its own, she could not help but find it lovely. She even wished she could take home a cutting to plant in one of the big blue pots beside the deck. It would look lovely, and would be safe enough contained there . . .

But there were undoubtedly laws against that. She told herself she would forget the plant, just as she would forget the woman who had introduced her to it.

Later that night, at home, as she was cleaning her teeth, she noticed a slight mark on her forearm. It was yellowish, like a bruise, and she fancied it was in the very same place where the long, pale fingers of the nameless woman had held her. Placing her own hand on it, she pressed gently. It was not sore. There was nothing to feel.

In the morning the mark had gone, and so had her memory of the woman's face, her voice, all the emotions she had so briefly and mysteriously aroused – everything about the evening vanished from her mind except the plant.

Fallopia japonica. Itadori. 'Takes away pain.' Tiger Staff. Japanese Knotweed. Himalayan Fleece-flower. Hancock's Curse. Elephant Ears. Monkey fungus. Mexican Bamboo. Sally Rhubarb.

On her way to work that morning she saw it:
In the untended garden of a seemingly empty house
In the forecourt of a shut-down petrol station
Beside the tracks between stations

At work, waiting for someone to get back to her, she idly searched the internet, learning some of its many common names, and saw photographs as bizarre as something from a disaster movie. There were entire monoculture forests of the stuff in parts of America – although, on the screen, out of context, it was just masses of greenery. More disturbing were the close-ups that managed to reveal the connection between this rampant, determined growth and ordinary human life. One showed vigorous, living spikes bursting through asphalt and concrete; another displayed what had happened to an abandoned car over the course of a summer. The one that haunted her was of a single tendril of green that had pushed through a crack and was now growing up the wall of someone's sitting room – *inside* the house.

She had a sensation as of ants crawling all over her, but it wasn't her body she was worried about, but her property. She had seen a patch of knotweed growing, flourishing, only a few streets away. What if there was more, closer at hand? She thought of how she sometimes pulled weeds from cracks in the pavement or anywhere else she might notice them, and dropped them into the bin without thinking about it. Her blood ran cold with horror. What if . . . what if . . . *she* was part of the problem?

When she got home that evening she went searching for it in the front and back gardens, around the decking, and underneath, along the pavement in front, and out back beside the garden shed. She spent so long outside in the fading light, hunched over and peering at every crack, cranny and growing thing that the children were embarrassed, and stuck their heads outside to hiss at her.

'What are you *doing,* Mum? Come back inside!'

'Stop that, you look like some mad old bag hunting for change. I'll give you a pound if you just come in now!'

Neil was scarcely more sympathetic than they were. When she said 'knotweed' he cut her off with an impatient sigh. 'What put *that* into your head? It's not even the growing season. If I saw it – and I would – do you think I am completely useless? Don't you trust me to deal with it?'

She was surprised: she'd understood that eradication was a task for professionals.

'Oh, that's such a con. It's a big business now – of course they don't want people doing it themselves. But as long as you are absolutely thorough, and understand what you're dealing with – especially when it comes to disposal – it's no worse than half a dozen other weeds. The problem started because, of course, it grows from cuttings, and people were careless. But it's absolutely not a problem in Japan, China and Korea, and it needn't be here.' Lecture over, he patted her back. 'Trust me. Japanese knotweed is not about to conquer London. Nor even our road. What set you off?'

She murmured something about the internet.

'Ha! First port of call for hypochondriacs and conspiracy theorists. Darling, next time you go surfing, stick to music videos and cats.'

She did not go looking for it, but it could not be avoided. She saw it everywhere she looked. Although not growing on her own property, it was so prevalent and so visible that she was astonished she had never noticed it before. It was such a pretty plant, too, but not in the showy way of brilliantly coloured flowers like rosebay willowherb or poppies that everyone knew. In its subtle way, it had transformed her world.

The flowers disappeared by October, and the leaves yellowed and fell, until by November there was nothing left of it but the bare, red-brown stalks that cracked and broke easily. Death was everywhere. Except for the artificial appearance of evergreen hedges and conifers, the natural world dressed itself in mourning.

Hannah felt hollow inside, an echo of the death she saw around her. This happened every year, but usually she managed to delay the onset of her seasonal melancholia by throwing herself into a frenzy of preparation for Christmas, shopping, cooking, decorating, entertaining . . . this time, she could not summon the energy. The children, fretting over exams or working extra shifts to save money for planned gap-year travel, hardly noticed. Neil, although concerned enough by her lethargy to suggest she needed a break – maybe treat herself to a weekend spa? or she could go visit her sister? – actually found having a low-key, inexpensive holiday period something of a relief.

All Hannah wanted to do was sleep, sleep, sleep until the winter came to an end. It would end, she knew.

Her mood changed, as she had hoped it might, with the season. Sometime in March, before Easter, while it was still cold and the trees were bare, she began to feel restless. She was compelled to leave the house – or, more problematically, her office – to go for a walk at least twice a day. Rain or shine, she craved fresh air, and the regular, repetitive motion soothed and revived her spirits. After only ten or fifteen minutes she was glowing with health, alive again in a way she'd almost forgotten. It was how she had felt a long time ago, when she was young and in love. And at the very start of her two pregnancies. But what was causing this absurd happiness now?

It was a little awkward, sometimes, having to come up with an excuse before rushing out; she was sure her co-workers thought she was having an affair, or had developed an addiction to gambling, drink, or drugs. And the need she felt to go walking, the craving she had for fresh air, *was* similar to an addiction – although it seemed to have no negative effects.

Often on her walks she noticed the skeletal remains of what had once been a blooming patch of *Fallopia japonica*. Earlier, she had found the bare, lifeless canes a depressing sight, but now, although not pretty, they marked the spot where new life was growing, little reddish snouts pushing through the debris.

In a matter of days they had become stalks several inches high, resembling fresh asparagus. They pushed aside anything in their way, cracking the old dead stalks as they rose. Nothing could stop the blind urgency of growth. Hannah saw several shooting up out of a crack in the pavement, forcing it wide, breaking the concrete a little more every day. While she was very glad it wasn't her driveway, she couldn't help finding a positive lesson in the sight. It said something about life, about the power of the natural world, and she thought it was good to be reminded of this at a time when people were so worried about how human beings were destroying the planet. Nature still had a few tricks up her sleeve, other ways of ensuring the survival of plant life in the face of almost any obstacle.

Her arm began to tingle and she rubbed it hard, resisting the urge to scratch for the third or fourth time that day. It was rarely a good idea to attack your own skin, however briefly gratifying it might be. She told herself it did not itch. And it didn't really – not quite. The sensation that had been plaguing her for several days seemed subcutaneous, as if it were the underside of her skin, and not the surface, that felt a tickle. She'd applied various lotions and potions she had on hand, but nothing worked, and it was probably pointless when she had no rash, no redness, swelling or any other sign save a faint, greenish shadow like the memory of a bruise.

She unfastened her watch – although it couldn't possibly be the problem – and was startled by how late it was. She had left the office what felt like ten minutes ago, yet two hours had passed. There was clearly no point in going back now.

She wanted to go home, felt it as an increasingly urgent desire, but when she reached the station, she went past, unable to bear the thought of going down the steps, of being underground, even for a short while. Eventually she managed to catch a bus that took her back to her area, and alighted when she was within a short walk of home. As she stepped down she noticed, with a thrill of recognition, the new growth sprouting at the base of the bus shelter.

The house was empty; possibly the children had already come and gone – she could no longer remember every detail of their schedules. Stripping off her coat, she dropped it on the floor, then took off her shoes and peeled off the hated tights. Unburdened, barefoot, she went through to the back, unlocked the door, unfastened the bolts, opened it and went outside, across the deck and down to the tiny scrap of lawn. It was pathetically small, the grass was patchy and faded, but it was *earth*. Home. She sighed with relief and wriggled her toes.

Now, without other distractions, she was able to attend to her own feelings, listen to what her body was telling her. The tickling sensation intensified, then became something sharp and chilly. She looked at her arm.

She saw, first, a thin line of blood, which in a matter of seconds became a gaping wound as flesh and bone gave way before the life-force within. The reddish-purple bud had pushed through the skin, and now grew before her eyes into an asparagus-like stalk. When it was six or seven inches high the tender green leaves began to unfurl.

Nothing could possibly grow so fast, and yet it was happening. Almost overwhelmed by a mixture of awe and pain, she felt other stalks erupting from other parts of her body. The resourceful plant had adapted to its new situation during its winter-long hibernation within her body, and had speeded its growth rate because, if it was not well established in minutes, rather than days, it was unlikely to survive.

If Neil came home while she was still recognizably his wife, he would try to stop it, he would do his best to kill the plant in the hope of saving her. And even through the fear and pain of the change, she knew that must not be allowed to happen. It was already too late for Hannah.

She wriggled and clenched and flexed her toes, digging them into the grass and then deeper into the soil, until they took root.

The Book That Finds You

This last story is a personal homage to Robert Aickman. I was eighteen the first time I read an Aickman story and still recall it vividly. I was a student at Syracuse University, alone in my dorm room as I read 'The School Friend' in the latest issue of The Magazine of Fantasy and Science Fiction. *Late afternoon darkened to evening outside as I sat in a lamp-lit circle, utterly absorbed by the seductively strange, deeply disturbing story, as unease turned to a dread that made me scream at the sound of a door opening behind me. It was only my roommate, of course, and we both laughed about it – but, although I did not realize it, that was a pivotal moment in my life as a writer. Robert Aickman joined my personal pantheon (Ray Bradbury, Theodore Sturgeon, Kate Wilhelm, E. Nesbit, Shirley Jackson, Harlan Ellison, Joyce Carol Oates) as a writer whose work I loved and learned from. Three years later I, too, was published in* F&SF, *and when I moved to London, I had Mr Aickman's address, and we made plans to meet – but it was too late. He was already very ill, and died soon after. But his stories, his influence on other writers, and even a type of story described as 'Aickmanesque' live on.*

THERE'S SOMETHING ABOUT A BOOK you find by accident, a book no one else seems to have heard of, a book that thrills and then becomes a part of you, when it's one you so easily might never have read at all – it almost seems like *it* found *you*.

For me, it was *Until the Stones Weep* by J. W. Archibald. The first time I saw that name and title was in cracked white lettering on the battered black spine of a used paperback, sandwiched between a novel by Eric Ambler and another by

Evelyn Anthony in the Mysteries/Suspense section of the Southwest Book Exchange, a narrow box of a place with a concrete floor, fluorescent lighting, and the pervasive smell (to me, always sweet) of old paperback books.

I pulled it out. The cover was crassly at odds with the ambiguously eerie title, sporting a hyper-real picture of a leering, warty crone with bloodshot eyes, extending a yellow, claw-like hand in a beckoning gesture. It didn't look like a crime story, but like something much rarer in those days before Stephen King had sold his first novel. I turned it over and read:

Mystery . . . Desire . . . Madness . . . Death . . .
Six Strange Stories of the Supernatural by a
Modern Master of the Macabre

'Mr Archibald can certainly make your skin crawl. His ghosts and half-seen monsters are as evocative as any by M.R. James.'

Dublin Herald

'A modern-day Poe, bringing fear and mystery into our modern world. No ghost-story aficionado should miss this treat.'

Sheffield Telegraph

'Better than H.P. Lovecraft.'

Evening Standard

I was fourteen years old. I'd loved everything spooky and strange since I'd discovered the works of Edgar Allan Poe at the age of seven. I'd read all of M. R. James, most of Lovecraft, and every genre anthology I could find, but I'd never heard of J. W. Archibald.

Of course I bought it, and read it from cover to cover

that night, to be rewarded by an uneasy sleep punctuated by nightmares. Those six strange stories – which I only half understood on first reading – made my skin crawl with a delicious, unreasoning terror.

I loved it.

The only problem was that there was no more, only those six stories by the writer who had shot to the top of my list of favourites. No one I knew had ever heard of him. As this was in the days before the internet, my means of searching were limited, but I tried my best, even putting through a request by the interlibrary loan service, without success. I never stopped looking, but I never even came across another copy of the book I had found. It was as if I'd made it up . . . or it had been made up, created in an edition of one, especially for me. I knew that was silly. *Until the Stones Weep* was a British paperback, published by Fontana in London in 1966; it was by a great stroke of luck that I had come across one of the few copies that had found their way to America, but there must be others; somebody else must know about J. W. Archibald.

And of course there *was* somebody else, living about two hundred miles away, but it took me another seven years to find him.

Everybody called him Tommy, a boyish name that went with the twinkle in his eye, his unruly hair, his whole attitude that life was a game. He was a collector who made his living dealing in second-hand books. His store was on South Lamar, in Austin; it hasn't been there for a long time now, but old residents may recall it. I only discovered it in my last year at the University, when I finally moved off campus to share an apartment and a car with my best friend, Maudie. Even though I went in there nearly every week – browsing more than buying – I was too shy to strike up a conversation with the good-looking man behind the counter.

One day Maudie said, 'We're going to Tommy's party tonight.'

'Who?'

'Bookstore guy.'

'What? Really? Wait, how do you know him?'

She rolled her eyes. 'Same way you do. I scored a copy of *The Doors of Perception* from him yesterday, and he invited me.'

I felt a clench of jealousy. 'Does he even know your name?'

She punched my arm. 'He wasn't hitting on me! He said, Be sure to bring your little sister.' She laughed. 'I don't know if I should be offended that he thinks I look older than you!'

Tommy lived in a small wooden house on a big lot on Enfield Road. His front room contained free-standing bookcases and wall-mounted shelves; elegant glass-fronted bookshelves side by side with the casual brick-and-board arrangements Maudie and I used. As soon as I saw all those books, I relaxed, and forgot everything else in my eagerness to browse.

And there it was. The book I thought was my own private discovery, in a stranger's collection. I stopped breathing for a second, and put my finger on the familiar wrinkled black spine, to be sure I wasn't dreaming, then pulled it out and stared at the familiar, ridiculous, hideous old witch.

'Don't let the cover put you off; the stories are much better than – '

'They're *great*,' I said fiercely, looking up with a frown into the face – smiling, interested, and very close – of the book's owner. I rearranged my own expression and said, 'He's my favourite writer, Archibald, but I've never met anyone else who's even heard of him.'

'Read anything else by him?'

When I only gaped, he led me into another room, where the walls were entirely covered in books. There was also a cluttered desk and a couple of chairs, one a leather recliner with a floor lamp beside it.

'It's a signed first,' he said, holding up a small, hardcover book in a plain red and white dust wrapper. 'So I won't let you take it away – in case you're tempted not to return it. But you can read it here – any time you like,' he added quickly as I sat down in his reading chair. 'I didn't mean right this minute; you're more than welcome to come back.'

'I'd like to look at it now – just to read a little bit,' I said. 'Please?'

His gaze softened; he gave me a sympathetic smile, and handed me the first copy I had ever seen of *The Secret Game* by J. W. Archibald and Sarah Anne Lyons.

'But it's – '

'A collaboration between two authors. Her second and his first published book, and the closest thing he's written to a novel. You know who she is?'

'*The Hound of God, The Servitors*, of course.' Lyons was a respected English novelist, and wife of another, even better known, novelist. I'd read one of her novels but had found it too dense with religious and literary allusions for my taste. 'But she's – '

'Married to Albert Baker, yes, *now,* he's her *second* husband, but after the break-up of her first marriage, she was Archibald's, uh, girlfriend.'

It was all too much. 'No! But he must be so old – much older than her, and – well, I thought he was dead! The way he writes . . .' Archibald's stories, while avoiding contemporary references that would absolutely date them, had always struck me as belonging to the world of the 1920s, if not earlier.

'I can see why you'd think that. His style is very old-fashioned.'

'But how old is he?'

'He's cagey about his age. He must be a good ten years older than Lyons – maybe twenty. She's, what, mid-forties now? So he could be in his sixties.' He told me – enjoying my astonishment and awe – that he had briefly corresponded with Archibald. He was about to get out the letters when he finally realized that my interest, then, was all for the book in my hands, and left me to read it in peace.

I spent the next two or three hours in a kind of fevered dream, so rapt in story that it seemed to be happening to me. I could hardly have said what the book was 'about' – I experienced it as a series of dreams and nightmares that flowed imperceptibly together. Incidents took place in London and Venice, in a Welsh village and on the Norfolk Broads, and, because I had never been out of Texas, as I read, the bleak stretches of Norfolk became the Texas coastal plains, the Welsh village was in the hill country, black cabs and red double-decker buses appeared on the streets of Austin, and the canals of Venice ran through Galveston.

The Secret Game was a novel in the manner of Arthur Machen's *The Three Imposters*; that is, a series of strange stories, loosely linked by several continuing characters. There were contemporary references that made it clearly a post-World War II production; mentions of bomb damage and rationing and to movies and songs of the late '40s. It was copyright 1950. In both style and substance it was easy to recognize as the work of J. W. Archibald. I was not familiar enough with Lyons's writing to guess how much she had adapted her style to his, but I wondered how they had worked together. The tone and style was so thoroughly consistent, it seemed the work of one writer.

When I finished that enchanted first reading and stumbled back into the front room, I found a much diminished party, and no Maudie.

'Your friend wanted to leave. I promised her faithfully that I'd see you safely home – when you're ready. I thought you might want to talk some more about Archibald.'

From the way he slightly slurred his words, I knew Tommy was in no condition to drive me across town, but I didn't care. I *did* want to talk about the book. We could talk all night, I decided, and drink coffee, and in the morning, he could take me home.

I was about half right. We *did* talk all night – not just about

The Secret Game and *Until the Stones Weep,* but about all our favourite books, and our shared desire to write, and our oddly similar childhoods – and drank lots of coffee, which he liked just the way I did, with plenty of half-and-half and lots of sugar – until, by the time we were left alone in his house, we were both buzzing with caffeine and the thrill of finding a soulmate. He was sober enough to drive me home by dawn, but instead we went to bed, to continue our conversation on another plane. And it turned out that our bodies connected as passionately as our minds. At one point while we were making love I fell into a sort of waking dream in which he was showing me one book after another, and they were all things I had been looking for, without knowing they existed, and he was giving them to me, to read and keep.

'Do you like this? How about this? No, wait, this is even better. This? Or this?'

I couldn't choose; I wanted them all, all at once. 'Yes,' I said, holding him tightly. 'Yes, yes, yes.'

After that, he never did drive me home – except to get my car and load it up with my things to take back to his house. *Our* house.

We had a blissful life together, for a while. Neither of us was terribly ambitious – although we had our dreams, and wrote stories that we hoped to sell, really all we cared about, besides each other, was getting by, doing the things we enjoyed, reading and collecting and talking about the books we loved.

My sister thought it was the least romantic affair she'd ever heard of. She couldn't believe I'd rather be given an aged, yellowing paperback book with a picture of a skeleton on the cover instead of a dozen red roses or a bottle of expensive perfume on Valentine's Day. But I've never liked cut flowers, and I'd rather choose my own fragrances. That wasn't just *any* crummy old paperback; it was an anthology that included a very rare, never-reprinted short story called 'The Chill Touch of Your Hand' by J. W. Archibald. She thought I was crazy for thinking that driving to Oklahoma City to spend the weekend looking through the books in every Salvation Army and junk store was more fun than the 'pampering spa weekend' she craved.

I'm not sure when or why it changed. I suppose it was a gradual thing, a distance that grew between us, a flame that burned out. At least on his side – I remember how shocked I was when, a month before what would have been our fourth anniversary of living together, he said, in that unmistakably heavy, resolute voice of doom those words all lovers dread: 'We need to talk.'

One week later, in a state of shock, I was living in my own one-bedroom apartment.

'Was there someone else?' Maudie and my sister both thought he must have been sneaking around with someone else behind my back. I did not think so. True, there was a new woman in his life before the month was out, but he'd always been fast like that.

Although of course I was miserable at first, the end of a relationship is not the end of everything. Other men found me attractive, and I had the freedom to pick and choose. And there were other things in my life. I had started selling my short stories – around the same time that I'd noticed Tommy's attitude towards me begin to change. Maybe the two things were not unconnected. My literary success did not amount to much – half a dozen short stories sold to magazines that paid less than five cents a word – but it was more than he had managed to do, and maybe he minded it more than he would say.

When I was twenty-eight, I came into an inheritance. I decided to use it to travel abroad. Friends of my family owned a flat in London I could use as a base for a month or two. London was at the top of my list – J. W. Archibald lived there. His reputation and career had received a boost with the coming of the horror boom, and he'd finally been published in America – thirteen of his old stories, and one completely new collection. An issue of *The Magazine of Fantasy and Science Fiction* with one of my stories also contained a brand new tale by Archibald, so I felt confident enough to call the magazine's editor to ask if he could give me Mr Archibald's address.

His voice changed when he heard what I wanted, becoming lower and softer. 'I'm sure he wouldn't mind, but ... This isn't for public consumption but ... he's not very well. In fact ... I don't think he's long for this world. He's moved into a friend's flat – he couldn't really manage on his own any longer.'

My heart sank lower and lower. 'I see.'

'But let me give you the address. You may as well write to him – I know he'd love to hear from you. I'm sure that if he's able, he'll write back.'

J. W. Archibald was dead before my letter could reach him. Two weeks later, I received a note on black-edged paper, signed with a name I could not decipher.

I was sad, of course, but the idea that I might meet him had never been real. And what could one brief meeting have added to my understanding or my pleasure in his writing? It was his words that mattered, the magic he'd created on the page. The great sadness was that there would never be any more, that he'd never write another story, *not* that I'd never been able to shake his hand and tell him how much his stories had meant to me.

Before leaving on my travels, I reread *The Secret Game* and all of the short stories. They were just as good as I remembered, haunting, disturbing, and puzzling. Multiple readings did not dilute their strangeness; rather, it seemed the more closely you inspected them, the odder they became. Even now that I was older and more widely read, able to pick up on his references (he was big on opera, architecture, and obscure nineteenth-century artists), some things remained opaque.

I arrived in London at the beginning of November. It was cold and grey and looked exactly as I thought it should. This was before London became a multicultural, international city with futuristic, gleaming skyscrapers, and enormous shopping malls, in constant flux. In those days, not so long ago, it seemed charmingly old-fashioned, a little grubby and run-down, but quaint; a city distinct from all others, like nothing I'd encountered except in fiction.

Although I was alone, I was too entranced by the novelty of it all to feel lonely. Living in a flat meant I could lead a normal life, shop and cook for myself and keep whatever schedule suited me. I walked all through the short daylight hours, sightseeing and storing up impressions, wrote in my journal and read in the evenings.

I'd brought only a couple of books with me, just enough to tide me over, for I anticipated the bookshops of London, where I was, as expected, overwhelmed by a variety of treasures.

On my first visit to Foyles, the new novel by Sarah Anne Lyons was prominently displayed, and that same day I read an interview with her in the *Evening Standard*, from which I learned that she was no longer married to Albert Baker. They had been separated for nearly two years, but the divorce was only now about to be finalized, having been waiting on the division of their property. Bert hated change, she said; he couldn't bear the disruption of moving, yet without selling their big house he'd been unable to give her half its value.

'It was much too big for him, of course, and he hasn't the least idea what has to be done to keep up a house, but he had become so stuck in his ways he was quite irrational . . . it was part of the reason I left him. I shan't be getting married again. When I was young, I seemed to feel I *needed* a man, to be complete, but now . . . now I find I enjoy living my own life. Rather like Lydie, in my new novel.'

The interview was a two-page spread, including a large picture of a very beautiful mature woman. On an impulse, I wrote a letter, care of her publisher, asking to meet her. I said I was a writer myself, and mentioned my sadness at the recent death of J. W. Archibald. I gave her my address, told her I did not have a phone, but would be in London for at least a month and available whenever it was most convenient for her.

The very next day, in the bargain bin outside a bookshop in Cecil Court, I saw a familiar wrinkled black spine with white lettering. The cover (that leering witch) was even more battered than on my own copy, but the pages inside were clean, and I could not resist buying it.

Standing with it in my hand, I had a sudden idea. Why not use Archibald as my tour guide? The places where the stories were set could provide my itinerary. After seeking out the London streets and buildings he mentioned, I'd go to the Norfolk coast, the Yorkshire moors, Wales . . .

I'd already purchased that indispensable guide, the *London A-Z,* and over lunch (in the Wendy's on Cambridge Circus – seeing it, I suddenly yearned for an American hamburger) I put the map book and a pencil on one side and began to leaf through my new copy of *Until the Stones Weep* in search of place names. There were none in the first story, 'The Trembling Leaf', which was set mostly indoors. 'The New Neighbours' likewise did not identify even the city in which its 'mid-nineteenth century housing estate for merchants and professional men' was located.

In the third story, at last, I saw some familiar names – perhaps a bit *too* familiar. I'd already been along Oxford Street, and Bond Street, and was even now in Cambridge Circus, but the next reference perked me up a little: *Notting Hill*, where a strange event occurred inside a house on a nameless 'side street'.

There was a tube station called Notting Hill Gate; getting there would give me more practice navigating the underground, and when I got there, I did what I was already accustomed to doing in any new area: walked around and looked at things.

I found a second-hand bookshop within five or ten minutes of walking away from the tube station, down what surely was a side street – it didn't seem to have a name.

A bell over the door jangled as I entered; the man behind the counter looked up, but left me to browse while he continued talking to someone on the telephone.

'Oh, they'll sell, but it wasn't a great haul. He was only having a clear-out. Moaning about having to get rid of *everything* for lack of space, but I'm sure he's paid for storage. There wasn't anything special . . . No. Nor that.

'Oh, yes, *some* signed firsts, but nothing really . . . Baker's no fool; he's a collector himself. Let me have all his wife's books – those loving inscriptions! Obviously couldn't stand to look at them again. You think? No, she's not collectible. Except that one with Archibald, and he didn't have that, of course. Uh-huh.'

My skin prickled as I eavesdropped shamelessly.

'Seven boxes – no cherry-picking. Probably only a dozen I'd really – uh-huh. Uh-huh. Downstairs. I'll price them this weekend. If you want. Ok. Sure. Listen, you know that bloke in Camden Town . . .'

I moved along the shelves, out of his sight, towards the back of the shop to the stairs leading down. Although there was no sign to invite customers to check out the stock on the lower floor, neither was there anything to say it was for staff only, so I descended, stepping lightly.

Downstairs it smelled of damp and dust and paper. The room had walls lined with metal shelving, double-stacked with books, and there were at least a dozen cardboard boxes on the brown and cream linoleum. The only lighting came from a single, low-wattage bulb dangling from a ceiling cord, and the corners were thickly shadowed. I took a step away from the stairs, then froze as one of the shadows moved. It looked like a man.

I opened my mouth to say something, anything to turn the sinister moment towards normality, but when the shadow reached the place where the light from the hanging bulb should have lit up his face and turned him into a person, there was no face. No longer a shadow, it seemed to be a life-sized figure of a man cut out of kraft paper, and it moved towards me too fast for me to scream – even if I had wanted to.

Then he was on me, arms wrapped about me, pressed hard against me; thin and light though he was, I could feel every naked, masculine inch of him. It was such an unexpectedly *welcome* pressure that I relaxed and melted into the embrace. I opened my mouth for his kiss, and arched my back and pressed myself against him, and as I did I remembered Tommy in our most intimate moments together, and the memory was so strong and physically irresistible that I groaned and lost myself in a convulsion of pleasure.

It was over in a second. Surely I had imagined it all, briefly overcome by the lingering effects of jet lag in the poor light and bad air of the room. But there *was* a man – I couldn't see his face, for he was standing with his back to the light, but he was there, blocking my way to the boxes I was so curious about, holding a book. The book in his hands was a small hardcover, and he pressed it on me, pushing it against my breast.

I caught hold of it before he could go farther, and quickly darted up the stairs. Although I knew I'd felt hands on my naked breasts, I was fully dressed for the London winter, and my navy blue coat was buttoned up to my collarbone.

The man behind the counter frowned when I thrust the book at him. 'Where'd you get this? I haven't had a chance to price them yet. Oh, all right – '

Although I really meant to return it, it was easier to pay him the pound he asked and go. It was already dark outside.

I rather wished I had let the man wrap my purchase, because the binding had an unpleasant, greasy feel in my ungloved hand, and for that reason I didn't like to put it in my purse.

The train was crowded. There was nowhere to sit, and I had no chance to examine the book I continued to clutch until I got home.

There was no lettering on the pale brown spine, no title or publisher's colophon. Inside, after two blank sheets, the title page:

The Rejected Swain's Revenge

'J. W. A.'

Below those two lines, centred near the bottom of the page, was a sort of symbol or device that looked like two letters intertwined, but I wasn't quite sure what letters.

Turning another page I found another two blank sheets; between them, a folded square of blue notepaper. Unfolding it, I recognized the handwriting from the letters Tommy had shown me years before.

My sweet Lady Anne,

I've done what I can, but it was never enough to please you. You were a hard mistress. Will your new man find life with you any less difficult, I wonder?

Something in the pages of this book may move you as my own caresses never could. I wish you joy of it.

With all my heart, I remain
Forever yours
A.

I was both disturbed and excited by this unexpected discovery and I wished more than anything that I had Tommy to share it with. He'd produced a bibliography of Archibald's work, and I was absolutely certain it had not listed 'The Rejected Swain's Revenge' even as a variant title. Could this have been produced by a private press? But then what had happened to the other copies? Why had no one heard of it? It seemed hardly possible that he had written, and caused to be printed, a book meant to be read by just one person, yet that is what I suspected.

Just thinking about reading it made me feel like a sneaking, spying, peeping tom – but how could I resist? I justified what I was about to do with the reflection that Archibald could not mind because he was dead, and Sarah Anne Lyons had not cared enough to take the book away with her when she left her husband – *anyone* might read it now.

Except, as I found as soon as I began to read the densely printed slabs of prose, it was hard to imagine anyone who would care enough. It was almost unreadable, an incomprehensible mess that reminded me of the automatic writing favoured by the Surrealists. There was no story and no argument. Whenever there was a sudden burst of clarity, it was to reveal a sexual scene, unusually graphic for the normally proper and tastefully suggestive author, and astonishingly unpleasant.

I flipped ahead, to see if things got any better, but it was all like that. I put the book aside, feeling soiled, and wished I'd never picked it up. (But had I been given a choice?) There were too many familiar turns of phrase for me to console myself with the thought that anyone other than Archibald had written it, but why? What had he thought he was doing? I wondered if he'd gone temporarily insane when his lover left him. He'd obviously regained his senses, because he'd been writing brilliant and mysterious short stories up until the final months of his life.

'Lady Anne' should have burnt it, I thought, with an irrational flare of resentment. She should have had more care for his reputation, even if she no longer wished to share her life with him. Yet I flinched at the idea of destroying it myself. It was a book, after all, and even if I neither liked nor understood it, it had been written by a very talented author.

Wrapping it in a shopping bag I stashed it out of sight in a drawer.

That night I slept badly. I woke frequently, heart pounding, convinced there was someone else in the flat; a man in my room, approaching my bed. The nightmares were connected to the book, but I could not think of how I could safely get rid of it.

In the morning, I packed my rucksack with clothes and books to last me a few days, took myself off to the nearest mainline station, and bought a ticket for the first destination that caught my fancy: Edinburgh. The Scottish city appealed to me for all sorts of reasons, not least among them that it had never, so far as I could recall, featured in anything Archibald had ever written.

The cold, wind, and icy rain did not bother me. I thoroughly enjoyed myself over the next four days, exploring the Old Town, seeing the sights and indulging in the bookshops – I even went on a ghost tour. I slept well at night and ate the hearty 'full Scottish' breakfast provided by my motherly landlady every morning, and went back to London feeling much happier, with one bag full of my dirty clothes and another full of books I had not been able to resist.

There was a letter waiting for me at the flat; a handwritten note on headed notepaper from Sarah Anne Lyons inviting me to call on her, and suggesting a particular afternoon – now just two days away.

That night I slept well, better than I had in Edinburgh. The simple trick of going away and coming back had given this borrowed flat the feeling of home. I did not open the book again, but told myself I'd been silly about it. All the same, I looked forward to returning it to its rightful owner.

★

Sarah Anne Lyons lived in a pretty, white-stucco-fronted house in a terrace near the river. She opened the door to me, gracious and smiling, and insisted I call her 'Anne'. Her beauty had not at all diminished with age, and she was even more beautiful in person than her photographs revealed. I felt quite overcome, almost in awe; she had that great charm and charisma that is the very definition of stardom.

Her sitting room might have been lifted from a copy of *The World of Interiors,* with its elegant, modernist furniture and white marble fireplace surround. Everything was black and white or shades of grey, including the framed prints on the walls, with a few perfectly judged touches of scarlet. There was no bric-a-brac and no clutter, nothing on the occasional tables but a white porcelain vase of red roses and an ebony bowl filled with apples.

The absence of books was especially striking, at least to me, but this was a room for entertaining visitors, not for curling up alone to read. Her office was probably lined with bookshelves.

While I was still gazing around the beautiful yet impersonal room, she brought in a tea tray, and we sat down to cups of Earl Grey and crisp little chocolate cookies, and had our chat. I hardly knew how to begin to speak to her – I felt like an uncouth visitor from another world – but she was very skilled at drawing people out, and before I knew it I was telling her all about my original, fortuitous, discovery of *Until the Stones Weep,* the effect it had had upon my own writing, how it had led to the relationship that I'd thought would be the most important in my life – 'but that's all over now'.

She had listened to my outpouring dispassionately. Now she put her head on one side and gazed at me with her dark, inscrutable eyes. 'Is it? Does anything – like that – ever *really* end?'

I stared back, unable to reply. I wanted to ask if she was speaking of herself and J. W. Archibald, but didn't dare.

She said, with a sigh, 'I suppose you want to know about *The Secret Game*.'

Rather timidly I nodded. 'If you don't mind.'

'Oh, I don't mind. I don't mind talking about Archie – not anymore. There were years – far too many years – when I wouldn't, when I wanted to forget . . . You see, I hurt him very badly. Of course, I was young, but that's no excuse for cruelty. I knew what I was doing, and there are always other ways of ending a relationship. I shouldn't be surprised – I wouldn't blame him – if for a time he didn't really come to hate me. Love can easily be turned to hate, you know; sometimes it's hard to tell the difference between the two passions. Whereas what I felt for him was indifference. That's a very hard thing for a lover to accept. But our relationship was never equal. He fell absolutely, passionately in love with me – really, with my looks. He wanted me, whereas I was never physically attracted to him. You never met him, did you? No, of course not. Even when he was younger, Archie was a very odd-looking man. Of course, what attracted me to him was not his body but his *mind* – he was just so clever! He knew absolutely everything about art, and music, and architecture, and so many other things. Knowing him was a great education – probably the best education I could have had; I was very badly brought up in that respect. So I was tremendously impressed by him, and eventually, although I was never in love with him *in that way,* he wore me down with the strength of his desire. We became lovers. He wanted to marry me – but that I would *not* do.'

She set her cup down in its saucer, the little click providing punctuation.

'All that is past. I am very pleased to say that we finally made it up. He forgave me, and we became friends again – just friends, but *really* friends – in the last year of his life.'

'This was after you'd left your husband.'

She shot me a look that made me think I'd gone too far, but

then gave a reluctant nod. 'Yes . . . Bert, the fact that I'd married him, as well as who he was . . . that was salt in Archie's wounds, so . . . although I like to think we still might have reconciled, you're right: the fact that I'd left Bert undoubtedly eased the way. Made it easier for poor Archie to readmit me to his inner circle.'

'When did he send you the book?'

It was clear from her look that she did not remember, so I prompted: '*The Rejected Swain's Revenge.*'

She shook her head slowly. 'I have no idea what you're talking about. The title means nothing to me.'

So I told her about the bookshop in Notting Hill that had bought seven boxes of books from Albert Baker. 'One was this very odd book. No publishing or copyright information. I think it must have been privately printed. I found a piece of notepaper tucked inside, addressed to "My Sweet Lady Anne" and signed "A".'

'No date?'

'No date. But because it was in with your ex-husband's books – '

She was frowning, the expression adding years to her face. 'Oh, it was too bad of him!'

'Archibald?'

'Bert!' She shook her head sharply, lips tight with anger. 'He must have intercepted it, seeing the return address. It was – unfortunately – just the sort of thing he would do. He was always jealous of my past, of any part of my life that did not include him. He was so ridiculously possessive. He didn't recognize the usual boundaries. He wouldn't stop at reading my diary or stealing my mail . . . and how dare I complain, unless I had something to hide.' She stopped herself from saying more. After a few moments, the tension in her relaxed and she managed a wry smile. 'One more crime to add to the ledger. Thank goodness, I don't have to put up with his spying and prying any longer.'

'Would you like to see it now? I brought it with me.'

'No!' Her eyes widened in alarm before she recovered her composure and said again but more gently, 'No, thank you.'

'But he meant it for you – '

'Whatever he meant by it, whenever it was sent, that time is past. It doesn't matter anymore. I'm glad that we were able to become friends before he died, and that's how I'd like to remember him – not as a rejected, vengeful lover, but as my friend.'

So I kept the book, although I did not open it again. It had not been written for me to read, and, crazy or not, I had a notion that my bad dreams had been caused by my trespass into its pages.

I spent some time travelling around England, France and Italy, but went back to Texas in time for Christmas, ready to settle down and write a novel. It was at a New Year's Eve party in Austin that I heard the news about Tommy.

The old cynic had finally been trapped into marriage by some young thing fresh out of college. They were having their honeymoon in Vera Cruz, but would be back home in another couple of weeks.

Why should I care if Tommy was married? I'd been leading my own life for years. I was over him. Why did it feel like a fresh betrayal, and the worst one; why did it feel like my heart was breaking? A line from one of Archibald's stories floated through my mind: the heart doesn't know what time it is.

I knew then that I could not live in Austin again, and made it my New Year's resolution to move. That very night I began asking about friends and acquaintances who had moved away to the west or the east coast, and when I had a handful of addresses, I wrote some letters. Within a week I'd learned that Maudie's best friend from high school, now living in Brooklyn, needed someone to help with the rent from March, because her present roommate was getting married. I applied for the position. The thought of living in New York was exciting; maybe I could get a job in publishing.

Before I left the city for good I mailed *The Rejected Swain's Revenge* to Tommy, with the original note from Archibald inside, and a Post-it note stuck to the cover saying:

Found in a London bookshop, from the collection of Albert Baker. Thought it would fit well in yours. Will repay close & careful reading.

I did not sign it (I expected he would recognize my handwriting) and I did not include an address, so it's not surprising that I never heard from him about it.

I scarcely gave him another thought as I was soon caught up in my new life in New York. But although I did not return to Texas for many years, Maudie kept me informed about what was going on. From her, I learned Tommy's marriage did not even last a year. It was not an amicable separation. Community property laws gave her a claim on everything he owned, and he wound up selling his business to pay her off.

Did I feel sorry for him? No. It was all his own fault. If he'd stuck to his position on marriage, as he had with me, none of it would have happened. Besides, I thought he'd bounce back as he had before. He probably already had a new girlfriend, and with his contacts in the book trade and his knowledge, everyone expected he'd soon open a new bookshop.

That did not happen. He went on selling books out of his house, even issued his twice-yearly catalogues, but people in town saw less and less of him – he seemed to have become something of a hermit.

It was only years later, when I was invited to a book festival in Austin, that I began to think of him again. The city was so changed, so much bigger and rebuilt I hardly recognized it as the sleepy, funky college town I'd known. The house where I'd once lived with Tommy had been knocked down, replaced by two tall, narrow townhouses.

I wondered what had happened to him, but my casual enquiries led to blank looks, and I did not pursue the matter.

I might never have known of his fate were it not for a chance encounter on my last night in Austin.

I was in a group just leaving a restaurant on Sixth Street when I saw Tommy walking towards us. He was so terribly changed by age, I think I recognized him more by his stance and loose way of walking than anything else. He didn't notice me; his eyes were cast down, and I did nothing to attract his attention.

It was what I saw when he went past that haunts me. There was someone walking behind him, so close it was unnatural, and a collision seemed imminent, yet because they continued in this manner for as long as I could follow their progress with my eyes, I knew it was deliberate, and Tommy well aware of, even allowing, this pursuit.

The person behind wore a long black overcoat – a completely unnecessary garment in the stifling warmth of the Texan night – and a slouch hat, which should have made him nearly impossible to identify. But what I *could* see – the parchment-coloured cheeks and chin, the long, incredibly thin, flat hands – and perhaps above all the odour, faint but unmistakable, carried to me on the faint breeze of his passage, of cheap pulp paper – convinced me that I had encountered him before, in the basement of a second-hand bookshop in Notting Hill.

The feeling of guilt for what I've done, what I've inflicted on poor Tommy –

Is it guilt that I feel? Or jealousy?